PERFECT LOVE

SNOWERS HOCKEY ROMANCE

EMILY BOW

CHAPTER 1

Calista shivered in the snowball-covered bikini as if the cottony puffs were made of real snow instead of fluff. How had she gotten here?

Dahlia jiggled an alternative puck-covered swimsuit. The three-inch black rubber spheres clanked together, warning of worse indignities to come. "You own the team. You pick the dancers' new costumes."

No. Frustration combined with the room's broken heater made Calista cringe. This was exactly the type of day-to-day operations she wanted to avoid. Not that she could have imagined this exact moment. Ownership wasn't finalized yet, and besides, wearing a dance team outfit couldn't be normal for any owner. The snowball-covered cups and bikini bottoms barely concealed her privates, and chill bumps rose everywhere else.

Why didn't the heat work in this conference room? She needed to take a look at the HVAC unit. Calista bounced up and down and tried to rub the cold from her arms. The snowballs shifted in an inappropriate direction, showing too much skin. She stilled, wanting nothing more than to change back into her own clothes. Hello, jeans and jersey on the end of the table, miss you. Calista fixed her gaze on her cousin. "You have Snowers shares too. You pick the dancers' costumes." She wasn't ashamed of the plea in her voice.

Dahlia looked from Calista dressed in last season's costume to the mass of black ribbons and plastic she threaded between her fingers—the proposed new suit. "It's complicated."

Really? There was a choice of two bikinis on the line. Calista arched her eyebrows. "Cotton or puck. Not that complicated."

Dahlia grimaced. "Willow will think I vetoed her puck costume because she came up with the idea. Going with the snowballs will make me look petty. Like I'm overturning her business ideas because she stole my fiancé." Dahlia's voice rose as suppressed emotions bubbled to the surface like an overheated Bunsen burner.

Calista nodded slowly. That was the best she could do to express sympathy at the moment because Dahlia's ex-fiancé, Dodo Applebaum, had never deserved her cousin. She couldn't decide what was making her more uncomfortable, pretending sorrow for their broken engagement or the puffy cotton snowballs bouncing against her C-cups.

Compassion made her stay, but her gaze slipped again to her clothes on the end of the conference room table. How much longer would she have to linger to show appropriate support? Calista fidgeted with her halter strap and eyed the door leading to the hallway.

Dahlia crossed her arms over her waist, hugging herself. "The executive office situation is straight up awkward. My new office is miniscule, but I don't want to have a desk outside Dodo's corner suite anymore." Dahlia blew out a breath. "Don't worry, we'll figure this out." She checked her slim platinum wristwatch. "I need to go meet Piper, sure you can't join?"

Love for her cousin and sister almost prodded her into going, but the thought of chatting about the costumes and the Applebaums for two more hours was more than her brain could handle. Calista held open her palms. "I have class." That fact was so embarrassing. She was supposed to have graduated in December, but she had to take one more class, a six-week intensive, before she could get her diploma.

She had only stopped by the stadium to watch the ice hockey team practice. Instead, she'd run into Dahlia and was now freezing her bits off. She should have refused to act as costume model, but when Dahlia had played the cheated-on, no longer bride-to-be card, she couldn't refuse.

Dahlia wadded up the black bikini and discarded it on the table. The pucks swooshed across the smooth surface with a speed that revealed her suppressed anger. "Thanks for modeling for me. I've decided I don't like either costume." Dahlia gestured in front of her chest. "Too immodest." She moved toward the door with a bounce in her steps, as if putting off the choice had lightened her mood. "Later, sweetie." She was out of there in a wave of her signature floral perfume.

The second the conference room door clicked shut behind her cousin, Calista let her smile drop. That was the thing with insincere smiles, they were hard to maintain. Missing practice to pretend sympathy had been difficult, because escaping an Applebaum wasn't a reason to mourn, but was a cause to celebrate, over a good game of hockey.

Were any of the players still on the ice? Was her favorite, Captain Ronan Stromkin? A giddy quiver shook her body. If she rushed and changed fast, she could watch him play for a few minutes before she had to jet to campus. Seeing Ronan would make for a wonderful day. Calista yanked at the bow behind her back and reached for her sporty blue bra.

The sound of a door opening came from the other side of the room, followed by a masculine voice, "Oh, eh. This isn't the women's locker room."

Calista froze. Right, because she was in a hurry and hadn't gone back to the ladies' room to change, she'd made an impulsive bad decision. She was standing in the team's conference room in itty bitty bottoms and a half-off bikini top. The cotton balls swung across her nipples, held up only by the strap behind her neck.

There were no words. No excuses.

Heat flushed her face, and Calista scrambled to

throw her hockey jersey over her head. She tugged on the hem, stretching the fabric as low as possible. She was not decent, but she was covered. She lifted her gaze to see who had entered the room.

Captain Ronan Stromkin!

CHAPTER 2

Holy hot hockey god—Ronan. Just turned twenty-seven, three years older than her, six-feet-one, shut-down defenseman, extraordinary, amazing—perfect. Ronan wore sneakers instead of ice skates, jeans, and a polo shirt the same medium blue shade of his eyes. That was good. If he'd been in his ice hockey gear, she'd have passed out from the power of this moment. As it was, wonder was shaking her knees. His light brown hair was tousled and damp, as if he'd just gotten out of the shower. It meant practice had ended. Dang.

Ronan's gaze took her in from head to toe then glanced around the room. "Unless you aren't alone?"

What did that mean? She had been with her cousin, but clearly, Dahlia wasn't here now. Calista opened and closed her mouth, but she didn't know what to say.

His gaze landed on the screen printed *twenty-two* across the front of her jersey. "That's my number. You came in here to meet me?" A high flush hit his cheek-bones. "I'm flattered. You must be a new dancer." He pointed his index finger at her chest and then up at his own hard pecs. "We're not allowed to date. Dancers and players, that is." His gaze stayed on her jersey, and he bit the masculine curve of his lower lip.

OMG, this was not how meeting Ronan had played out in her fantasies. She was supposed to introduce herself to him as a fan. An admirer who recognized his genius on the ice, or as the potential new owner, one who'd assure him he was the star of the team, the best of the best. Tell him how lucky they were to have him on their roster, praise his speed, tout his skill and his control. More compliments blossomed in her brain, shutting down her ability to speak.

Ronan looked torn, but he stepped forward. "Your jersey's caught." He gently untucked her bunched sleeve. His fingers were warm and careful against her elbow.

Sparkly tingles shot from the point of his touch through her chest. What wizardry was this? He'd strung electrical currents to her nerve endings and made them dance. He was controlling her neurons the way he controlled the puck on the ice. This man was magic.

His fingers lingered, and he trailed them down to her wrist. "Your skin is so soft." Ronan spoke as if he were in a trance. "I'm flattered," he said again, sounding bemused. "But I really can't." His gaze dropped to her bare legs, and he tapped his fingertips against her wrist as if he couldn't lift them off her. "We can't." He repeated as if she'd argued. "I mean we could—." Ronan closed then reopened his mouth, like he wanted to finish the sentence but at the same time knew he shouldn't.

Confusion and awe warred within her. What was happening here?

Banging sounds came from the door behind him. Letting her go, Ronan scrubbed his hand over his face and backed toward the exit. He jerked his body around and left.

Calista grabbed her clothes and scrammed.

Her three classmates were using the university classroom furniture as intended, Calista was not. She sat on the floor to disassemble her desk using her core tools: screwdrivers, a drill, and a wrench. Calista took the desk's frame down until every bolt, screw, and base part lay in a semi-circle around her. Fun. Fun. Fun. Her body buzzed with the energy of solving a mechanical puzzle.

In the darkest corner of the room, Vivien played on her computer, pretending she wasn't hacking, living her bliss. "What do you know about the Mer-bar?" Vivien asked with her jacket's zipper tab in her mouth, which caused her question to come out garbled.

Olivia, who'd come in early, had a sunny spot by the window. She was reading through a sheaf of papers, which looked like legal contracts. Olivia straightened the starched edge of her rounded Peter Pan collar. "You're in a class for geniuses, and we get extra points for actively socializing with real humans. You tell me, what do we know about a bar?"

As the only lawyer in their group, Olivia could make a solid point. Score one, Olivia. Too bad the class wasn't destruction, hack, or zinger 101. They'd ace it.

"I've been to a bar," Vivien muttered. "Two of them."

The fourth and only male member of their group, nicknamed Artie for his Artificial Intelligence ambitions, jotted in a small black notebook. When Artie finished, he dropped his pencil on top of his family-sized bag of beef jerky. Leaving both behind, Artie moved from his desk to the floor. He inched toward Vivien, as if by moving slowly Vivien wouldn't see him crawling toward her.

Should she say something?

When Artie was a foot away from her friend, he used a yellow measuring tape to determine the length and width of her llama-topped slippers. Vivien either didn't notice or chose to ignore him.

Calista held her tongue.

Next, Artie, still on his hands and knees, maneuvered to the window and measured Olivia's pale pink flats. Olivia noticed him, checked her phone, and made a note on her legal pad.

Artie pivoted toward Calista's sneaker-covered feet last.

The yellow tape measure rose above her toe, clearly measuring her size eights, and whirred back into its casing.

To be honest, Artie creeped her out when he did things like this, but kicking him in the head wouldn't get her the social points she needed to graduate. Calista wasn't sure what would. "I don't understand this class." She projected her frustration with Artie onto her statement about the university making her do this special project in order to graduate.

Olivia rolled her hazel eyes. "Project Genius was the best I could negotiate after you burned down a lab. Vivien hacked. Artie did his unmentionable act, and, I may have been too blunt during my oral exams. Maybe. I'm not saying whether I was or I wasn't, but here we are. We've got to figure out the best angle to succeed because we all pass or fail together."

Group project. Each of them gave a shudder.

Calista knew she had underexplained the fire. That failure didn't mean she lacked people communication skills as the dean had said. The pressure of the moment had simply caused her to go temporarily mute.

"Did you have to add in that whole we'll be punctual and not skip rule?" Vivien asked.

"I had to give them something to show we're disciplined." Olivia tapped her pen atop her clipped stack of papers in a steady staccato. "Look forward, not back. Here's my angle. I'm going to suck up to the professor. Hint that I could offer him free legal counsel." Olivia spoke quieter. "What about you guys?"

Calista didn't answer, still caught up in Olivia's phrasing. Burned down a lab? Please. They'd only had to replace the ceiling, no one had gotten hurt; and the most important part, the bit that they never mentioned, was that she'd improved their Bunsen burners. The chem lab's flames burned hotter and higher than any other within that cost range. Mechanical re-envisioning wasn't something Calista could explain, she'd learned that early on, so she had buried the urge to try.

This desk required only a simple repair and no fire. Minor welding would have helped by lengthening the metal, but she could imagine her classmates' faces if she fired up a torch. Hah. *And the dean thought she didn't consider consequences.* Calista added washers, steadied the wobbly leg, and bolted the end to the tabletop. After three more, she righted the desk and checked the top with the level. Excellent.

Vivien didn't answer Olivia either. "Back to what I was saying." Vivien spun her computer around so they could see a mermaid swimming on the display. "The Mer-bar is a Canadian club where women swim inside a two-story aquarium. Here's where the process gets murky. I can't tell if they lure men to them like sirens, or if men pick them out to buy them a drink like dating days of old."

"Hmm, misogyny under the water." Olivia straightened her legal pad and flipped the page. "Many potential lawsuits there. Tell me more."

"Misogyny?" Vivien tapped on her keyboard, making the image zoom out. "Depends on who's picking." She used a defensive tone and crossed her arms over her chest.

"Mer-MAID. It's a derogatory term about virgins." Now, Olivia sounded like a lawyer. Well, she always did, but when her tone grew lofty, Calista knew legalese was coming. "Maidens can only be virgins. They have scales from the waist down, ergo, they can't get their legs apart. We're promoting the myth that men want untouched women."

"Are you listening, Calista?" Vivien asked.

Calista smushed her lips together. Of course, she was, sort of. Why did people turn to her when the talk pivoted to virginity like her status was scrawled across her forehead by an industrial marker? All three of them had taken Dahlia's purity pledge, not just her. "Um hmm."

"Opinion?"

A tank which essentially held multiple human-sized fish. Where to start? "What's the tensile strength of the structure? It'd have to be see-through for the partner-selection aspect to work, no matter whether the men picked the women or the women picked the men. Glass? Some type of industrial plastic? Imagine the floor joists alone to hold that many gallons."

Neither Vivien nor Olivia responded. First, they prod her for her thoughts, and now they leave her hanging. Typical. Calista let them marinate on her ideas and bolted the seat back against the frame.

Artie didn't volunteer an opinion, and none of them prompted him for his thoughts. He was back seated in his chair, where he wound wires through a tube, while chewing on a large strip of his peppered beef jerky. The half of the meat strip that hung from his mouth bobbed, and his teeth made a scraping sound against the hardened beef.

Seat complete, Calista flattened one palm against the writing surface and the other against the seat-back. She tried to make the structure wobble. Nope, steady as titanium. She slid onto the chair like a normal student and took out her notebook. Now, she could brainstorm contributions for the class. Something she would have done already if she hadn't been distracted by replaying her meeting with Ronan in her head. She could focus.

Calista drew four squares on the page and connected them with arrows. The four of them needed to work together, share, interact, contribute, and present the project.

The fact that they were all solo workers had been brought to the attention of the dean. However, to make up for their supposed transgressions, and a lack of course credits that utilized groups, they'd complete a project under the supervision of Professor Terrence. Show the university that they could work as a group without imploding, then the university would stamp their seal upon their sheepskins. Hah, as if her having these guys in the room would have saved that lab's ceiling. She diagrammed four people fighting over one fire extinguisher.

"Calista." Vivien was staring at her over the top of her laptop, and she sounded impatient.

How did people chitchat and concentrate on their work at the same time? Ah well, she had other gifts. "Hmm?"

"Do you even want to know why I'm asking about the Mer-bar?" Vivien snickered, and the llama-eared hood of her jacket slipped over her brown eyes. "And they think I lack social skills."

Heat flushed Calista's face. Using herself as a barometer, it wouldn't take much to call anyone a social butterfly. She was an unashamed homebody, worker, and hockey-watcher. One hockey game had tens of thousands of people in the stands alongside her. Surely that counted as being incredibly social during hockey season. On average, that made her more social than most, but she truly wasn't tracking the hidden meaning behind Vivien's small talk, so maybe she had a smidge to learn.

"Calista," Vivien prompted.

Vivien was on about this as if the Mer-bar had personal meaning for her. Calista rolled her pen on her notebook. "Sorry, yes, big water tank and you don't know about the structure. Is this for a birthday rental?" Had they all forgotten Vivien's birthday? Heat flushed her face. She needed to set up a calendar that gave her an electrical shock, and not just a discreet notice, so she wouldn't hurt her class-mate's feelings when she got lost in her work. "Do you want me to calculate what size you'll need? Or how many gallons will fill a tank you've rented?"

Vivien turned away. She typed faster with her attention on her monitor. All they could see of her was the back of her hoodie, which had big llama eyes and a protruding pink llama tongue. "I don't need your calculations. I want you to ask me why I brought this up."

And give up the puzzle? Nope. That would be admitting defeat. Calista could do this. Was the answer less obvious? More of a segue into another topic? "You want to buy a fish tank? Saltwater or fresh? Buoyancy matters." Calista raised her legs to the top of her desk and leaned back, pleased to note the furniture remained steady. This relaxed, feet up position was superior for theta-wave producing brainstorming. "What kind of fish?"

"Did you or did you not, ask me to help with the Snowers ice hockey team?" Vivien spoke like she was giving her a clue.

Calista snapped upright and dropped her feet back to the floor as if the desktop had turned to slick ice. Her insides buzzing, she braced her sneakers on the linoleum, ready for something awesome. "This is about the Snowers?" Calista tried to portray a cool countenance, but she couldn't say the team's name without revealing her enthusiasm.

"Did you buy another professional ice hockey team that I'm not aware of?"

"No." Calista answered the question she knew had been rhetorical. Olivia and Vivien had both helped her with the onslaught of paperwork that had come with the contract to purchase Austin Snowers shares. Management of an organization required a head lawyer and a computer expert.

Plus, Calista trusted Vivien and Olivia. Not to get to the point evidently, but to ensure her investment ran smoothly. Hiring a great team was how she'd avoid any day-to-day demands. That's how Dad ran his auto shop. He paid well, offered his staff career growth, and they stayed. That allowed him to work on his exotic car obsession mostly undisturbed.

"You told me to work with Dahlia on organization requirements as needed." Vivien tilted her laptop and showed a picture of a frozen rink. The sound of ice cracking filled the room as the image shattered down the middle and the players ran through.

"Cool." Calista's heart beat harder at the sight of hockey images. "Dahlia actually has experience there. She worked in the front office before I accumulated the shares for the acquisition."

"Wasn't she fired?" Olivia chipped in the question, not to be snide, but lawyers liked clarity and didn't hide from difficult facts. "Just saying."

Sort of. "Not for performance." Dahlia had been let go because she'd stopped dating Dodo Applebaum, the former majority owner. That sounded bad, so Calista didn't share that part. Dahlia's dismissal last month didn't reflect her qualifications at all. Calista untangled the sentences in her mind. "Dahlia works there again, now." And Dahlia would remain in the head office if Calista kept control of the hockey team. If Calista failed with her bid for ownership,

Dahlia would likely have to leave again. Dahlia had lost enough—her man, her planned future, her job. Calista could get the last one back for her permanently. If Calista didn't screw up. The pressure mounted in her brain and her heart. She shoved the idea off; she could do this.

Calista owned seventy percent of the stock. The fact that she had majority stakes seemed mathematically clear to her. But the other shareholders, the Applebaums, were fighting the purchase, and no matter what, they still held thirty percent and a minority vote, unfortunately. Unless she could think of a way to get them to sell their shares.

"I set up internet alerts to chart the players' activities." Vivien spoke with careful, slow language, which implied Vivien may have searched forbidden websites. The unspoken word *hacked* hung in the classroom. "These alerts have given me privileged information."

Olivia drummed her fingers on the desktop. "Tell me everything, but only in terms of *what* you found, not *how* you found it."

"Friday night, at 10:00 PM, a number of Snowers players have passes for the Mer-bar." Vivien raised her arms to the sky. Her hood fell back, catching on one of the messy horns her dark brunette locks were styled into. She flattened her palms in the air as if she had completed an Olympic routine instead of taking half an hour to get to the point.

"Sirens, shots, and suckers? Sounds like a lawsuit ready to happen. Dahlia won't like that. Given her push for positive social media, she'll take away the players' purity points." Olivia's hazel eyes glinted as she processed all the potential pitfalls, but her voice held more relish than warning. "How are you going to make those rowdy men act right while out of the country? Are you going to cancel their admission to the Mer-bar? Is that what this is about?" Olivia tilted her head and her brown hair and swung against her collar. "Honestly, as long as the bar has adequate consent forms, the Snowers' organization won't have a problem, legally speaking."

Calista needed a third friend who knew P.R.

Vivien repeated her victory arm gesture. "Wrong, my herd." With one hand, she pointed to herself. With the other, she held up three fingers. "I got us tickets so we three can go to the Mer-bar and revel."

Oh. Calista shook her head. Nope, that was not her idea of a good time.

Vivien stared at her with a knowing expression, clearly ready for her refusal. "Let's just say one Captain Ronan Stromkin has a ticket."

Electricity shot through Calista, and she did her best not to flush, though she knew her eyes were widening and her mind was changing.

"We're going." Vivien hummed their purity pledge motto, "No wedding, no bedding."

Olivia rocked her shoulders to the rhythm and chanted the second verse of the purity pledge the three of them had all taken last autumn. "No gold band, we just hold hands."

Calista didn't love the third line, *I do, or we don't,*

so she simply chanted the final verse to show she was in on the plan. "No marry, no cherry."

"No marry. No cherry." Vivien said solemnly and held her computer so they could easily see the screen. A mermaid holding a large ticket faced them. A fishing net held by a buff fisherman hovered just above her head. "I've secured our entrance to the Mer-bar, Friday night, 10:00 PM. Pack a passport and a bikini, geniuses. Friday, we jump into the mermaid tank."

Her own ticket to the Mer-bar? A chance to see Ronan again. Calista smiled. This time, she'd form words in front of him. She'd articulate all that she had wanted to say back when she was near naked and mute back in the stadium conference room. Excitement rose inside Calista, and her grin evolved to giggles. Yes, redo, version two, clothed and articulate. Sign her up to take on the tank.

Olivia blinked and said nothing.

Silent was not Olivia's usual mode. What was she thinking? Probably, *international lawsuits begin with one ticket.*

Artie made furious marks in his scientific notebook.

A thousand questions tangled inside Calista's mind. She opened her mouth to talk bikinis and share her puck versus snowball costume adventure with her buddies.

The professor came in.

Calista shoved her comments back down. Dang. They'd just gotten their conversational flow going, and he'd interrupted them. They didn't need super-vision, oversight was stifling them.

The professor went to the head of the room, flipped open his laptop, and his name populated on the smartboard—Professor Terrence. He was a hand-some man with a lean build and overlong blond hair. Ah, she knew him. She hadn't realized her special project's Professor Terrence was Professor, *"call me Terry"* who she'd met at the Renaissance fair via Piper. Professor Terrence had been one of Piper's English professors.

Olivia and Vivien sat up straighter and exchanged a glance.

He was good looking. Sure, he was no Ronan Stromkin, but he was worth staring at. This class might not be so bad after all. Could he skate?

The professor nodded at them. "I'm Professor Terrence." His British accent came out clearly, as he said his name.

Calista and her two female classmates nodded back. Artie didn't look up from his wires.

"In the future, you will likely work for corpora-tions, interact in boardrooms, participate in trainings, and chat at water coolers. At minimum, in your future jobs, you'll be expected to share status updates. Proper English, social awareness, and solid communication skills matter. That's what we're building here. You will work together with minimal supervision and present a final project, which I will grade."

Despite the cool accent, he was boring her.

Couldn't he simply quote some Shakespeare at them? At least she could tune that out. Calista could see why Piper had never been into him when she was in his class. He had a jawline worth looking at, though. Not that genetically fortunate bone structure mattered.

Skill mattered, as did dedication and ambition, like how Ronan had been traded from a top Washington team to the underperforming Austin Snowers. Had that made him pause? Nope. Ronan had shifted into high gear and propelled the Snowers to the top of the league. For the first time in her life, her local team had a shot at the Cup all due to the leadership skills of one man, Ronan. Who was also very handsome and the total package. Sigh.

Professor Terrence pulled up their names on the board. "Let's start with Olivia Hammond, JD, LLM. Aiming to finish her Doctor of Juridical Sciences degree."

Olivia got to her feet and held out her arms in one of her lawyer stances. "Career choice is critical for everyone. One wrong move takes years to recover from, decades even. To that end, I researched the professors here to see how you all got to Sage Hill, this top tier university, in the great state of Texas."

Olivia wasn't kidding about sucking up. Calista herself didn't need to. Piper had aced Professor Terrence's class. She'd ask her sister for the inside scoop. Did he love regurgitated lectures or scholarly rebuttals? Piper would know. Her sister peopled well, and Piper would share her knowledge. Though if Professor Terrence brought in that communal water cooler he'd spoken of, that would not go down well. Olivia was finicky, and Artie was definitely the type who shoved his water bottle all over the spout, not that she'd seen him use a communal cooler. Ronan could lift a water cooler with one arm.

Professor Terrence straightened his posture.

"I did research also," Vivien jumped in. "In fact, I looked you up personally." Vivien lifted her laptop in both hands, so they understood she meant online. The mermaid on the screen opened her mouth and released an audible spray of bubbles. Vivien shoved the lid down. "I poked at the school's Human Resources database, but when I landed on the payroll platform, I backed out, realizing that looking would be..."

"Wrong?" Calista asked, realizing she needed conversation points too.

"Illegal?" Olivia suggested.

"Disheartening," Vivien said. "Teachers should make so much more money than they do."

Wow, thought she'd said she didn't look.

"Kissing-up was my idea," Olivia hissed in a whispered aside to Vivien.

Vivien shrugged. "Compared to what professional hockey players make..." Vivien whistled loud and low. "Professors should get food stamps."

Professor Terrence drew back in a British rejection-of-other-humans stance. "Your name?"

"Vivien Durand."

"Vivien Durand, who would like a bachelor's

degree in Computer Sciences from Sage Hill University, also the youngest of the group, I see. Thank you, Vivien. Moving on. Calista Amvehl, dual doctorates in mechanics and innovations, your turn to update the group, please."

CHAPTER 3

Hmm, Calista glanced at her open notebook with the four squares scrawled on page one. That drawing wouldn't impress him. The professor was there to guide them, so she'd share her background and see if he had any ideas. "According to most of my professors, my specialty is spotting problems and fixing them."

Artie popped his head up. His shaggy dark hair and wrinkled t-shirt were the opposite of the professor's pressed shirt, a vest, black slim-fit trousers, and carefully slicked hair. "Tell him about the desk." Artie jerked his body side to side, demonstrating a shaky platform.

Good one. Calista touched the edge of her desktop. "The leg wobbled when I first came in and sat down." She pointed to her tools on the floor. "No longer."

"You fixed a desk? And you want PhDs from Sage Hill?" Professor Terrence shook his head as if Calista wasn't understanding the class. "You all have a lot to learn from Arthur. He presented his robotics project idea via email before I even arrived."

Yeah? That didn't sound like teamwork.

Vivien pinched her lips together, and Olivia shot Artie an annoyed look.

Calista tilted her head, but when she saw her two friends staring at Artie, she realized his nickname was an abbreviation of his first name, Arthur, not an abbreviated form of his major in Artificial Intelligence. She didn't admit her ignorance, because social skills 101 had to be *learn a teammate's name*.

"A.I. is the future," Professor Terrence said, nodding approvingly at Artie. "Your choice of major is brilliant."

Olivia frowned. "One chair leg was definitely shorter than the others."

Artie jerked his body back and forth as if they hadn't understood his first demo. He gagged on his dried beef strip, coughed, and stopped moving. "Mermaids can't open their legs."

"Right." Professor Terrence wrinkled his brow, but half pretended not to hear Artie, and focused on Calista. "You're a prodigy, and you think you should get credit for fixing a wonky leg that could be steadied with a five p, cardboard pub coaster?" Professor Terrence shook his head. "Don't answer that." He held up his palms. "That's why we're here. We'll refine your ambitions."

Was that why she was here? The char marks on the lab ceiling flashed through Calista's mind.

Professor Terrence looked from Calista to the smartboard. "Amvehl?" He said her last name again. "Any relation to a Piper Amvehl?"

Did he not remember meeting Calista at the Renaissance fair? Their interaction had been brief, and men didn't typically remember her, not the way they did Piper. Sigh. Whatever. "Piper's my older sister." Calista made an invisible checkmark in the air. "She introduced me to you during the Tudor history scavenger hunt."

"Ah, yes." Professor Terrence's eyes gleamed. "What's Piper up to?"

Dating Mikah, Snowers offensive defenseman, number sixty-five, quickest on the ice. Living with him. Calista's heart wrenched. She missed Piper being around the house. Career-wise, Piper was eyeing PhD programs, and still loving Tudor England. Which part of that did Professor Terrence want to know? Calista opened her palms.

"Tell Piper I said hello, and to stay in touch." Professor Terrence moved to the door. "I understand it's early days, but as a group, you need to develop a clear project that you can successfully work on together, and most importantly, articulately summarize. Carry on." He left.

In his wake, silence hung in the room. Was being articulate the most important? She'd bet the next person who sat in this chair wouldn't care if she described the leveling process. They'd just be happy to be balanced. Calista checked the clock. They still had another hour to go. She could normally lose track of time when focusing on a project; a whole day could pass before she looked up. But she was feeling every minute of this two-hour communication lab. Calista drew another square on her notepad and wrote their full names inside. She could do this. "Didn't realize your name was Arthur." Calista offered the verbal branch to Artie. "What do you think is the best way to pass this class?"

Artie shrugged, lifted his tube of wires, his bag of jerky, and headed to the door.

Calista eyed the exit, wishing she was more of a rebel too, but she stayed put. "Why does Artie get to leave early?" Would telling on him help or hurt her score with Professor Terrence?

A group of Snowers dancers accompanied by Willow also had tickets for the Mer-bar tank at 10PM. Calista, Olivia, and Vivien had intentionally arrived late because Calista wanted to maintain her anonymity during this excursion unless she got to meet with Ronan. They hurried into the Mer-bar's dark interior. The change of going from freezing Canadian winter to the heated interior of the bar had them all yanking off their coats. Excited nerves jittered through Calista at this special opportunity. They were doing this.

The hostess, wearing a maple leaf-covered sarong over a red swimsuit, checked their tickets and showed them to the changing room, decorated in turquoise colors from the sparkling tiles to the locker-covered walls, and up to the ceiling. The décor made it feel as if they were in the aquarium already. Fun. She'd have to do something like this at the hockey stadium, like make a tunnel of ice for the fans to walk through.

For tonight, she and her friends had each worn their swimsuits under their street clothes so changing didn't take long. Calista wore a light blue sporty bikini, Vivien a white one piece with big strategically placed llama eyes, and Olivia a peach, high-cut tank-ini. They were ready to go.

Calista shoved her clothes and purse into a locker and rubbed her hands together. Ronan would be here tonight. She hadn't told anyone about her and Ronan's first encounter. She hadn't described their meeting in class because the professor interrupted. She might have done it on the flight up to Canada, but when she ran the replay in her head, she didn't think she came out that well. *He said you couldn't date...and what did you say?* She didn't want to explain that she had pretty much said nothing. Plus, there were no words to describe the tingles and sparkly sensations he'd caused. She touched her fingertips to her wrist. Her fingers failed to spark the same sunburst reaction.

Her friends put their things away too and moved over to the gear table. On a higher level, Calista knew she and her friends shouldn't be at the Mer-bar, at all; she knew that because she'd kept this trip secret from her cousin.

Dahlia was all about improving the team's reputation and nudging the guys to appeal to a family-friendly audience. Mer-bar parties would not qualify.

Plus, Calista intended to own the team, and frolicking inside a mermaid tank would not be a good look. On the other hand, if ever there was a time when she could attend a big social event for the players, unnoticed, this was her brief window. Before any huge official takeover confirmation occurred, this was her shot.

Not that there needed to be a huge dramatic announcement, an email would suffice. The didn't care who signed their checks. They only cared that funds filled their accounts. Dahlia had an MBA. She'd make sure everyone was paid. That had to be in MBA 101. Pay the people. No one cared about the name on the signature line. Calista shrugged on a harness holding a small oxygen tank and grabbed a pair of flippers.

Olivia eyed the scuba equipment and stepped from foot to foot. She didn't select anything.

A display rack would make the choice easier for her, one with three tiers. The chill seeped into Calista's bare feet. Maybe Olivia's feet were physically cold. Heated tiles would be a nice upgrade in here too.

Olivia shivered. "It's so decadent to be in a swimsuit in January."

"In Canada, maybe," Vivien said. "I've swum plenty of times in the winter back home in Austin." She looked at the exit. "I hope the aquarium's not too crowded."

Calista didn't care about crowding. Only one name on the tank list concerned her—Willow.

Willow had stolen Dahlia's man, and she'd done the same to Piper last Valentine's when Piper had been dating Dodo's brother Warren. While Calista was happy enough to have the Applebaum men cut from her family tree, she hated the disloyalty. Not just on the men's part, but on cheating Willow's too. Willow had been Dahlia's friend and sorority sister. Plus, Willow would know Calista, and that she shouldn't be here. This had been in the back of her mind since she scanned the attendee list back at the hotel. "Willow's here. What if she causes drama?"

Vivien grabbed a pair of goggles and spit on the lens. "Willow won't even recognize you."

"How can you say that?"

Smiling, Vivien circled her hand in front of Calista's face. "Mask, mouthpiece. Your whole face will be obscured." Vivien pointed to the mouthpiece and stared flat-eyed at her before holding the cleaned goggles in front of her eyes. "You need a breathing apparatus, because this place doesn't actually transform you into a mermaid. You know that, right?"

Hah. If she had a mermaid tail, she'd swish it. "I am tonight."

Olivia giggled.

"If they can't see our faces," Olivia rubbed her arms, "how are men even going to pick us?"

Vivien shrugged. "Their system must work. Sells out every weekend. I had to bump three people to get us on the list."

Oh. Calista did not need to know that.

The interior door, with the picture of a staircase painted on the front, opened. A platinum blonde Mer-bar hostess came in. She was dressed in a white swimsuit covered in red maple leaves, same Canadian theme as the ticket taker.

The hostess held the door open with her hip. Beyond that was darkness broken by a wavy, light blue glow. "They're ready for you. Have fun. And at any time, if you have any concerns, don't wait for a guy to scoop you out with a net. Just swim to the top." The hostess pinched her nose with one hand and waved her other arm in the air in case they didn't know the word swim. "Have fun."

Olivia widened her big hazel eyes and tapped her flippers against her palm. "Um, I thought there would be more instructions."

The hostess kept up her smile. "Instructions are on the website. You ticked the box that you read them when you bought your tickets."

Olivia's lawyer's stance was at odds with her beach-day appearance. "What you said about swimming to the top, I didn't plan on swimming. I thought there'd be a ladder, and I could hang out on the rungs."

"Nope. If you're not picked, you swim to the top. You three are gorgeous. You'll get scooped up." The hostess snapped her fingers, showing off her acrylic nails painted white with red leaves on top. "Like that." She leaned harder against the door, widening the opening.

Heck, yeah, water play and Ronan. Calista stepped forward.

Olivia wiggled her hands. "You see, technically, I can't actually swim."

Calista stopped and turned back to her friend. That should have come up before now. Like back at the classroom when they first heard about the bar, or on the plane, even at the hotel, or on the drive over.

The hostess's face twisted. "I'd have to check with my manager on that one."

"Eep." Vivien grimaced.

Calista swiped her hands one over the top of the other. "Just hang at the bar."

Olivia's shoulders sagged in relief. "Yeah, I'll do that." She dumped her flippers back on the table and headed to her locker.

"Your call." The hostess shrugged. "No refunds." She turned to Calista and Vivien. "The tank awaits."

Calista and Vivien stepped out of the room and onto the dark blue painted stairwell. Seashell wall sconces lit the way up the concrete stairs.

The hostess nodded. "The most important thing is to have fun. And don't mess with the fish."

Calista paused. "Fish?"

CHAPTER 4

Vivien stopped beside her and turned back to the Mer-bar hostess. "I have questions."

The hostess giggled. "Our sea creatures have their own two-story swim tube inside the tank, separate from you girls. They can't get to you, but that doesn't mean they want their habitat riled. But don't worry, they're totally sealed off. You two just have fun."

"What marine life is in there?" Vivien's brown eyes sharpened. "Vertebrates? Invertebrates? Bony fish, jawless fish, cartilaginous fish? The online consent form said nothing about swimming with sharks, or eels, or…"

The hostess shrugged. "It's just fish."

Thinking about the exchange, Calista had questions too, mostly about stability and the material strength of the fish container tube. She resisted voicing them. Except… "How do you feed the sea creatures if they're totally sealed off?"

The hostess's chipper smile dimmed. Not the first

time Calista had seen that impatient expression. She thought Vivien's questions were worse.

The hostess curved and lifted her hand as if raising an airplane window shade. "We open their hatch when there aren't swimmers in the tank. They roam, clean the water, and eat their dinner."

More questions bubbled to Calista's mind. The hostess wouldn't be that annoyed, curiosity was healthy. "How do you get them back in the tube?"

The hostess stepped back until she held the doorway with the tips of her fingers. "That's all the time I have down here, I have to escort the first group of fishermen to their fishing pier now. If you want in the tank..." She pointed to the flight of stairs with her free hand, "You'll run up those steps, and dive in."

Calista opened her mouth to ask the names of the fisherman in the first group, but the hostess released her hold, and the door swung shut, closing off their view of the locker room.

"Good luck you two." Olivia yelled from the other side.

Calista climbed the first step. "Not as informative as I would have liked."

"Agreed." Vivien trailed her, thumping her flippers against her thigh as she climbed.

As they reached the halfway landing, muted musical beats became audible, and portholes appeared. The round windows provided brighter light and a view of the tank. The aquarium was a semicircle that faced the bar and backed up against the wall where they stood. The two-story tank was exactly like the pictures online, except for no mermaids. Rocks covered the aquarium floor, and human-sized fish toys were spaced throughout: a rock archway to swim through, wavy green plants, a clam, and a treasure chest against the back wall.

There were fish in the central tube as promised, vibrant, multi-colored, constantly moving, and contained.

Looking through the tank, a rounded front wall revealed the club. The first floor held customers rocking out on a dance floor. Pulsing, circular blue lights floated around their bodies as if the customers were amid bubbles. The second level held booths with people having drinks, while the same blue lights bounced around them as if they were all in the aquarium together.

Interesting.

Calista continued to climb, and the echoes of giggling feminine shrieks came from above accompanied by loud splashes.

Vivien rubbed her arms. "That must be the group ahead of us going in."

Calista nodded. They continued on and reached the top. The last step transitioned to a square platform with a waist-high half-wall. The only visible worker, a man wearing a white t-shirt and red swim shorts, was leaning over the top, staring at the women in the water. "Welcome to the tank," he said, without looking away from the dancers. Beside him, a stack of fishing nets on extendable poles were propped against the wall. The rods were twelve feet in length and each ended with a wide webbed net, big enough to scoop up a human.

Calista wiggled. Wild mermaid adventure ahead.

The concept was self-explanatory, go over the ledge and into the water before the guests, who'd bought fishing tickets, climbed up from the bar area and fished for a mermaid. Calista leaned over the wall, and the plastic faux wood edge pressed into her waist as she looked down.

Inside the depths, ten or so Snowers' dancers, wearing puck bikinis, helped each other reach the rocky floor. Once the last one landed, they went into an underwater version of their daytime dance routine with synchronized shimmies and high kicks. On the other side of the glass, onlookers stared in at them.

Vivien fiddled with her oxygen tube. "That's a lot of eyeballs. And I don't just mean the fish."

"No marry, no cherry," Calista said, though the words didn't really fit the moment.

A blue and yellow striped slim fish swam to the top of the central tube and opened its snout revealing rows of pointy teeth. He took a gulp of air and circled the top lazily.

Vivien shook her head. "Nope, I'm out."

"Oh." Calista wavered and looked down at the tank again.

Beyond the glass, club guests turned to stare at a group of physically stunning men coming into the bar. The Snowers ice hockey players had arrived.

Calista caught her breath, but she was only

looking for one. Ronan. There. His build was unmistakable even through the distortion of water and distance. Her heart picked up, beating hard in time with the pumping pulse of the music. She slipped flippers on her feet and climbed atop of the ledge. Kneeling there, the rough plastic bit into her knees and the water in front of her bubbled.

"Wow. Go for it, aqua woman, you do you." Vivien backed toward the host and removed the harness holding her oxygen tank. She offloaded the O2 and set her flippers by the worker. He didn't look up. "I'll find Olivia." Vivien saluted her. "See you back at the hotel."

Calista nodded and waved. She put her mouthpiece in and dove forward into the cool Canadian Mer-bar water.

CHAPTER 5

The water closed over Calista as she dove deeper into the mermaid tank, initially chilly, but warming once she acclimated. Keeping her body in a straight line, she used her arms to push against the current. Here, the full silence of being underwater replaced all the club noise. Her senses narrowed to the pull of her muscles, water flowing over her skin, and her loose hair that touched her arms. She swam toward the back, down one story, then two. She did a lazy flip and slowed, hanging above the rocky tank floor.

This was really cool. Despite her bravado, Calista didn't move to the front glass wall. She was here and that was enough. Calista swam to the treasure chest and climbed on top of the coins. From there, she kicked her flipper-clad feet back and forth and took in the scene distorted by the goggles and water.

The Snowers' dancers performed hip thrusts to the awe of the onlookers shoved against the glass wall. She couldn't see Ronan from this angle, but most of the guys standing in the closeup viewing area were players. The previous guests must have ceded room for them. Canadians were hockey fans, made sense. The players she'd already met personally stuck out first:

Saxon Etterwahl, twenty-two years old rookie, 6'3", jersey number eighty-three. Position sniper, still finding his way, but he showed great promise. His eyes were as large as the fishes as he took in the dancers' antics.

Kiernan Kelchier, twenty-six years old from Boston, 6'1", jersey number thirty-six, playmaker. Unexpected moves, and crowds loved him. He winked at one woman while nodding to another, and waving at a third. Piper said containing him would be like wrapping a present with glitter paper and trying to not get any sparkles on her hands.

Liam Velhausen, twenty-six, 6'2", jersey number fourteen, Canadian, nice. He was pointing at various spots on the glass, high then low. From this viewpoint, Calista couldn't tell whether the women or the fish had his attention the most. Goal tenders were like that, alert to everything.

Calista didn't know what her exact agenda was. Sometimes diving in without a plan could result in incredible innovations, other times, it left her feeling awkward. She put the fake coin down and picked up one of the prop gemstones, a pearl the size of a beach ball. She weighed the orb in her palms. The opalescent surface shined under the water.

This would look even better inside the giant fake

clam over there. Did the shells close? She could climb between the top and bottom shells and be a totally incognito creature in there, peeping out at everyone; or that might draw attention. What was that painting? Aphrodite on the half shell? That would be her, hah. Nah. The stunning dancers drew all the guys, not her.

Being on the treasure chest was a great spot. She had a clear view of the fish. They swam down and nosed the seal over their release hatch. What time did they get freed tonight? The zebra fish looked especially hungry.

As long as Calista kept her gaze on the fish or over the heads of the dancers, she was good. If her eyes dropped, she caught a view of entirely too much of the dancers' underwater backsides. Their thong-wearing bottoms were topped by a black puck. The look was not working for her. Guess she did have an opinion on the dancers' costumes after all. She shouldn't have doubted Dahlia, those suits needed to be replaced.

The water current wound her hair over her upper arm. Calista brushed the strands back. She should have gone with a braid like the long-haired dancers had done.

Only one dancer had short hair. Her razored pixie cut spiked up in the water as if she wore a spiny black sea urchin on her scalp. Not a dancer, Willow, big cheat.

As if Calista had telegraphed her judgement through the waves, Willow pivoted, bent her knees to her puck-covered chest, and scanned the tank by moving her head left to right. She stilled. Her gaze locked onto Calista.

Willow shoved her hands forward and kicked into a horizontal swim position. With sharp strokes, she headed toward the back of the tank. The cheat came to a stop in front of the fish tube, blocking Calista's view of the exit hatch. Willow planted her feet and threw her arms out straight, like a starfish. After Willow steadied herself, she flipped her hand over, holding out her palm and widening her fingers. She rolled them in a circular motion, indicating she wanted the faux pearl gem that Calista held in her palms.

Willow craved what didn't belong to her. Shocker.

Calista's heart punched in anger about far more than the faux pearl. This woman had hurt Piper, then, not learning from her mistake, she'd hurt Dahlia. Calista kept her breathing steady, pulling in the correct amount of oxygen.

Willow deserved to be denied what she wanted for once. Calista tightened her grip on the smooth gem and shook her head.

Willow reached over and snatched the pearl away.

Calista's empty hands drifted to her sides. WTH. Her muscles tensed to rise, and Calista forced herself to maintain composure, because no one needed a scene. Calista bit her teeth into the rubber of her mouthpiece and resisted the urge to take the pearl back. The crowd near the glass wasn't only hockey players but other partiers too; neither her sister nor her cousin would thank her for causing a public spectacle. She was a lady. She made her posture relax like she didn't care.

Willow spun back toward the front, floated her legs out behind her, and mermaid kicked her way to the center of the dance line. Once in place, she shook the pearl over her head like she had won the Stanley Cup. She followed that with a pirouette. The movement and pearly glow drew extra attention her way.

This was not Calista's scene; she should go. Calista rose.

A movement in the crowd caught her attention— Ronan. He shifted away from his group and followed the glass tank around to the side. He walked, while looking her way, until the wall stopped him from going any further. He was mere feet away. All that colossal manliness right there.

Calista's heart fluttered like the blades on the faux fern that brushed against the glass. She swam forward and waved.

Ronan flattened his palm on the wall. Calista swam to him as if he was reeling her in. She fitted her hand against his with only the thick, smooth glass between them. His hand was so much larger than hers, no wonder he had stellar control of his hockey stick. What a man. And the best part of this moment? She could stand here in silence because her oxygen tank mouthpiece didn't allow speech, and it didn't matter that she didn't have the right thing to say. Score.

The bad thing about being voiceless was that she actually had things she wanted to say to him. She wanted to express her admiration over how he'd dug deep at the last game and coordinated the effort for a win. She wanted to hear about how he grew up, who coached him, and how he excelled in so many aspects of the game. He had speed, charisma, and control. He was a wonder to watch, perfection. An underrated player who was about to breakout big, but for now, only she seemed to recognize that Ronan would become one of the greatest who ever played. She shivered and pressed her fingers harder against the glass.

Ronan grinned, showing a nice smile and a sparkle in his blue eyes.

He must sense her appreciation for him; he was spot on. He was extraordinary. She tapped her fingers on the tank wall as if she could convey her admiration in morse code.

Ronan pointed to his chest, then up, and arched his eyebrows.

Calista looked up.

He was indicating the fishing pier.

Oh, this was that moment. Ronan wanted to scoop her out of the mermaid tank and talk too. She nodded enthusiastically, gave him two thumbs up, and kicked her flippers back with her legs together in a mermaid emoji pose.

Ronan winked, made a fishing reel motion, and left her. He walked back around to where his fellow players stood. He tapped on the shoulder of a few of the men and pointed to a doorway, then he disappeared from view.

Calista kept her gaze upward. Minutes later, Ronan was at the top of the pier, accompanied by Dodo, Liam, and Kiernan. Kiernan went right to the edge. He held his left hand out with his fingers curled inwards around an imaginary rod, and with his right hand he made forward circles, as if he were manning an imaginary reel. He bucked his body back and forth as if deep-sea fishing against a fierce swordfish. Liam clapped him on his shoulder in encouragement and shared humor.

While those two hovered at the ledge, Ronan disappeared from view and returned with real fishing nets. He handed them out to each of the men, and the four of them lined up at the pier. Not hesitating, Ronan lifted his pole up and over the edge. The end lowered into the water, then Ronan maneuvered the net in Calista's direction.

CHAPTER 6

Calista waited patiently for Ronan's net to reach her. A few of the dancers saw what was happening and looked over. Several rocked their hands as if they held pompoms and were cheering her on. Cute, their friendly gestures made her smile around her mouthpiece; they definitely deserved better costumes.

Willow, who'd been spinning with her pearl prize, paused. She clutched the gem to her chest, floated her body forward, and mermaid kicked with her legs together. She was heading to the back of the tank again.

Great, have all the jewels and the coins. Calista was abandoning her treasure to the women remaining with only goodwill toward them.

Willow stopped in front of Calista; she tucked the pearl against her side, pointed to herself with her free hand, and made a number one sign.

What did that mean?

Willow jabbed her index finger toward the surface.

Did Willow want out of the tank? All she had to do was swim up. Calista waved her hand upwards like *have at it*.

Willow pointed to her chest, made a hashtag with her fingers, and a number one again.

Ah, got it, Willow wanted to be the first scooped out of the tank. Dodo was up there. He could fish for Willow. No way he'd beat Ronan in any athletic competition though, even fishing. Willow would have to take Dodo's tardiness up with him directly, another Applebaum failure. Calista was not getting in the middle of their super healthy dynamic. She had her own ride to take. She shrugged.

The net was almost here. Giddiness rocked her body. All the times she'd tried and missed out on having time with Ronan, here was her opportunity. Ronan extended the pole far enough that the end waited in front of her waist.

Eagerness spun through Calista, but oddly so did the purity pledge. Make him work for it.

Calista hopped to the side.

The net followed her with a flatteringly smooth swish.

Okay, that was enough playing hard to get. Calista drew in a deep draw of oxygen, filling her lungs, and clasped the sides of the net. She twisted her body and hopped in. The coarse mesh of the small round hammock bit into her skin, but the sensation wasn't uncomfortable, and to her own credit, the maneuver had been performed with a touch of grace. Success.

Ronan lifted the pole, and she began rising. Calista was moments away from actually getting to speak with him. Her heart rate increased. Yes, netted by Ronan. She hoped Vivien was still here and catching this on camera, because she'd make the video her screen saver. Calista gave a quick two pumps in the air imitating Vivien's favorite celebratory motion.

Willow swam, keeping level with Calista, and made the number one sign again. Willow pointed at Calista and arched her hand palm to back, over and over, indicating Calista should jump out of the fishing net.

Annoying. Calista shook her head. She couldn't help herself; moving slowly, using both hands, Calista made a hashtag with her first two fingers, and then a number one with her index finger. Calista turned her finger inwards and pointed to her own chest.

Willow reached out and latched onto Calista's wrist with one slim, cold hand. With her other, she shoved the pearl behind Calista, dislodging her position. Simultaneously, Willow kicked her petite legs up and pushed against the underside of the net. A pinched wrist, hard flippers against her back, then the three-pronged approach forced Calista out of the mesh basket. Willow immediately released her, and

Calista drifted toward the rocky bottom. What was happening?

Above her, Willow situated her narrow butt into the net, and threw the pearl down in the direction of Calista's head. The currents slowed the white orb, and Calista dodged the round gem, moving easily in the water. She put her hands on her hips and looked up, no clue what to do now, and too surprised to even be fully angry.

Willow hung in place as if Ronan had stopped lifting the pole. On the pier above them, the guys were all laughing, except Ronan. Ronan dropped the pole back into the water, extending the length, lowering Willow until her flippers touched the rocky aquarium bottom. He'd given her back to the tank. Willow was now within a foot of Calista but still sitting in the net.

Calista reassessed the situation.

Willow wasn't dealing with sweet Piper or delicate Dahlia. Just the thought of how Willow had done her family wrong gave Calista the strength to move. Calista swam up to Willow, grabbed Willow's arm, and jerked her from her perch.

Willow came forward, but the rope basket did too, because the puck at the backside of her bikini had gone through the netting like a button through a hole. The basket inverted, holding Willow in place by the backside of her puck swimsuit. Willow hung there, arms and legs out, paddling just above the rocks, but going nowhere, like a crab being lifted from the water.

Hmm, without her tools, Calista couldn't cut the ropes and free Willow. Not unless Willow wanted to remove her bikini bottoms, which was almost happening now, and Calista didn't want to see that.

Ah well, Willow had won this round, or her costume had. Calista pressed her lips against the mouthpiece and held out her arms, palms up. Fine, go up first, Willow.

Calista would follow. If the guys were allowed a second catch, Ronan could fish for her again. If the men only got one turn, would one of the other guys give her a lift up? Or would they go after their own prizes? She didn't have enough information to know, and she didn't want to be uncaught, unchosen, or unwanted, the tuna left behind. Her battered ego shuddered.

Willow reached backward, got hold of the frame, and got back inside the net. She swiveled to get comfortable.

Calista backed away.

Willow made another number one sign and scrunched up her petite frame so she could fold her bent knees inside the hammock and tuck her red-painted toenails into the webbing. She was going nowhere.

Guess Willow would be chatting with Ronan on the platform first.

Ronan had his trophy fish, though he'd netted the wrong class.

No.

Calista was not cool with giving up and had a

narrow window to talk to Ronan. This was her shot, not Willow's. Calista kicked upwards, out of reach of Willow's short arms, and grabbed onto the stick. The pole jerked with the weight of two women and angled down.

Ronan began lifting, and the weak aluminum bent with their combined weight, like a straw lifting two heavy lemon wedges from a glass.

Willow waved her hand at her in a jerky motion, indicating Calista should let go.

Hah.

Calista could, that would be the gracious move. Like when some late attendee at the yoga studio shoved her mat right against Calista's, and Mom had her scoot over to make room, but this wasn't a Zen moment. Her pulse was amping up, not mellowing. Calista narrowed her focus on the problem. She hadn't even begun to use her advantages, two of which were tenacity and a knowledge of mechanics.

Calista ran her palm along the metal pole until she felt the ridge where the extension fit inside the base. Tapping her fingers along the top, she found the white button that connected one end of the pole to another, the same as on her pool cleaning equipment. She pressed down. Nothing happened at first, and then the bottom of the pole holding the basket loosened, disconnected, and sank, carrying Willow to the seabed.

Satisfaction floated through her as a small piece of her world righted. Calista clutched the net-free pole, and Ronan lifted her. She was going upwards at a smoother pace now. She let Ronan do the work, her shoulders relaxed, and breathing calmed.

Willow gained her flippered feet, the net stuck to her backside. Fists clenched, Willow looked up and around, and then at the fish tube. Willow moved there, ran her hands against the side, hit the feeding hatch, and jumped back.

What was Willow doing? Calista tightened her grip.

The newly released fish swarmed into the water, circling Willow's body, and then darted outwards. The multi-colored sea creatures filled the lower tank in an instant. Their speed and momentum were relative to their sizes and ability to wiggle.

No. Calista shook her head, and revulsion jolted through her.

The dancers, who had been high kicking in a chorus line, stopped and formed a protective group huddle.

Calista couldn't stop swiveling her head. So many fish. This was the oddest moment of her life. More surreal than when her financial advisor had told her there were Snowers' shares for sale, and she had put in a buy order.

The water swished over her with increased agitation. Calista paddled with her free arm and kicked. *Please pull faster.*

Willow swatted at the water and backed up to the glass wall, her movements jerky and angry. She reached behind her and struggled to detach the net from her backside, looking like an awkward tennis player.

Customers surged forward to peer into the tank, camera's high. Willow's efforts were comical and despite all the fish, and an urge to get out of the tank, Calista's lips were twitching.

Above, Ronan was still reeling her up, and the guys beside him had the freedom to laugh. Liam had his hand over his mouth, his shoulders rocking. Kiernan was pointing and leaning so far over the side, he was in danger of falling in. Around her, colorful fish swam near and too close, ending her humor. She wanted out, and kicked harder, straining her muscles to move.

The worker, leaning over the tank, shook his head and waved his arms upwards, signaling everyone inside the tank to swim up and get out.

All the dancers were kicking their flippers, heading to the surface. With their strong legs, they were fast. The whole crew reached the top just as Calista did, their hands, arms, then heads broke clear of the water. The dry, chilled air hit Calista's skin. Around her, there was a mad scramble by the dancers to climb out of the fish-full water. The men at the top were using both arms to pull the women from the tank.

Ronan focused on Calista. He braced the pole against the pier and reached down, gripping her upper arms. With his big, firm hands, he lifted her out of the water and settled her onto the thick railing.

Cold air fully washed over her, and Calista

grabbed the rough ledge. She swung her flippered feet around, so her back was to the water, and she faced Ronan. With his supportive hand on her elbow, Calista scrambled over the ledge and upright.

Chills wracked her body. The music from the club boomed through the air. Above that came the high soprano screeches of the dancers' exclamations. They were all shoved together on a platform too small for this many people. Calista wanted to strip her goggles which were fogging up and take out her mouthpiece like the others were doing, but she didn't want to reveal her identity in the middle of a crowd like this.

Dang it, Calista had wanted to speak with Ronan, but not in front of everyone. She kicked off her flippers.

"Hi, I'm Ronan," Ronan said in a deep voice.

Pleasure flashed through her and Calista reached for her mouthpiece, but the crowd, the noise, and the situation stole her words, and she dropped her hand. Before Calista could think of a way to ask to speak with Ronan privately, a dancer shifted and bumped the pole, causing the end to clatter, and the side shoved into Calista's hip. Ronan released her to move the equipment to the wall.

Good thinking, a multi-million-dollar player tripping because fishing gear was left out would not look great on her ownership bid. The best thing to do was get out of here.

The worker raised a large canister. "Take a scoop of their feed and toss the pellets in. Watch your hands if you want to keep your fingers."

Nope, but great distraction. This was her break. Heart pounding, Calista jetted to the exit.

Downstairs, Calista did a quick shower and an even faster change of clothes. She was escaping while she still had her anonymity.

CHAPTER 7

Ronan waited for the pretty dancer outside the women's dressing room. He dropped his head back against the wall and shoved his hands into his pockets. The Snowers paid him millions to keep his eye on a three-inch puck going a hundred miles an hour across the ice. He rarely failed. Yet, here, he'd lost a whole freaking human. He'd turned away for half a second and the lovely blonde disappeared. Women usually waited for him, but his intriguing mermaid hadn't.

Sure, she'd been a touch red-faced at the fish free-for-all, but she hadn't had to leave the pier without him. The chase was stirring, but Ronan wanted to let her know he wasn't that man, only wanting the unattainable. He was a stable guy who wanted a loving partner and a traditional home life. Didn't most women like that?

He'd been thinking about his blonde since meeting her in the conference room. His body warmed at the heated images. He'd made a mistake that day too, treating her like she worked in the front office and was untouchable. She was a dancer. He could work their dating out with a simple HR disclosure. If the relationship failed, he wouldn't be traded to a team across the country. He had to get out of his own way and not let his past smash this opportunity.

The door to the dressing room opened, and the blonde backed out. Ronan's heart tripped like when he was a rookie, and he'd taken the ice at his first professional game. That sensation had been a mix of excitement, passion, and anxiety. He'd never had a meeting with a woman to rival it.

First, he saw her fan jersey, with his name on the shoulders, nice. His lips curled up. Ronan liked women who knew their own minds.

Next came a hint of her vanilla shampoo from her golden wet hair. He breathed in. Sight, smell, what other senses would she delight before the night was over? His body tightened like he'd never been this close to a woman. Wow, he had it bad. She'd gotten under his skin with her unusual combination of being extremely forward and unexpectedly evasive.

She was turning his way now. Each of her movements drove his pulse higher. Her creamy skin was flushed pink. He wanted to be the cause of her glow. She was like a female version of his favorite ice cream held out of reach on a hot Texas afternoon. Come closer.

The dance beats thrummed through him. *Get her*

to leave with him. Stop, he had discipline, he could work this right. *Get her name. Get her number.*

She stopped. The door swung shut behind her. "Hi." Her face pinkened further, and her light green eyes sparkled. She tugged her wet hair from the neckline of her jersey and smoothed the wet strands.

"Why, it's *my catch.*" Ronan said, as if he were surprised to see her there, though it was obvious to them both that he'd been waiting for her.

She grinned, and the curve of her pretty lips showed a hint of her white teeth. "Sort of."

True, she'd caught him more than he'd netted her. He wanted those lips and teeth on him tonight. Would he get that chance? Ronan took his hands from his pockets and loosened his stance. "What happens now?"

"You're asking me?" Her voice squeaked on the last word. "I've never been here before."

Sure, that's cool, he had this. "I wanted to get your name, get your number, and give you mine, if you're interested?" He knew she was.

His mermaid rattled off her digits with flattering speed.

Adorable. Ronan couldn't help smiling. He took out his phone and sent her a quick text of a fishing pole emoji so she'd have his number. She grabbed her phone, checked the screen, and giggled, her tone melodic, surprised, and sincere. Ronan wanted to run his thumb over the curve of her bottom lip and touch the sound; instead, he hit enter to add her to his contacts with a mermaid emoji. He needed her name.

Kiernan popped over from down the hallway, his mischievous teal eyes bright and locked onto the mermaid. "Hey, Cal-pal."

She shook her head at the nickname.

Ronan's chest tightened. "You know each other?" Ronan kept the question on an even note. Past was past, but he didn't love the eager glint in Kiernan's eyes. That boded trouble on and off the ice.

Kiernan looked at him like he was an idiot.

Ronan's shoulders tensed.

Kiernan shifted his gaze back to the gorgeous blonde. "Cal-fish?" Kiernan kept trying with the nicknames.

Women found that crap charming. Ronan wasn't a woman. He breathed in deep. She was *his* catch.

His mermaid pursed her lips and shrugged. "Just Calista." Her voice was quiet.

Kiernan raised his hand and snapped his fingers. "Cal-owner?"

CHAPTER 8

Hockey news slammed through Ronan's brain at the unusual name. *Calista? Calista Amvehl? Possible new owner of the Snowers?* She'd bought a ton of shares in one unexpected bulk purchase, and now the lawyers were getting rich sorting out the mess of terms. Ronan's heart thumped against his chest in a bad rhythm. No, he had to be wrong.

He wasn't.

His blonde dancer was an illusion. Calista Amvehl was the epitome of front office. The one beer he'd drunk lurched through his gut. His body urged him to back away as if he were being shoved toward the penalty box by two refs.

The dressing room door opened again. Despite his mistake, Ronan took Calista's elbow and tugged her clear of the swinging door, and Calista came straight to him with zero resistance. Ignoring the soft feel of Calista's skin that urged him to curl his fingers inwards, Ronan dropped her arm.

Behind her, Dodo's girlfriend, Willow, exited the dressing room. Willow wore a dancer's puck costume though she wasn't a dancer, and tank water dripped from her lean body. She was Dodo Donovan's woman and a perfect example of the troubles that came with mixing business with pleasure. She was one of those women who liked to stir up problems where there were none. Give her this pond of drama and who knew what mess she'd twist up.

Willow eyed the three of them standing there in the dressing room corridor. "Calista." Willow sounded neutral. Her gaze took in Calista's wet hair, and she put her hands on her hips. "Who sent you? Dahlia or Piper?" Her voice hardened on the other women's names.

"Neither." Calista shifted from one sneaker to another and hugged her coat to her chest, concealing his number.

Calista's answer didn't reveal her end game. Why was she here at all? Was she currying favor? Getting off on sneaking around? Getting off on players? Oh shit. Ronan's heart stopped. He needed exactly none of this. The front office could keep their fuss. Ronan's career was on an upward trajectory, one that was about to get him traded back home to Washington. This was exactly the wrong kind of heat to throw onto his life.

"Just checking things out." Calista's answer was lame, but her voice was lovely.

Willow looked between her and the two men. "I suppose that makes sense. Anyone can come to these things, they're not exclusive. We're all here to increase the fanbase." She laughed. "Unless you're here to put forth one of Dahlia's silly purity initiatives?" Her voice was full-on mocking.

Calista's shoulders edged up. "Dahlia did ask me to check on the dancers' new costumes." She paused. "I agree with her, they don't work."

Willow's dark eyes flared. "And you think you get an opinion, why?"

Hidden layer woman jabs were flying, and Ronan just wanted away from the drama; whereas Kiernan looked amused, like he couldn't wait for the catfight to escalate.

Even back here, away from the main club, they were drawing attention. Two brunettes, nice-looking, but not dressed for the club scene or as hockey fans, joined them. One wore a wool suit with a high neck blouse underneath. She'd buttoned her rounded collar all the way up to her chin and had a sharp critical look in her eyes. The other he'd describe as quirky with her llama jacket over jeans. Neither was his type.

The llama-chick bounced up to Calista. "Found you." She eyed Kiernan up and down. "Met you in Vegas."

Calista turned to her friends. "This is Ronan." Calista looked up at him and gestured first to the llama-wearer. "This is my friend, Vivien. She works with computers." She pointed to the other woman. "Olivia, friend and attorney."

Ronan hated how much he loved the sound of his

name on Calista's lips. She spoke like he was *her* favorite flavor of ice cream. He ran his hand through his hair. *He was not doing this.* He'd nod in greeting and jet out of there.

Willow put her hands on her hips and stepped forward, although the radius was already tight. "In case you forgot my name, I'm Willow." She was pointing out that Calista hadn't introduced her.

Vivien jerked her thumb toward the aquarium. "What a sea creature swamp. That was something."

Had to agree with her there. Fishing on the Sound was one thing, here at a club, pulling up a mermaid that turned into a human-sized mistake—traumatizing. If Calista had ruined fishing for him, he'd be pissed, more pissed. Ronan controlled his breathing; he'd leave and not think of her again. He'd think of Washington, of going home.

His former GM had been reaching out more frequently. His stats were there and enough time had gone that Washington could ignore his past front office mistake. He couldn't screw up now, not again, and definitely not in the same way by dating a woman in management.

"Great to meet two fans." Willow gestured to Olivia and Vivien, and then turned back to Calista. Willow cupped her hands around the pucks concealing her boobs. "But I'm not one to be so easily distracted. These costumes are garnering zillions of likes on my social media."

Vivien made a thumbs down.

Olivia touched her rounded collar. "They're too on the nose."

Willow tensed as the women didn't shy away from disagreeing with her. Her gaze scanned the way the two were dressed. "You're not exactly our target audience." Willow huffed out a laugh and waved a dismissive hand at the trio. "Fashionably awkward, party of three."

Huh.

Willow pointed at Calista. "I will be talking to Dodo about this."

Vivien raised and lowered her hoodie's zipper, flashing glimpses of a white one-piece swimsuit. "Calista is the owner, not Dodo Applebaum."

Calista held up her palms in a slowdown motion.

Willow rolled her eyes. "Is she? Dodo explained how that was all a paperwork mix up, easily correctable."

Ronan strongly hoped so. Not that any of this mattered, Calista wasn't for him. He had no opinion on management fiascos, his mind was already on catching a cab back to the hotel.

Olivia's eyes narrowed. "As Calista's head attorney, I beg to differ."

Willow's bravado faded a touch. "We'll see."

Why was he still standing here? He had the discipline to stay away from Calista and her games. Ronan edged around them. "Excuse me." He left.

❄

The evening had been so bizarre. While climbing into her hotel room bed, Calista's phone rang with an incoming video call from Dahlia.

"Can we talk?" Dahlia used her soft voice.

Calista flinched as the worst question known to humankind came her way. Calista made a noncommittal noise, stacked the pillows how she liked them, and untucked the top sheet from under the mattress. She propped the phone up so her cousin's lively face appeared face level. Even at this hour, Dahlia was put together, her hair in a sleek high pony, tied with a ribbon that matched her long-sleeved, peachy-pink pajama top.

Dahlia continued without her fully agreeing. "My team news alert says, *'New Owner Pulls Plug on Fishy Fan Adventure.'* Something about you yanking the dancers from an aquarium?"

"Not true." Calista shoved at her messy, still damp hair as it was giving away her adventure and filled her cousin in on her activities at the Mer-bar.

Dahlia opened and closed her mouth through the retelling, and when Calista was done, she grinned big. "Let me focus on the important part. You're saying, new dancer costumes are in order?"

The dancers and fans deserved better. Calista nodded. "One hundred percent."

Dahlia clenched her fists and made a happy clicking sound, like a parakeet who'd just found new seed spread around her newspaper. "You will not regret this. I'll have mockups ordered by the end of the week."

❄

Back in Texas, Calista sat curled into her favorite stadium seat, breathing in the cold from the ice, and darted her gaze around the rink. Watching the Snowers run practice drills was amazing. Her body thrilled at the action, and her mind emptied of the trillion thoughts racing through her neurons. Without the clash of the sticks and swish of blades on the ice to clear her busy mind, she'd explode. Nothing compared. Having seen the Snowers play had been everything growing up, taking her from high strung kid to almost normal. Now she got to watch ice hockey several times a week, in person, which made her relaxed and happy. Add in the thrill of seeing Ronan, whew.

The players huddled in their end-of-practice rundown with Coach. This was the best. Mood both soothed and elated, Calista rose to her feet and grabbed her backpack to leave for campus.

Dodo Applebaum came down the stadium aisle toward her.

Drat, she'd lingered too long.

CHAPTER 9

"There you are." Dodo's hearty, good-old-boy voice suited his clothing choice of starched button-down shirt and creased khaki trousers. "I heard that you watch the games from here sometimes."

Calista had season tickets and saw all the games from here. She didn't say so though. Guess she didn't need to buy season tickets anymore, but she did like these particular seats. Seating improvements would be a good use of money and would help ensure all the fans had a great experience. They could make family zones with room for kids to squirm about and add in big recliners. Calista mentally added these to a list to toss to her cousin for follow up.

Dodo hooked his thumbs into his belt loops. "Wanted to pass along the rundown on some things that need doing. Thought you could handle them, because Dahlia always goes on about her mechanical genius of a cousin. Plus, you wanted in, right?"

Calista tilted her head. What was he talking about?

"The locker room shower pressure is inadequate. It's like those poor boys are standing under a tree limb during the rain. Drip. Drip. The guys are always complaining about that, and don't get me started on the visiting teams' whining." He sighed big. "Of course, as a girl, you can't go in the locker rooms. You'll have to hire a man to handle that chore."

Dodo spoke as if he had intended to do the plumbing work himself. Calista could see his soft manicured hands from here. Nothing wrong with that, until he'd implied he was more capable than her to fix something. Her hackles rose. No one who knew her threw down like that. Hmm, that was the point. He didn't know her at all. She calmed back down.

"There's more, if you want to hear about the real behind-the-scenes work that a stadium and team like this requires."

Dodo was trying to put her off her ownership bid, but Calista didn't fall for his crap. Plumbing, pipes, infrastructure, there could be a thousand reasons for low water pressure: debris, pollutants, minerals, or leaks. She said nothing.

Dodo eyed the number on her jersey. "Twenty-two fan, huh? Captain Ronan's staying at my old bachelor pad."

Her heart picked up at the mention of Ronan's name, but she did her best not to let interest show on her face. Why was Ronan renting?

"What had he said?" Dodo snapped his fingers.

"Oh, yes, sunroom sheetrock damage. You know how those guys party, walls get broken." He looked at her empty hands. "Shouldn't you be writing this down?"

He'd said two things: low flow and wall damage. She didn't need a spreadsheet.

"I'll have my secretary send you a comprehensive rundown." Dodo made a gun finger at her and pulled the trigger. "Don't say I never gave you anything." He left the way he came.

Calista started along the row to the aisle, moving slowly, so she wouldn't catch up to Dodo and have to walk out with him.

The sound of blades on ice made her turn. Kiernan skated up to the half-wall lining the front row not far from her. He had his helmet off and his dark hair was sweat-dampened. "Hey, Cal-cat."

Hmm, he hadn't teased Piper with nicknames, not that she'd heard, then again, men treated her sister differently than they did her. Sigh. Piper had womanly skills she didn't possess. That was life. That made her the best sister for Calista to have. What did Kiernan want? Calista had delayed too long as it was, she needed to get to class. Calista shook her head.

"Like my moves?"

Kiernan was an extraordinary talent, and he knew it. Calista grinned instead of heaping praise on the hotshot. She climbed up a step.

"Hey wait, the guys have questions about your takeover."

Calista paused. Takeover. She rolled the term in

her mind but didn't know him well enough to discern if that was a jab or praise. Piper would have known before the last syllable left his mouth. Not knowing how to react, she didn't.

Kiernan shuffled in place as if he couldn't keep still even after the hard practice. "About this whole *'who owns us'* business, and *'what does our futures look like?'*. That kind of piddling stuff. The things people worry about, right?"

Ownership was definitely an awkward term. A million thoughts spun through Calista's head. But she didn't have time to string out a hundred words, much less process all that was going on in her brain regarding the team purchase.

Dahlia knew more about operations, so she'd be the best person to answer Kiernan's questions. Besides, Dodo still owned a percentage, which meant they couldn't make changes right now anyway. Most critically, her ideas had layers and layers, like a honeycomb. Which side of the hexagon did Kiernan want to know about? "I have class."

"Catch you later then," Kiernan said easily.

The email from Dodo's secretary populated as Calista was walking into class.

There were no assigned seats, but they'd gravitated to the same spots as if there were. Vivien was in her usual spot, hunched over her laptop, Artie wasn't there, and Olivia was at her desk by the window.

Calista showed Olivia the to-do-list email from Dodo's administrative assistant. "Could plumbing or drywall be our class project?"

Olivia lowered the blinds, lessening the bright sun that made screen-viewing a challenge. "Anything could be. Is one of these a good choice though? Arguably."

Did her classmates want to spend the next six weeks discussing plumbing? Calista did, but the others should get a vote. "I want to speak with Dahlia about how we should work everything." Plans needed project management. Calista was better at the big ideas and the actual fixing, not with triage and vendor management. Plus, the whole thirty percent Applebaum vote was a problem, blech. "Can you go with me in case Dahlia needs any legal ideas for us to take action?"

Olivia hissed out a breath. "Yes. Honestly, Dodo should not be contacting you directly. What he's saying on the surface isn't what he means, he'll trick you." She pointed to her own chest. "Correspondence should come through me."

Calista couldn't agree more. "I'd love for you to handle that stuff."

"I want in." Vivien popped up her head. "The more I know, the better."

How did Vivien stare at code and still follow what happened around her? Maybe Vivien could teach her that during this project. Hmm, this special class might be worthwhile after all. Not new-stand-seating-at-the-stadium valuable, but still.

Sneakers screeched on the linoleum out in the hallway, and then Artie reached his arm through the doorway. He braced himself, leaned back out to the hall, and rolled in a cart containing at least a hundred wires swirling over the sides. His project suggestion must be untangling the mess he'd made. Not fair, he got an equal say on the project. They should include him more. Calista smiled encouragingly. "We're talking about doing stadium improvements. Would you want a voice on that type of project?"

Artie threaded his fingers into the wires and stared at the tangled mess as if it held the answer to her question, then he went through a rotation of moving each of his fingers up and down as if he were playing a piano or maneuvering a puppet. At no point did he answer her.

Calista was actually fine with going forward without him. However, Professor Terrence wouldn't be okay with excluding others during teamwork time. She made her question easier. "Artie, do you have any thoughts?"

Artie canted his head. "How tall are you? You look about the same height as Vivien and Olivia. You're like triplets. I'd guess, five-six?"

Ew, creeper was right.

Dodo called the meeting for the next morning. Calista, Olivia, and Dahlia sat in the conference room facing Dodo, who sat at the head of the table, along with his lawyers who were a trio of middle-aged suit-wearing men.

After the round of introductions, Dodo leapt in. "Let's be reasonable, ladies." Dodo's lips morphed into an ingratiating smile, and he smoothed back his fair hair. In his early thirties, he knew his best features were his salon-streaked locks and his expensive dental work. If Artie had joined them, he could argue that Dodo was at least two percent artificial.

Dodo went on, "I was shuffling funds, a mere ten percent. Temporarily. At the same time, Warren discovered I was seeing his ex, Willow."

TMI alert. Dodo should be the one taking a course on business communications. Calista felt her eyebrows arching but couldn't help her expression.

Dodo darted his gaze briefly to Dahlia, who he himself had been engaged to at the time of his indiscretion. "In a temporary moment of anger, Warren dumped all his Snowers' shares. Had I known that we were losing the controlling majority, I would never have risked my own shares. Not with the small amount we'd let go to the public already. You see my point." He sounded very reasonable. "I never meant to have the team stolen out from under me."

Calista had wondered how the shares had become available. Now she knew. She didn't appreciate the term *stole* though. Olivia would get him for that.

Olivia shrugged one shoulder. "Our point is Calista purchased seventy percent of the Austin Snowers ice hockey team. That makes her majority owner with named shareholders Dahlia Amvehl and Piper Amvehl."

Dodo's primary lawyer lifted his index finger. "Seventy percent divided by three named partners. Sounds to me like Ms. Calista Amvehl owns significantly less than Mr. Donovan Applebaum's thirty percent."

Dodo's second lawyer chuckled. "I was no math major, but those numbers sound right to me."

"Hold your calculators." Olivia yawned. "Look at how we structured her purchase, as a singular organization, one entity, seventy percent."

Dodo lifted his palms. "I've explained our pickle to a family friend, a judge, so you know his opinion is sound." He gave Olivia a pointed look, as if the shine from her new diploma was obvious. "Now, he couldn't give me direct advice or an exact prediction, no more than if that groundhog is going to get next month's weather right. But after talking with Judge Johnston, Jimbo, if you know him like I do, well, just so there are no surprises, what I've done is file the paperwork with the court to review the contract and correct the mistaken sale. I mean, if I weren't running the show, and my GM left with me, as he would, the whole shebang would fall apart. What are the players' opinions on all this? The league will care, and the portion of the company that's public, well, those board members will care. What's best for the Snowers?"

Calista flinched. She had been trying to tune out the legal wrangling, but Dodo could take the

Snowers from her. Her skin chilled, forming an icy shell, and she fought off the implications. It was that or hyperventilate.

"The sale is done," Olivia said, looking unimpressed enough to help Calista calm down. "All your filing does is prevent us from moving forward with our progressive ideas for the stadium."

"You can't simply assume ownership of a professional men's team. The league must be involved." Dodo shook his head. "You ladies need a better understanding of how the real world works."

If Calista lost the shares, would she still get a chance to fix the plumbing as a special project? What did this mean for her season tickets? For Dahlia? Despite her desire for control, her trillion thoughts spiraled outwards from there, and she couldn't move or articulate any of them.

Dahlia's face turned red, and she made a strangled noise. She understood the threat of what was going on. Why were she and Dahlia the only ones flustered? How was Olivia so composed? Olivia could teach her that trick during special class. After this experience, she may need multiple remedial tutorials on workplace communication, the university was right.

Dodo turned to his former fiancée. "Here's what we propose. Arbitration. We can work things out while the front office continues our same smooth operations. Of course, Dahlia, sweetheart, will maintain her position. She can even have her old office if she likes."

Her old office was adjacent to his. Dahlia's head jerked and she found her voice. "I'm fine where I am now."

Dodo's primary lawyer got to his feet and put his gray legal pad in his briefcase. "We'll get the paperwork corrected, and this little lady," he pointed to Calista, "will rake in a hefty profit. You'll have to give me some of your savvy stock tips." His colleagues copied his motions and murmured jovial agreements.

Calista wanted a shower.

Dodo edged his hand toward Dahlia's as if he wanted to pat the back of her hand. Instead, he flattened his fingers on the tabletop.

Calista did not feel sorry for him. He'd made his bed with Willow and lost Dahlia through his own poor judgement. How had Dahlia dated him? Sure, nice-looking billionaire, fit. Guess she could see the appeal to some women, but not sane ones because in the end the bride would still have to honeymoon with Dodo. They'd fight over hair gel and tooth polish then sue the hotel. What a life.

Dodo nodded. "Good meeting. Glad we all agree, we'll continue running as is, let the courts sort out the issues. We voted those judges in, right? Let them do their jobs."

The next morning, Calista paced the hallway in front of the men's locker room. Her thoughts were on pipes and the articles she'd read on plumbing. The urge to go in and have a look pulled at her. The players weren't here yet, maintenance had the keys. Why couldn't she go in?

Duh. Any of the players could arrive for practice early and make it weird. Meet the new owner, she's a peeping Tom. She needed an official escort. Mikah could show her around. He was going to be her brother-in-law if his relationship continued to flourish with Piper.

Calista moved into the adjacent conference room and sent Mikah a text. *"I'm in the conference room, but I want to see the inadequate pipes. Can you let me in the players' locker room when you get here?"* Reasonable request, done. She fired up her laptop, projected pipe diagrams onto the big screen, and lost herself in plumbing charts.

Not an hour later, Mikah arrived—with Ronan.

CHAPTER 10

The two superstars came in together, well before their practice time. They wore street clothes, had frowning faces, and tight jaws. Their tense expressions were more common for them when they were on the ice. Calista wiggled her shoulders, wishing they were out on the rink now. That said, they were both here which helped her out.

Two birds, one stone. Mikah could get her in to see the plumbing, and she wanted to speak with Ronan and clear up how they met. She had his phone number, and the vague sense that she owed him an apology but hadn't known where to start. Calista shut her laptop, gave the two men a small smile, and waggled her fingers at them. See, she had social skills.

"Hey, Calista," Despite his expression, Mikah spoke with the soft voice he used the few times she'd seen him with his sister Lily. "Dodo's pushing the team to take sides in this ownership battle, and you know I want to keep my position." He rubbed his jaw, looking like a model going for a thinking pose. Piper hadn't simply fallen for a handsome guy, Mikah was a star on the ice. His career mattered. "I have to stay out of this as much as I can."

True. Mikah, through no action of his own, was caught right in the middle of the ownership battle. He'd started dating Piper before any stock news broke and this had been sprung on him. Heat flushed Calista's face. She owed him an apology too because she'd put him in this situation. "Sorry." She rotated her hands in front of her as if holding the world. "About all of this."

Mikah's face softened. "That's okay. Now, about your text, Captain here will give you a quick look around the locker room while I take some ice time. You two, just give me a minute to change." He went through the interior door into the locker room.

Calista looked at Ronan from under her eyelashes, and her heart shimmered. "I didn't think it through when I texted Mikah. Piper told me he's always one of the first players in. I didn't think he'd need to contact you." Was that part of the chain of command? She'd have to ask Dahlia. "I certainly didn't mean for you to have to come to the stadium early."

"When the owner calls, we jump." Ronan's voice held a dispassionate note he hadn't used with her before.

Calista's lips tightened, knowing her words were inadequate. She'd called this one correctly. Ronan wanted an apology. Calista pushed her laptop away and rolled her chair back. "Sorry." Ugh, not all that she wanted to say. "I mean, sorry about how we met." Her face bloomed hot. They'd met right here with her half out of her dainties. He'd touched her elbow and made sparks flutter under her skin. She took a breath. "Sorry. I didn't make my name clear from day one when we met. I was never a dancer, just doing Dahlia a favor by trying on the costumes." There, that was better. Her shoulders loosened.

"No problem," Ronan said easily, though his blue eyes didn't warm.

Wasn't her identity communication failure the reason she should be apologizing? Was there something more? Something less? "I—"

Ronan backed toward the exit. "I've got to make a call. I'll step outside. Meet you here in ten." He left.

The whole scene made Calista feel bad inside, more guilty than she thought she should feel, but she couldn't shake the uncomfortable crawly sensations. She sat back down, cradled her laptop with her arms, but didn't open the lid.

Five minutes later, Mikah came through dressed in his gear and left to take the ice. Fifteen minutes after that, the door to the locker room opened again, and Ronan stood there dressed in his practice clothes, with skates on.

Holy hockey gods, he looked amazing. Snowers blue was his color. He was the best thing that ever happened to her hometown team. Happy hormones flooded her body, and Calista held in a small moan. Would it be weird to ask for a selfie with him?

Ronan leaned backward, holding the door open. Calista rose and headed to him. She slowed when she neared him to relish their height difference, more pronounced because he wore the ice skates. Amazing, Ronan Stromkin, right here, in front of her, in uniform. He was history about to happen. He was the stuff retired jerseys and Stanley Cups were made of. Hockey coaches would study his moves in the future. Fans would be his for a lifetime. Would saying any of that be appropriate in this moment?

Ronan shifted on his feet. His expression didn't invite her to share her thoughts. She'd seen him up close before but not in uniform. This was taking out her knees. They needed statues made of all the players, as Piper had suggested, but especially Ronan.

Realizing, she was moving at a bizarre snail's pace, Calista picked up her speed and entered the locker room. Fluorescent lighting and the overwhelming scent of industrial bleach made her nose twitch, and Calista did her best not to sneeze. The air filtration system could use a definite upgrade.

Inside was a bunch of light blue and white metal lockers and bench seating. The long narrow room curved to the left. Logic told her the showers would be back there, and she continued around with Ronan following her. There was a strip of showerheads placed high on a long-tiled wall and a floor with drains. Nothing luxurious, nothing worthy of ice hockey athletes. Calista shook her head. "Not much privacy."

"We're used to it."

Dad had showers at the garage. Their showers were individual long cubicles. Wouldn't take that much space to do that here. Would probably have to lose the conference room to get it done, or maybe they could open the opposite wall. She needed to see the building's blueprints. Calista kept her thoughts to herself, because taking down walls would require the judge to stamp *sold* on her takeover.

Wouldn't it? Dodo had told her to address the plumbing. She could ignore the part where he took it back. Dodo was wishy-washy, look at his dating life. She'd show she could do her part improving the stadium, while the lawyers scrutinized the paperwork.

Ronan pointed at the showerheads. "Poor water pressure. It's worse on the visitors' side, or so the guys say. Dodo calls that stadium strategy."

Make visitors uncomfortable? Mom would never agree, and Calista didn't either. The best needed to play the best under equal conditions, that way they could all shine and elevate the upcoming game by feeling great. If the visitors' locker rooms were worse, that embarrassment benefited no one. Those men gave her team an opportunity to rise to their highest levels of play. They deserved to be treated as respected guests, at minimum. Calista frowned. "Do you think that's good gamesmanship?"

"No." Ronan's voice was flat and his answer unequivocal.

Calista hadn't thought he would. No guy at his level needed a shady advantage. She nodded in satisfaction, Ronan knew what was right.

Ronan turned on three showerheads at the end. Nothing happened. "These don't work, you have to get down here fast or you're third rotation."

"I can fix it." To what level was yet to be established. Calista pushed her hair back and ran her brain around the hours in the day. This was a busy week for her between paperwork, business meetings, and school. Because her term was short, she had to be there every weekday and twice on Thursdays. Nothing she couldn't handle though, she wasn't even working part time at the auto shop. Right now, her parents wanted her to focus on finishing her degrees. School wasn't intense, but its rigid, be present, be on time, don't burn down the building, created its own restrictions. Calista worked to untangle her thoughts so she could explain that despite her schedule, the Snowers were a priority, but then the locker room went quiet and dark

One minute the fluorescent lights buzzed in the background, the next moment, they were thrown into total below ground blackness.

CHAPTER 11

Calista squeaked, and her pulse picked up. Not that she was scared of the dark or couldn't handle flipping a breaker. It was the unexpected nature of the change, and the totality of the blinding darkness that surprised and pulled the weak sound from her.

Calista stood very still and felt for her phone. She whirred on her flashlight app and directed the beam on their feet. Her sneakers looked small beside Ronan's skates. She roamed the light the length of his skate blade while mentally calling herself creepy like Artie. She couldn't help it though, she wanted to know his shoe size. Dang, instead of learning skills from her friends, Artie was rubbing creeper off on her. Blech.

"That's new," Ronan said. "Did you pay the light bill?"

His teasing comment took away the eerie atmosphere, and Calista relaxed. "Nope." Her phone whirred off. She hit the power button again and got a few seconds of illumination before the light wavered. "I have a low battery. Where's your phone?"

"My locker." Ronan's answer came to her in the darkness. He shifted and his skate guards clattered on the floor as if he were going to turn and walk away. One stupid fall and he'd be ruined for the season.

"Wait." Calista moved and got in front of him. She kept hold by keeping one arm stretched behind her. "I'll go first, just tell me which way."

Ronan put his free hand on her shoulder. "Why?"

Calista appreciated the weight of his grip, as if he were steading her. She'd lain in bed every night since the Mer-bar thinking how easily he'd plucked her from the tank. She'd have to watch him workout sometime to see what he benched. That would be normal for an owner, right? She couldn't stay in her own head, she needed to answer him. He wanted to know why she was leading. "If we hit a bench or something, I don't want you to fall and injure yourself."

"Is that the owner speaking?" Ronan's voice was tight again.

"The fan." The sincerity in her own words was unmissable. Calista wanted them to go back to how they'd been before. Not that she could put a word on their earlier interactions, but they'd been easier, as if he'd wanted to move closer to her, not farther away.

"Well, that's sweet. But not happening." His voice softened a degree.

Calista valued that small change and shifted to

face him, though she couldn't see him. They breathed together in the dark, and neither of them moved.

The lights flashed on, and they both blinked against the biting fluorescence. They were standing closer than she expected, but neither backed up.

"Sorry, wrong switch, I'm not peeking." Dahlia's voice came from the door. "I'm looking for Calista." Dahlia didn't wait for a reply. "I know you're in there. I have some more mockups of dancer's uniforms ordered."

Calista toyed with the idea of not answering. If she moved behind Ronan, Dahlia wouldn't even see her, he was that big. Where would that reaction fall on the good communication scale? A zero. Calista sighed and couldn't help the small pout forming on her lips, but she let her feet carry her away from Ronan and toward Dahlia. She rounded the corner with a small goodbye wave his way. Better set her cousin straight now, so she didn't miss practice later. Calista followed along the benches to the exit. "I'm not modeling them for you."

Dahlia came into view just outside the doorway. She wore a pretty wool business suit in Snowers blue and grinned her bright smile. "That's not what I need from you. The order status reads delivered, but I can't find the shipping box." Her voice dropped to teasing. "Did you hide my package so I wouldn't make you try them on?"

"No, I do need stadium blueprints though, for a separate reason, not to find out where to hide your stuff." Calista joined her cousin in the hallway, and the locker door snapped closed behind her. "Nice suit, great color."

"Thanks." Dahlia tilted her head. "I'll look into getting you the blueprints." There was a pause, and then Dahlia said, "I actually will need you to try the suits on when I find them."

"Nope."

"I'd ask Piper, but she's staying out of the changes for Mikah's sake, at least until all the ownership questions are settled."

Complex mechanical breakdowns were much easier to solve than the problem of how to resist the plea in her cousin's voice, and Calista found she couldn't tell her straight up *no*. "I'll think about it."

Dahlia's phone beeped, and she tilted the screen toward Calista. "Dodo copied both of us."

Dodo's message read, *"The office is fielding tons of emails with questions regarding ownership. Let's put that down with a team meeting this afternoon, 2PM, men's conference room. Calista Amvehl can explain her position to the players."*

Nope, Calista shook her head though Dodo obviously couldn't see her.

"I don't know about this, but we'd better go because it won't look good if he documents his attempts for us to work together, and we're no-shows." Dahlia chewed on her bottom lip, marring her peach lipstick. "I don't like it though. Can you get your lawyer here?"

CHAPTER 12

Calista's lawyer Olivia couldn't make Dodo's impromptu meeting, but Vivien said she would come, and Dahlia assured her she'd handle the presentation. So while Calista watched practice, Dahlia prepped slides. Her MBA was paying off, unlike the special project class Calista was attending.

After practice, Calista met Dahlia in the hallway so they could go in together.

Dahlia drew in a deep breath, then reached out and squeezed her hand, before opening the door and going in.

There, Calista paused. It was moves like that, that small reassurance her perfectly self-possessed cousin knew she needed, that thoughtful touch of companionship that killed Calista, and she knew she'd end up trying on the new dancers' costumes, if her cousin asked again. Calista moved into the conference room already crowded with players. The guys had just finished practice. All had shower-damp hair, and they wore street clothes. The clash of masculine colognes was pleasant. The only ick factor was that Dodo sat at the head of the table, one leg crossed over the other in a casual pose like he owned the place.

Dahlia went to the left of the screen, so she would present while Vivien turned the slides. Vivien sat in the corner clicking on her laptop and the slides projected. Not that Dahlia couldn't handle a computer, but should Dodo's crew try and hack and derail, Vivien would take them down. Calista moved to stand by Vivien, which happened to be near Ronan's chair.

Calista kept her gaze off him and sank down crisscross on the floor beside her friend. From this angle, she could see expensive tennis shoes under the table, most in motion. These high energy guys weren't made for long meetings.

Would they blame her for this or Dodo? Hopefully Dodo.

Where she'd sat put Ronan directly in the chair in front of her. Which wasn't why she'd picked this location, it had just worked out that way.

Ronan spun around and rose. "Take my seat."

Aww, sweet, Calista motioned to the laptop at Vivien's side. "I'm helping Vivien. Thanks though." She wasn't. Ronan sat back down.

Vivien used an app on her computer to dim the lights, and the first slide came into focus. The simple text had the team's name and meeting date.

Dahlia waved. "I'm Dahlia Amvehl. I've had the privilege of meeting everyone, and you may have met Calista previously, but I'll take this opportunity to introduce her. Calista Amvehl is the owner of seventy percent of the Snowers."

"That's still to be confirmed," Dodo said.

Dahlia gave him a tight smile. "And this is Vivien Durand, our IT expert. We don't want to take a ton of your time, but we do have a few highlights for you guys." The energy in the room shifted as the men went from awkward guys who wanted out to a team showing patience. Good job, Dahlia.

The hallway door opened, Willow popped into the room wearing a red mini dress. She walked through the light beam and went to Dodo's side. Jerry, who'd been in the seat close to Dodo, hopped up and moved to stand by the wall so Willow could take his place. He had Dodo's coloring, but in a lighter hue. He was like a pale shadow of Dodo.

Willow sank down and adjusted her short skirt without thanking him.

Dahlia's cheeks pinkened, visible even in the low lighting. She swallowed and clicked to the second slide. *Team Improvement Ideas.* "I'll jump right in. We've seen less use of the chauffeur app than expected, and I wanted to remind the team that this perk is half the price of any other ride service. We want to make sure you get home safely."

Willow rolled her eyes. She leaned toward Dodo's chair as if to speak privately to him. "And track their every move." Her aside was audible to the entire room.

Hmm, that was how corporate rideshare GPS worked.

Cousin Dahlia took the heckling head on. "Sorry, did you have something to add, Willow? I know you're not against our providing sober drivers?"

Willow shrugged one shoulder and then adjusted her scarlet bra strap under her neckline. No one had said she didn't know how to be appropriate. "I'm here to look out for the men's best interests. A counterpoint is how we improve, right?"

No matter how reasonable the statement, contrary opinions flooded Calista because Willow had been the one to pose the question.

"Your comments are more contrarian than helpful." Dahlia straight up called Willow out.

Vivien gave Calista a side-look, as if to ask if she'd heard that. Calista shrugged and wrapped her arms around her knees.

"Dodo and I just want to understand the full picture." Willow placed her hand on Dodo's armrest. "Is the discounted ride a part of the purity app or not?"

The guys groaned at the word *purity.*

The rideshare was totally a part of the purity app, Dahlia was busted. Though what was up with the men's rejection? What was wrong with saving themselves for a higher ideal? Calista needed a friend whose specialty was biology to explain men's resistance to good sense. Though not all had resisted, according to Dahlia, a number of men had questions about the purity process.

Dahlia glared at Willow without responding because what could she say? Yes, the car service app was contained within the purity app portal. No marry, no cherry, no free ride via the BlackBerry.

Vivien elbowed her and projected a display of cherries dancing. The men in the room laughed.

"I'll continue." Dahlia nodded at Vivien who turned the slide.

Liam looked at the clock. "Sorry to interrupt, but you said this would be short. How much longer? I have a massage appointment." He rolled his big shoulder and rubbed it with his right hand. "I hate to be late."

Jerry snickered.

Kiernan rose and edged toward the door. "I have an appointment too, at the bar. I'll make use of the free ride. Thanks for the reminder."

Dahlia clicked to the next slide and an image of the stadium appeared. "We want your input on what renovations are needed." She spoke quicker, as if to get her words out before all the players made excuses and left.

Kiernan hesitated.

"You can't hold up all the guys, they earned their free time." Willow held out her hands. "Couldn't you email this?"

Vivien pursed her lips and nodded at Willow's solid point. They needed Olivia here to argue back.

The most obvious would be that it was Dodo who called the meeting in the first place.

Willow turned to look down at Calista. "Unless Calista has something to say to everyone?"

Everyone turned to look at her.

CHAPTER 13

Geeze, no. Calista had nothing to say to the group, that's what she had Dahlia for. Calista felt her face blanch and her eyebrows arch. She shook her head and made big eyes at Dahlia.

"There you go," Willow said, as if Calista were agreeing with her.

Dahlia rubbed her middle finger across her forehead. "Fine, I'm a team player." She faced Dodo. "How do you normally handle group decisions?"

"Starter six," Dodo said. "The rest of you men are dismissed."

There was a mix of grumbles, a few yelled questions wondering what would change, and a number of happy departures, until only the six starters remained: Mikah, Captain, Rookie, Jerry, Liam, and Kiernan.

"You know, I'm staying neutral," Mikah said. "So, I'm not staying."

No one contradicted him, and he left.

Dahlia jumped in before anyone else left. "Questions about change are welcome." Dahlia highlighted the image of the Austin Snowers venue. "How can we make the stadium better for you? We have ideas, but we want to hear yours first." There. Dahlia had the right tone and the right words.

Calista nodded, now they were on track.

Dodo got up. "Why don't we make this more convivial? Take our group up to the smaller conference table outside my office? Have drinks."

All Dodo's suggestion had done was remind the guys of small discomforts like thirst, make Calista want a lemonade, and interrupt Dahlia's flow. If they had a long, low, minifridge in here, Dodo wouldn't have been able to derail Dahlia's presentation. Calista made a mental note to order one.

"Great idea, Dodo." Willow nodded. "The conference table in my new office will be perfect. I'll order refreshments. These boys did just get off practice, after all. We were being thoughtless keeping them in this room."

"I could use a drink," Kiernan said.

Jerry was still standing, although after the other players had left, plenty of seats had opened up. Jerry clapped Dodo on his shoulder. "You know you've got my backing on whatever issues arise. I have full faith you know what's best for us. I don't need to be there. Consider my vote yours."

※

Ronan opted to take the stairs up to the executive offices. Starters needed to focus on their game. The fact that they'd been called upstairs to meet with Dodo and Calista in an owner pissing contest irked him, but at least the guys would get their questions answered. Once this situation was resolved, they'd clear their minds of these distractions and focus on the upcoming game.

He went in. The room smelled like new leather and old money.

Liam, Kiernan, and Rookie followed him, each having given their all at practice. All of whom should be enjoying their hard-earned down time. Instead, they were dealing with front office issues.

Mikah had it right, opting out. Even Jerry thought of a way to skip. If those two were smarter than him, he should rethink his captainship.

Calista was already seated. Adrenaline surged and his muscles tensed. When he ran into Calista, he felt like he'd been slammed into the boards. His reaction to her was over the top primal. The more he was around her, the more he wanted his hands under her jersey, and her intense focus on him, only him. He shoved the tension down.

Calista was sitting to the right of her cousin Dahlia, the one who'd been engaged to Dodo and always wore high-end business suits. Oh, she was gorgeous like Calista but in a salon luster way. Dahlia didn't cause any reaction for him other than a desire to avoid the front office. Not like with Calista, who'd snuck under his radar before he knew who she was.

Ronan blinked and shifted his mental game. What he meant was, he had wanted a date when he'd thought Calista was a hot dancer, but that wasn't who she was. He took a seat at the opposite end of the table, as far away as he could get, until he could make his excuses and escape. The other three men were milling about. Dodo and Willow hadn't made it yet.

Saxon sat beside him. His rookie eyes showed how over his head he was up here. "I don't understand, we're supposed to meet Dodo. Where is he?"

The other players didn't echo the question because they recognized Dodo's shitty powerplay. Dodo was making them wait.

Liam took a chair on the other side where he would have a view of the door. "My legs are killing me, I knew I shouldn't have gone after those extra sprints."

"Yeah, you should have." Kiernan moved over to the private bar. "I believe Dodo promised us a drink." He examined the selection. "No point in going into a house made of candy if you don't have a lick. Am I right?"

Dahlia examined her French manicure and looked torn. "Not sure we should."

"Scotch. Scotch," Liam chanted, stating his preference and egging Kiernan on. The Canadian was the match to Kiernan's dynamite. On the ice, that power and intensity were unbeatable. Off the ice, these two were too much for normal society.

Kiernan's hand hovered over the bottles. "So,

Canadian." He paused, tilted his head up, and went for the crystal bottles contained behind a gold rope. "Top shelf private stash, anyone?"

Dahlia opened her mouth, as if to spout out a purity protest, then she shrugged, and made a *whatever* moue with her lips. She walked over to the heavy desk that used to be hers and looked around. The bulky furniture had been moved to the corner to make room for the addition of this large conference table. On top of her former desk was a long name plate that read Willow in red letters. Dahlia didn't touch that. She went behind the desk and lifted a shipping box. Frowning, she raised the air bill to eye-height to read the address. Mouth tight, she pivoted and placed the box on the center of the desk calendar. She grabbed a hockey stick-shaped letter opener and sliced into the packing tape. She tossed a telling gaze to Calista.

Kiernan lined up a set of tumblers on the table in front of the empty chair by Calista, standing a touch too close. Kiernan poured like a pro. "Ladies first."

That looked like trouble, he'd head it off. That was one of his duties as captain. Ronan rose and took the empty seat beside Calista, pretending not to see Kiernan smirk at him. Kiernan slid the full glasses across the polished black granite top as if they were pucks. He got them into the nets formed by the attendees' hands. Lastly, he served Dahlia who was removing bubble wrap from the shipping box.

"Thanks." Dahlia drank the liquor in a long

swallow and winced at the taste. "I'll arrange drivers for us with the app." She motioned for a refill.

Kiernan accommodated her, then he took the open chair down by Rookie.

The guys at the table drank their own drinks in an amber-warmed silence, only broken by Dahlia's unpacking, which had a solid anger. Ronan had enough ex-girlfriends to recognize the tension in her moves. If he had to guess, there was a yet-to-be-returned engagement gift inside.

Kiernan leaned down the table to offer him a top-off. "Captain goodie two-twos?"

Clever idiot, playing with his jersey number. Why not? Ronan waved his fingers toward his glass in agreement.

Dahlia carried the opened box to the head of the conference table. "New options for the dancer costumes have arrived."

He'd guessed wrong there.

Dahlia braced her palms on the box and leaned in. "While I've got you here. You guys can vote on which you like best."

Kiernan nodded. "I want a piece of that."

Calista took a drink. "I'm not putting them on."

Images of the last time he'd seen her in the snowball bikini, and half out of it, flooded his mind and tied his tongue. Ronan swallowed. He wanted that again. This time he'd look longer, though looking had not compared to touching or breathing her in. Her fragrance was vanilla-scented excitement, and her skin the softest he'd ever felt. He'd barely touched her. What did the rest of her feel like?

"Of course not, the guys will get the idea without a model," Dahlia said, her voice easy, her composure returned. "I ordered three designs." She held up the first one, a full body suit with a jersey design that went over the torso and hockey pants on the bottom.

Kiernan shook his head hard. "That's putting me off my drink."

Liam made a thumb's down, and Rookie followed the gesture.

Ronan didn't bother to vote because the majority had spoken.

The next was a bat bra. The bat was Snowers blue, each wing covered a breast and the bat body rode facing up over the bra clasp. The bat concealing the bikini area faced up also. Bats were a symbol of Austin.

Kiernan made obscene finger gestures. "Is the bat going into the cave or out of the cave?"

Dahlia threw the bat back in the box. "Come here, Calista, you make things look nicer."

Ronan held in a groan. Yeah, she did.

Calista wiggled her wheeled conference room chair left then right, her face flushed a pretty pink. "Nope."

Dahlia gave her begging eyes with irises a shade darker than Calista's.

Calista's shoulders slumped, and she rose.

Ronan's heart started an out-of-control rhythm. Was she going to put the suit on?

CHAPTER 14

Calista moved beside her cousin, stiff and uncomfortable.

Ronan wanted to caution her about being suckered in by others, but he couldn't help wanting to know what was about to happen.

Dahlia held white bootie shorts and a cut off jersey against Calista's body. Glittery white letters spelled 'SNOWERS' across Calista's chest and the jersey's hem ended just under her boobs.

Yes. That one. Ronan bit down on his bottom lip. Dahlia was right. Against Calista's curves, mere fabric took on new life.

Kiernan whistled and gave a thumbs up. "That works for me."

"I wouldn't say no to that," Liam agreed.

The urge to fight them rose inside Ronan. He took a drink instead. Drinks had saved many a friendship.

Saxon nodded with big eyes.

Ronan's fingers curled into a fist. He wanted to

punch him too. None of them should be looking at her with anything other than professional distance.

Calista slipped back to the table and sipped her Scotch without meeting their gazes.

Dahlia mushed her lips left and then right, undecided.

"Let's let the bar choose," Kiernan suggested. "Have the dancers wear those next time we go."

"Oh, yeah." Liam agreed.

Dahlia looked upward and nodded thoughtfully. "Not a bad idea."

"It's not?" Kiernan asked, even though the idea had been his.

Dahlia nodded. "We'll have all the fans wear costumes they create. That will generate enthusiasm, investment, and increase our social media traffic. The winning designer will get season tickets." She held up the mini jersey again. "This will be our backup outfit. Calista will wear it."

"No, she won't." Calista's voice was smooth and pleasant even with the refusal.

Dahlia shrugged. "Fine, I'll ask one of the dancers to volunteer." She smiled. "I like the idea of a vote instead of owners deciding."

"Who is the owner, exactly? Applebaum or Amvehl?" Rookie got daring on second-glass bravery.

That was the question of the hour.

Kiernan moved around the table, refilling all the glasses until the Scotch bottle was near empty. "What's in a name?" He had shiny teal eyes and a flushed face at this point, and he'd reached Calista.

Calista covered the top of her glass with her hand, so he skipped her. Calista poked her finger in the cut grooves of the glass.

Ronan gave up trying not to look at her.

Calista lowered her chin to the tabletop and stared at the half inch of golden liquor remaining in her glass. Her gorgeous hair fanned out around her. "Amvehl. Am-vehl." Each time she said her own name, she altered which syllable she stressed. She was a touch tipsy, this stuff was strong.

"Stromkin." Ronan said, for absolutely no damn reason he could think of. "Strom-kin."

Calista, keeping her chin on the table, tilted her gaze to his, and her light green eyes brightened. She smiled, as if he'd given her roses and spoken to her in a private language.

Ronan's heart thumped. Ridiculous to be flattered by her admiring gaze, he breathed in and out, holding her look. He had to get out of here. He forced his gaze away and rose to his feet.

Liam got up too, accidentally blocking Ronan. Liam leaned against the table and stretched his left leg out behind him. "Seriously, stop me next time I try and catch Mikah's speed record. Eh?"

"I got you, bro," Kiernan said. "But I say you could have gone faster."

Dahlia motioned to Calista. "Show Liam a good yoga stretch for his hamstrings."

Calista rolled from her chair to the floor. She

pushed up on her palms, ass in the air. Her hair tumbled forward, and her body formed a triangle as her jersey slid down revealing taut abs.

Ronan couldn't move to go; instead, he angled his head for a better look.

Liam copied her, his body big and awkward. Nothing to look at there.

Calista exhaled and stepped one foot between her hands and raised her arm, lifting her torso upward, and twisting her hips to the side.

Damn, Ronan's body tightened like he was the one stretching. Look at her hamstrings.

The door clicked open and Dodo bounded in unaccompanied by Willow or the promised refreshments. "Thanks for waiting, important call, couldn't be helped. You men know how it is." Dodo took in the scene, but his eyes glued to the empty Scotch bottle. Dodo rounded on Dahlia. "You know my father gave me that Scotch for a special occasion."

Dahlia pinched her lips together and shrugged. "Sometimes people make choices they shouldn't make." Her voice was pointed. "And I'm not the keeper of your whiskey collection."

Liam collapsed on the floor. "That's so hard, but my legs feel better, thanks. You're too good to me, Calista."

"They were behind the rope." Dodo said, as if a tiny, velvet-covered cord equaled Fort Knox and Vatican level security.

"A rope could mean anything," Saxon said, not without apology. Rookie logic helped here. "I thought it was highlighting and displaying the bottles available to drink."

Kiernan shrugged one shoulder. "I didn't even see a rope."

Liam covered his eyes from where he lay on the floor and didn't get up. "I saw a rope two drinks ago. I don't see a rope now." His speech slurred, and his Canadian accent thickened. Ronan would be sure to pour him into the purity ride share.

Calista popped up and wobbled on her feet. Her face was blushing, and her green eyes were big and innocent.

Dodo rounded on Calista. "As a part of the executive team, if temporarily, you should know to set an example."

Ronan stepped forward.

Dodo went on, not realizing how close he was to being smashed. "Don't think I won't inform my attorneys that you're up here drunk off your ass with the team."

Calista twisted her torso toward Dahlia. "Am I on my ass?"

"Nope," Dahlia said.

Calista spun back and nodded confidently.

Dodo moved a foot closer to Calista. "You keep taking my things. Those bottles were clearly marked."

Dodo was twice Calista's size. Thought he could bully her? Red mist settled in front of Ronan's eyes. He held his body tense and breathed slowly so he didn't lose it.

"What rope?" Calista muttered, repeating Kiernan's lame excuse. "I didn't see a rope."

Her response struck Ronan as funny, and he laughed, so did Kiernan.

Their laughter made Dodo's face flush red.

The guy was still his owner, that calmed Ronan's humor. He needed to keep his head down so his future trade went smoothly. Calista could defend herself.

"You lot, out." Dodo pointed to the door. "You're banned from this office."

Dream come true. Happy to comply. Ronan hooked Liam's arm, helped him up, and out the door.

They headed to the elevator as a rowdy chuckling group and crowded in.

Liam hung back. As the broadest shouldered guy, he could be hyper aware spatially, they all could, given their height and builds. Kiernan pressed and held the open-door button. The elevator doors buzzed, having been ajar too long.

Kiernan grabbed Liam's arm. "Make room." He yanked his teammate in.

Ronan shifted so his back flattened to the wall. Though there was room between him and Calista, who was in the corner, he did his best not to get any closer. Even from here he could breathe in her vanilla scent. No player should know what his team owner smelled like. He inhaled deeper. Or felt like. He'd never ever felt such soft skin, not ever. His fingers clenched, and he lifted his arm over Calista's head and flattened his palm to the side wall before he did something stupid like touch her.

The doors closed and the elevator jerked into motion. Calista wobbled.

Ronan moved his hand from the wall to the small of Calista's back to support her. She didn't look at him, but she leaned into his hand. Her waist was curved just right, and he couldn't make his hand drop off of her.

CHAPTER 15

Ronan couldn't take his eyes or his hand off of Calista as the elevator descended.

"Banned from your own old office. Do you want your office back?" Calista asked Dahlia, who stood in front of her.

Was Calista being supportive or troublemaking? Ronan found himself curious, though none of this was his business.

Dahlia stared straight ahead and shrugged. "I definitely don't. It's attached to Dodo's office suite."

Calista tilted her head, and her silky hair shifted against her back. The strands brushed his hand, triggering X-rated images. "It doesn't have to be. I need the blueprints."

Dahlia snickered.

"How can he ban us?" Calista sounded confused, but her voice shifted to worried. "It's only from that one office, right?"

Ronan wanted to hug the concern in Calista's voice

away. He kept his gaze on the numbers of the descending floors. To his left, his teammates were talking about the bar they were headed to next, but his attention was on the women's conversation. He should have kept his distance and taken the stairs. He curled his fingers inwards, not caressing Calista, but holding firm.

"Dodo's not banning us from the stadium, the ban is from his office and Willow's." Dahlia reassured her cousin.

"Oh, no, we can never go in his office again." Kiernan said in a sing-song voice. "Or at least thirty percent of it."

They all laughed.

Calista's posture eased, and while Ronan appreciated his teammate lightening the mood, conversely, he was a touch jealous that Kiernan had been the one to make her smile.

The elevator reached the ground floor.

"We'll make your current office better," Calista said to her cousin.

"While the lawsuit is in play, we're limited to the changes that Dodo signs off on." Dahlia reached forward and held the door-open button. "That's not necessarily a bad thing, we don't want to misstep while we're in the middle of negotiations."

The Canadian got out first and braced his big arm on the elevator door to hold it open for the rest of them to exit.

Calista still looked concerned.

Ronan wanted to take her back to his place and

kiss her until her stress melted away, and her expression changed back to the one she usually looked at him with—happy excitement—like he was king of the ice. Holy hell.

Calista moved forward, and it took everything for Ronan to let his hand drop as she walked away.

"Drink, Captain?" Kiernan asked.

Better to have a drink with the guys than to do something stupid like follow Calista and ask her out. "Why not?"

Kiernan reached behind his back and revealed he'd taken a second liquor bottle from the special stash.

Late the next morning, Ronan swore he could smell vanilla lotion at the ice rink, which was impossible. Calista was in the stands, but at the other end of the stadium, simply watching practice. He was huddled with a bunch of practice weary men. She wasn't luring him over. He was being an imaginative idiot. Probably because he'd dreamed all night of her in the mermaid tank luring him in.

Coach waved to get their attention. "Ain't going to lie, men, a change of ownership is not convenient right now." Coach stood in front of them, telling it to them straight like always. "But we play the puck that drops."

The dancers filtered onto the other end of the ice.

They wore puck bikinis, black round circles that barely covered their assets.

Willow was in tow and managing them. She lined the dancers up in two groups.

The men around him shifted to get a view beyond Coach, and their heads tilted left or right depending on their positions.

Willow dropped her arm and the dancers at the front of the line laid on the ice on their frontal pucks. The women behind them grabbed their ankles and lifted them, spread, as if they held wheelbarrow handles.

His eyes widened. They were going to freeze off the parts of their bodies they liked to shake.

Then they were in motion.

Coach jerked his thumb over his shoulder as if the twenty-three men in front of him were unaware of the barely dressed women behind him. "Who's in charge of scheduling? You know how I feel about people on the ice on my time."

Kiernan nodded rapidly, his gaze glued to the dancers. "We legit need to know more."

"You know what I mean, focus, men. Hockey. Puck. Rink." Ronan turned to Mikah. "You've got an in with the Amvehls. What do you know?"

Mikah sliced his gloved hand in front of his chest. "I'm not doing this, I'm not the go-between, and you don't want me to be."

Coach gave Mikah a nod, freeing him from the conversation. "You're excused, Czerski."

Mikah skated off to the locker room.

Fair play, Mikah was dating Piper Amvehl. The Amvehls and the Applebaums could hash out ownership privately. Otherwise, Mikah was stuck in the middle like an expensive wishbone with a multi-million-dollar contract. Front office was messing with more than just his game.

Saxon's eyes never left the other end of the rink. "I saw the email about Willow's promotion to head of dancers' activities. I don't even know what that is. Do we need to get her a congrats gift? Should I go ask?"

Kiernan put his gloved fists on his hips and spared a glance at the rookie. "Dude, Willow's part-nered up with Dodo. For shits and giggles, let's say you do get her a gift. What's that say if the new owners are the Amvehls? Sorry, Dahlia, your ex dumped you for Willow, but I bought Willow a three-quart Tupperware dish with my bonus, can I get another bonus next year?"

"Shit," one of the guys in the back said.

Yep, succinct and captured exactly where they stood, they needed to keep their skates out of this.

Saxon took off his helmet as if he needed more air. "I didn't get Willow any kind of dish. Is that what you guys are getting? Just saying, let me go in on it."

Ronan drew in a deep breath. The men needed him to lead. "This will get worked out. We stick to the ice and leave the Applebaum-Amvehl mess to the courts."

He could feel the guy's tension ease. He'd given them good captain-worthy advice. He was thankful when he got it right.

"No, man, I can't take it." Saxon clapped his gloves together. "If ownership changes, will we keep the same positions? I hate change. Is she going to pick us off, or let us make our mark?"

"I just need time," Havard grumped, his Norwegian accent making the words difficult to understand. "This had to have happened during my slump?"

See, that's where this kind of disruption went off the rails. One missed puck had become a slump in Havard's mind. His superstitious attitude could be catching and derail their progress. Ronan tensed, knowing he had to put this down, now.

"I tried speaking with Calista the last time she was at practice," Kiernan said. "She blew me off for class." He frowned. "Chicks never blow me off." He turned to Liam. "Is this how you feel all the time?"

Liam sniffed the air. "They can smell the purity pledge on you."

"They do not." Kiernan stuck his nose in his own armpit. "I didn't swear to the pledge, bro. I said, I was *thinking* about taking it. Huge difference."

Saxon's hazel gaze darted left then right, almost as fast as Liam's tracked the room. "We need answers, man."

"You know we're not getting answers from those women. The Amvehls have left us nothing but a mess. I don't even want to speculate what they're up to." Jerry arched his eyebrows at Coach. "Am I released, Coach?"

Coach dismissed him with a short nod.

Kiernan switched his gaze to him, his captain. "If only there was some way to know who Calista would talk to."

"Like a sign," Liam said, egging Kiernan on. Liam circled his hand in front of his chest. "Some sort of symbol."

"Too obscure." Kiernan pointed to the back of Ronan's shoulders. "Spelling out a name would make it so much clearer."

Several guys snickered at their antics. They could see from here that Calista wore a jersey with Ronan's number on it, the giant twenty-two was hard to miss. The men looked at him expectantly.

Calista probably wore his jersey to curry favor off the back of Ronan's reputation. Her manipulative move didn't seem to disturb his teammates the way it did him, but not everyone saw the whole game in front of them. Some guys excelled at one power move at a time. Calista wearing Ronan's jersey was causing him no small amount of hassle. Next, they'd be accusing him of receiving favoritism. Had that occurred to her?

No hope for it, Calista had strung him up, though, seriously, as long as management did their thing, and kept the players out of the drama, all would be good. "Front office is going to do what they're going to do. We stay clear, keep our focus on the ice, and on the game."

"Come on, Captain." Saxon skated closer. "Please, man, find out something for us."

Crap.

Calista had left him no out. Even with the distraction of the dancers, the guys were focused on ownership issues.

Ronan schooled his face and pulled on a pleasant expression, not letting them know this task got to him. He'd take care of their worries for them, he had no choice. It was his job.

He skated over to Calista.

CHAPTER 16

Calista needed to go, or she'd be late to class, and being on time was part of her social contract with the university. No skipping, and no tardiness allowed, all to show Professor Terrence and Sage Hill University that she was professional, worthy of their higher degrees, and capable of being released into the wild without tainting Sage Hill's renowned reputation. But Ronan was on the move.

His epic speed and smooth balance made the others look like hobby skaters.

She wasn't the only one to notice. Several of the dancers' heads turned from their positions belly down on the ice.

Ronan was skating up to the wall in front of her. He waved for her to come down.

She could spare a minute. Calista moved into the aisle and eased down the steps to the wall surrounding the rink.

His eyes and lips were tighter than the other

times she'd been close to him. In fact, Ronan wore the kind of expression that shut down the words inside her. Calista was sensitive enough to recognize his tension, despite what being in a special class implied about her lack of awareness. She just didn't know how to spin this moment in her favor. Dahlia and Piper could have handled any of these guys in their sleep. Not her.

"My position is captain of the Snowers, as you know." Ronan's voice was easy, but his words lacked a greeting. Still, he was here, one-on-one with her, but at the same time, making his job clear.

She'd expect nothing less from a man with his cumulative point total since joining the Snowers. A less assertive man would never achieve what he'd accomplished in so short a time. "Calista Amvehl, Snowers fan." Her voice was soft, but she was pleased to hear it didn't waver. Sure, she'd erred by not solidly introducing herself when they'd first met, and barely being able to talk to him since, but that hadn't been intentional. She could get tongue-tied sometimes, everyone did. How'd he like it if she surprised him when he was wearing nothing but a puck? And since then, their interactions had been complicated.

They stood there in silence.

Did he want another apology? Would that fix this? Should she leap in with her praise about his practice performance? Would that be welcome? She just didn't know. At least he'd come to speak with her alone, in person, and in front of everyone. Bold move, that's the kind of gutsy guy he was. Her heart did a full rotation. He was amazing.

Ronan pointed back to the team. "I've explained to the men that front office actions are out of our control, that we shouldn't concern ourselves until we need to. But there are loads of rumors flying around, and the men can't keep their noses out of them. They sent me over to get some answers. Fair?"

Answers? Tension tightened inside of her like an overwound engine belt. There was nothing confusing about her owning seventy percent. What more of an explanation did they want? Calista didn't know what to say. "I have to go to class."

Ronan stared at her, his jaw tight. "Let's start with the jersey you're wearing. You can see where that puts me in an awkward position."

Calista shook her head, her feelings starting to hurt, making her face feel hot and her chest tight. Thousands of fans wore his jersey. She looked at him, questioning his opinion with only her expression.

"When you only wear my number, the display makes the guys believe I'm your favorite. That I'm less vulnerable than they are for any upcoming changes, and that my position is secure while theirs is at risk."

"You are my favorite player. You're not at risk."

His face started to soften, and then his jaw hardened. "It's creating tension." His voice was firm. "A good start will be for you to nix my jersey."

Stress wound through her, and she hooked a finger in her neckline to pull it out an inch for some air. "You shouldn't tell women what to wear." Not knowing what else to do after relaying that basic truth, and needing to go to class, she left.

The next day, Calista couldn't resist going back to the rink to watch training wearing one of her number twenty-two jerseys, despite the fact that yesterday had left her feeling bad, maybe because of it. She'd been up all night replaying her interaction with Ronan, and she wanted practice to wipe those thoughts away.

Calista yawned and curled into her stadium seat. She wrapped her arms around her bent legs and placed her chin on her knees. She sank into the sounds and the motions, letting go of thoughts and her sense of time and place. She lost herself in a dreamy alternate reality until practice ended early.

Ronan again skated up to the half wall in front of her seat and waved her down to him.

Ronan Stromkin, the ice hockey wonder of their generation, the soon to be recognized super star, the man whose touch caused curious flutters under her skin.

Just like yesterday, Calista couldn't make herself leave. She rose to her feet and moved down the aisle until she was as near to him as the wall would allow. She wore his jersey right to his face and cocked her chin.

"Sorry about yesterday's interaction. It was..."

Ronan worked his jaw. "Less than productive." He gestured between them. "Let's start again." His expression was pleasantly neutral. "Let's keep it simple. I'll call the guys over, let them ask their own questions. I'll keep them down to a mild roar."

Nightmare, and not in her wheelhouse. Dahlia did the big group presentations, not her. "I have class." Calista shouldered her backpack.

Ronan stayed put. "Sage Hill?"

Calista paused before answering. "Yes." Calista hated how she sounded like she wasn't sure. She'd met Ronan a bunch now and should be more at ease in his presence. How many more meetups would it take for her to be chill around him? She stepped backwards and went up a row.

"Impressive university."

"Thanks."

Ronan froze, and until then she hadn't realized he'd been in motion. "How old are you?"

"Twenty-four. Two weeks ago."

His expression eased. "Happy belated birthday. I turned twenty-seven in November."

She already knew that. Was he biding time until the guys skated over and threw questions at her like she was the team spokesperson? Nope. Was he wanting to criticize her favorite jersey again? He could try. She was learning to separate the man from the player. "I can't be late."

"Right." Ronan smiled readily. His charisma that had won him the captainship full-on display. "How about I swing by campus after practice? Drop me a pin, we'll get coffee."

Her stress eased. Everything about that sounded perfect. "Okay."

Calista yawned. She wanted to leave class early and meet Ronan before she became too tired to be an engaging coffee partner. Conversation wasn't her strong suit at the best times. Leaving early was so not her either. Ditch class for a guy? This was a special class though, and no denying Ronan was an incredible man among men.

Speaking of men, Artie was showing progress. His tangled wires and metal scraps were taking the shape of a robot. His transparent tube was now shaped like a slender arm tipped with fingernails painted dark red. Following up from there, the tan rubber skin had a bendable elbow and ended at a partial shoulder balanced above a pair of wheels. The way he'd balanced the tube, the arm stuck straight out, with the fingers about three inches from the floor. He revved the wheels and the fingers shook.

"Wheels?" Vivien looked up from her laptop. "I don't think you know how human anatomy works. I can find a website to show you."

"Don't offer a man stuff like that, he'll misconstrue your intentions." Olivia's voice strangled off, and her eyes widened. She was staring at the door.

Calista followed her gaze and swiveled around.

Ronan had joined them.

Her heart thumped.

Ronan was leaning against the door frame, with one foot crossed over the other, taking in their group.

No guy had ever looked that sexy and imposing. He was larger than life, hardened muscle and talent. Her senses came alert. He was magnificent.

How did they seem to him? Did they appear normal? Calista tucked her hair behind her ears and did a quick intro for Artie who he hadn't met.

Artie kept his gaze on his robot's arm.

"Hey." Ronan greeted him in a friendly voice. His being in her real world shook her, like a fantasy becoming real. Or, more likely, as if she'd disappeared inside of one of her daydreams. She squeezed the strap on her backpack to ground herself.

Ronan arched one eyebrow. "I know I'm early, does coffee still work for you?"

Calista nodded and shouldered her backpack. She moved toward Ronan without looking at her friends and with zero thought of making him wait. No one should ever make him wait.

Suddenly, there was a whirring noise and something cold and immovable wrapped around Calista's ankle. She stumbled.

Ronan reached for her and she clasped his arm. Light crisp hair, solid muscle, zero give.

Calista steadied herself.

Ronan didn't even jolt at the weight of her. He was crazy stable. Her clumsy trip hadn't thrown him off at all. Hockey players had the best balance of all men in the world, and his was the best of the best.

Her gaze dropped to what had stopped her progress to the exit.

OMG.

CHAPTER 17

The red-tipped fingers on Artie's eerie robot arm had hooked Calista's ankle. The partial robot held her in place. "Unhand me." Geeze, she sounded like one of Piper's Tudor heroines, but there was no other apt phrase that fit her intruded-on situation. "Now, Artie."

"Diameter," Artie muttered out as if he were commanding the robot to measure her ankle.

"Let go." There, that was more modern and clearer.

Artie stared at his controller. "Working on it." His tone was defiant.

The robot fingers creeped up her calf an inch.

Vivien's gaze pivoted between Artie and the arm. She shifted her laptop. "How are you controlling that? Let's talk code."

Artie said nothing.

Olivia snapped a picture with her phone and jotted on her legal pad.

Calista tightened her grip on Ronan's arm and shook her foot. The robotic fingers moved an inch higher. "Come on, Artie, I got no sleep last night." She yawned. "I need coffee."

Artie didn't answer her. He adjusted a knob on his controller, which was black and triangular like a high-end gaming joystick.

Ronan's expression went from easy-going to hockey fierce. He met her gaze with serious blue eyes. "Want me to handle this?"

Calista found his expression hot, and well worth the inconvenience she was experiencing with her lower leg. She tilted her head. "What would that look like?"

"I grab that arm and beat Artie in the head with the wheeled end."

Calista snickered. Violence should never be funny. She couldn't help her lips twitching, though.

The whirring revved louder, the mechanical fingers opened, releasing her, and the Artie arm wheeled back to its owner.

Excellent.

Calista shook out her foot, and she and Ronan left.

Only moments ago back in class, Calista had thought she'd give anything for a nap. Seemed like Ronan was just the shot her system needed. Reenergized, she barely kept herself from skipping as they made their way to the ground floor coffee shop.

Ronan reached around her and grabbed the door handle. "That happen often?"

Calista tilted her head to him. "Which part?"

"Assault?" Ronan's voice was dry, but his use of the term didn't waver.

Calista waved off his suggestion. "Artie's working out the kinks on his robot."

Ronan made a masculine sound of disbelief but didn't contradict her. He opened the door, and the aroma of coffee beans wafted out. Exactly what she needed.

Ronan paused and let Calista go in front of him. The coffee shop was packed. The machines were brewing, and the baristas moved at measured speed.

The hoodie-wearing student in front of them checked out Calista. His gaze stuck to the number twenty-two across Calista's chest. Long moments passed as the guy stared without moving his eyes.

Dude, he was standing right there beside her. Pissed tension wound inside Ronan. First Artie, now this prick.

The guy jerked his gaze away.

Ronan let out the breath he was holding and tried to shake off his reaction. Despite the tough reputation of hockey guys, he wasn't short-tempered. The universe just seemed to be messing with him lately, especially where Calista was concerned.

The dude tugged his hood back and lifted his chin at a competitive angle. He assessed Ronan to see which of them had the upper hand on the steal-the-woman versus keep-the-woman meter.

Dude had no clue.

The guy did a double take. "Ronan Stromkin. Dude, that game last week, epic." He drew out the epic and yanked out his mobile phone and tapped on the screen. "Can I get a selfie?"

If he stopped eyeing his date...companion. Grrr, where had that slipup come from? Ronan looked at the fan. "Sure."

This was the type of situation where Ronan's dates got weird. Some women hated having to share him, while some women loved the attention, until they realized none was on them. Never simple, it always resulted in his having to make it up to them.

Calista smiled. "I'll grab a table. Will you get me a coffee?"

Ronan nodded, and she left him for a corner spot.

The dude threw his arm over Ronan's shoulder and held up his camera. As happened with this type of event, the one guy's actions drew the eyes of everyone in line. That, combined with the fact that last week's game had been a blowout, led to Ronan doing a meet-and-greet with what seemed like every co-ed in the coffee shop.

The good thing with hockey, was that in their heavy gear and face shields, Ronan could mostly go around without being recognized, but not tonight. Was Calista going to be pissed this was taking so long? Fair play, most dates would be. They wanted to go out with a hockey star, then hated the drawbacks of fame, not to mention his demanding travel schedule.

Date? Why did he keep thinking that word?

This was not a date, Calista was the new owner. She was probably thrilled he was chatting with the fans. Or she was annoyed. He'd find out, and he'd handle her either way. He finally got their two coffees, tipped the barista, and joined Calista at the corner table.

Calista had rested her forehead on her arms, and she didn't look up at him.

Clear enough, she fell in the angry companion category. Ronan could handle a sulky woman. He squatted beside her. Was she going to ream him out in a whisper? Play passive aggressive and not look him in the eye? She might technically own seventy percent of his career, but he was no pushover. "Calista?" His voice was firm.

Calista shifted, softly grumbled, but didn't move.

Sulkier than most.

CHAPTER 18

Ronan touched her, stroking her silky long hair away from her face, and repeated her name louder, firmer. "Calista."

Calista jerked up and rubbed her eyes; a slow smile curved her lips. "Did you get me a cookie, too?"

Oh. His chest rose and fell. He hadn't known she was hungry. "Just the drink. Were you asleep?" That was a first, he could put that on his dating profile. Dating him was better than a sleeping pill. He didn't share the self-deprecating thought, though he did mentally kick himself again for thinking of her as his date.

"No." Calista's gaze darted away from him and returned. "Yes, sorry, I was out cold." Calista grimaced and took the coffee from him. She pried at the white lid. "Thanks."

"Why are you so tired?" Ronan hated the images

that came to mind of some other guy keeping her busy all night.

Calista shrugged. She got up and grabbed sugar and creamer and stirred both into her coffee. She didn't meet his gaze. "Got wrapped up in a special project last night. By the time I realized how late it was, I thought it would be easier to just stay awake than to sleep for two hours and have to respond to an alarm."

"Special project?" Not his concern. Ronan was trying to become less entangled with the front office, not more. He shook his head. "Sorry, not my business."

The doorbell clanged as two women hurried inside, giggling. They looked around, ignored the line, and came directly over to him. "Can we get a selfie?"

These interruptions happened at times too. Fans put the word out on social media, and more fans seized the opportunity to come and meet him. He and Calista were going to have to leave if they wanted a private conversation about the changes in the organization.

"I'll take the picture for you." Calista held out her hand and took the women's phones.

The women wrapped their arms around his waist, and Ronan smiled graciously. Then, with practiced ease, he thanked them and sat back down.

Calista gave their phones back and joined him. Had she taken the photos to be nice, or to control the social media?

"It's not normally like this." Ronan rubbed his jaw. "But fans post and more come. We should probably head out."

"Yeah, okay." Calista sounded disappointed then covered her yawn with her palm. She stared at her cup of coffee and then at the trash can, then she dumped it.

She'd only taken two sips. "Was the coffee that bad?" Ronan took a drink of his own bitter caffeine. The brew didn't compare to Seattle coffee. He should take her to his favorite place up town.

Calista shrugged. "If we're not hanging out, I'm going straight to sleep."

Whoa, their *hanging out* had at no point been on the menu. He didn't correct her word choice though, women rarely liked that. "Got ya." Ronan took another drink.

Three more coeds came through the entrance looking around instead of hopping in line.

Ronan led Calista to the back door.

A customer came through the exit and stopped. The vest-wearing man was looking at Calista and not him. He pointed to his watch.

Calista winced and hurried out without saying anything to the man.

When they got clear of the outside tables, Ronan asked, "What was that about?"

Calista adjusted her backpack. "Professor Terrence pointing out I'm not in class. He's overseeing my group's special project."

This was the point where most women would

normally volunteer more information. Comment on the man's looks to make him jealous or jump into flirty banter to reassure his ego, not Calista. She walked quietly beside him, making him wonder what she was all about.

They continued along the path, an easy stroll in the crisp, dry January air.

Winter in his hometown Seattle never looked like this. Ronan missed the lush green misty views. Then again, there was a lot to be said about the year-around bright sun and the clear blue skies of Texas. He'd appreciate Austin while he was here, especially because he'd be moving away. As soon as the offer came in, he was gone, no matter who won the Applebaum-Amvehl fiasco.

Of course, if his teammates were secure in their positions, they'd take the news of his leaving better. Ronan could at least get that much information for them. Whatever the word from the front office was, he'd tell the news to them straight, not leave them anxious and unknowing like what was going on now. Ronan automatically headed toward the parking lot where he'd parked, but realized that Calista could have parked clear across campus. That could work, he'd walk her to her car, and they'd have twenty minutes to get the team's status pinned down.

Ronan's stomach chose that moment to crunch, reminding him that he'd burned a concession stand's worth of calories at practice and needed to refuel. All this coffee was doing was burning a hole in his gut.

He tossed his cup into the nearest bin. He had to do this part carefully. "I'm hungry, you wouldn't take it wrong if we grabbed a bite, would you?"

"How could I take food wrong?" Calista sounded bewildered. She kept going right beside him though.

"Let me take this back a step. Which way are you parked?"

Calista pointed to a student lot in the direction of visitor parking.

"Got ya. Now, as to dinner, you're the new owner. The only way our dining alone together would be appropriate would be with the whole team there or with people in suits present, pushing to get me the best terms and highest salary, while your attorneys push back. That's how interactions between the front office and players go."

Calista blinked. "Do you need money? My check-books is the glove compartment, or I can use an app."

"I don't need your money." Ronan pressed his lips down, crushing a forming smile. He did not want to find that offer endearing.

They crossed onto a lot and Calista went to a mid-size SUV in Snowers blue. Nothing fancy or new, but in perfect condition. He'd heard that her dad owned an auto repair shop, so the safe ride made sense. What the mid-price range vehicle didn't fit with was that she owned the team. She should have a chauffeur, bodyguard, limo, or, at minimum, a luxury vehicle.

Questions about her bit at him. He liked to understand situations and take them down to their base level, but he was trying really hard to not be curious about her as a woman. If he asked, she'd get the wrong idea. He didn't want to get sidetracked or send a mixed message, even though her vanilla scent and intriguing personality were luring him in.

Calista chirped open the door and tossed in her backpack.

Ronan checked the backseat for her. A gym bag and rolled up yoga mat lay on the floor. The rest of the space was empty. The light blue color of all her gear was the exact shade of the Snowers uniforms.

What kind of workout did she do beyond yoga? Calista was slender, but strong. He resisted asking the personal question. This was not a social meeting; this was business, and he shouldn't have to keep reminding himself not to be curious about her. "I really do need to get the team's questions answered, so we can move on. We could do that over a meal."

Calista took a hair tie from her gear shift and put her hair up.

The golden strands swirled into a curvy knot that begged to be released. That mass of hair, in the sunset, on his pillow would be something to see.

Calista nodded. "I could eat."

Got ya. "I don't want to run into more fan interruptions or be seen on social media speaking privately with the new owner. You wouldn't take my meaning wrong if I asked you back to my place?" In this light he noticed the shadows under her eyes. Was he being a jerk to keep at this with her? He couldn't make himself take back the question. The sooner he got answers and the sooner he could establish more distance between them, the better for him, because what was good for his career was to distance himself from her. He had the discipline to make that happen, after he got his answers.

Calista seemed to have a million thoughts behind her clever green eyes. She said, "Drywall."

That was no answer as to whether she felt comfortable going back to his place. Man, she was dragging him in, and he wanted to explore her obscure comment. "What?"

"I need to look at your drywall. It's on a repair list Dodo gave me." Calista tilted her head. "Like the locker room plumbing. Your drywall or the plumbing could be my special project for class." She looked at him consideringly. "Is there six weeks' worth of drywall damage at your rental?"

Calista spoke in riddles, making him itch to ask about the six-week project, but the team's questions had to go first, not his interest. "Nope."

"Too bad." She climbed into the driver's seat.

Okay, typically, classes weren't that short, except during summer, nor did they run over winter break and have only four people. He resisted asking for more detail.

Calista toyed with her keys.

Dad swore that a man could learn a lot about a woman by paying attention to the small details on her everyday objects. Calista's keyring had a miniature Snowers hockey puck. Expected. A small Swiss army knife. Interesting. And a sparkling silver ball with a seam. That he had no clue about.

Calista arched her eyebrows. "Dodo said you guys had a party."

"No." Ronan was more of a one beer, call if you need a ride kind of guy. Weird of Dodo to blame a party. Not the case, and odd of Dodo to put his rental house repair issue off on Calista. Not that Ronan cared how management divided up their responsibilities. Still, he would have preferred not to share the story of the wall damage with Calista, and now he had to. Shitty, embarrassing memory. "My ex threw a shoe at my head. The stiletto stuck in the wall. No big deal."

Calista blinked rapidly. "Easy patch then." She ran her thumb over her miniature puck. In a whisper, she asked, "What did you do?"

He liked her low voice. He'd confess a lot to that voice. "My ex-girlfriend was a frenzied ball of over-reactions. It's why we didn't work out. I'm a no-drama guy. When I walk away, I'm done."

"Ah."

He liked that sound on her lips entirely too much. His groin tightened, begging him to make her echo the sound all night long. He mentally kicked himself. Calista owned the team. He'd just told her about his love life. That was not the kind of story a man told his boss. He should have shrugged as if the cause of the damage didn't matter. They needed to get going and get his teammates' concerns over with. Ronan backed up a step. "You're okay to drive? Not too tired?"

"It's not far, right?"

All the properties the Applebaums leased to the guys were near the stadium. Ronan shook his head. "I'll send you a pin with the address." What did this ownership change mean to his lease? Didn't matter. He would soon be traded and this would be a non-issue for him. That was what was great about renting through the organization, flexible terms allowed for his breaking his lease early.

Ronan shut her door.

Calista gave him a thumbs up.

Cute. He shot off a text to her with his address, ignoring the mermaid emoji he'd saved with her contact number back at the Mer-bar. He'd been meaning to change that. Later. He backed away and headed to his truck.

Calista parked in the driveway of Ronan's rental. The modern two-story house was well kept from the outside, and the lawn manicured.

Ronan waved her in from the garage.

She was entering Ronan's private sanctum. Calista walked toward him too tired to feel as overwhelmed as she would have at any other time. She eyed the garage walls with a curious gaze. All three sides held racks full of sports equipment, but no tools. "Where are your tools?"

Ronan pointed to a small plastic box, the basic kind of kit department stores put on sale during the holidays.

Calista twitched. The one in the hatch of her SUV was bigger. How did he fix things? Hmm. Calista followed him in through the garage door.

After the drop zone, there were more modern lines. The high ceilings were impressive and the open concept suited the space, as did the minimalistic cool décor, a large black leather sofa and square ebony coffee table. Very masculine. She'd never been in a bachelor pad. This was very cool, very good for expanding her knowledge of the opposite sex. Could she ease this into conversation during class? She'd totally get social credit for being in Ronan's house if not actual points.

Ronan's phone rang. He glanced at the screen. "Sorry, got to take this. Make yourself at home." He gestured to the dining table off to the right and went out the back door to a sunroom.

Curious. Why couldn't he take the call in front of her? Olivia believed when a man did that, he was cheating. Lawyers were cynical like that. Who was on the other line that he was hiding? Instead of going to the dining room, she sank on to the sofa. Comfy. She'd just lean back for a second and puzzle out the answer.

Her eyes drifted shut.

❄

Ronan wanted to punch the sky, everything he wanted was coming to fruition. GM Olson had just straight up said that when he renewed his own contract with Washington, he would move forward with acquiring Ronan's contract. Washington was within his reach. He strode back in with confident steps. The way things were going he'd snag his answers from Calista and get her on the road with a takeout bag before he dug into his evening meal solo. Win-win-win.

The house was quiet.

At first glance, it was as if she'd left. Then he saw her on the couch. That mass of blond hair, that creamy skin, long legs, sleeping beauty. He gently brushed her hair back from her face. "Calista?"

She was out, her breath rose and fell with an even rhythm. Calista couldn't drive home this tired. He could call her sister, but Piper hadn't struck him as the discreet type, and he didn't want her in his business.

Mikah would pick Calista up, but Mikah was trying to stay out of management drama. Getting involved was the opposite of what Mikah wanted, and Ronan respected that.

Ronan could take her home. Then her car would be stuck here, and he'd have to arrange another meeting to get her ride back to her. How to simplify this? He touched her cheek. Her skin was warm and soft, crazy soft, like the petals in the rose garden back home. Hockey. Puck. Rink. He got his head back on. "Calista." He spoke louder this time.

Calista's eyes blinked open. The clever light green was fogged with sleep and incomprehension.

Yep, no way he'd put her in a cab. "I don't think you should drive. I can take you home. Or I have guest rooms." Grrr, the stupid words were out before he could stop himself. He'd just invited the new owner to spend the night.

CHAPTER 19

Calista didn't move from the couch. "Sleepy." Her voice was almost incoherent.

She could stay over. He'd do the same for any of the guys who passed out on the couch. He'd toss a throw over them and let them sleep it off right there. Calista wasn't a guy though. Her phone was on the entry table with her keys. Ronan went over, pocketed her cellphone for her, and returned. He lifted her into his arms and carried her up to the guest room. Her weight was light, her body soft and curvy. Holding her in his arms was the opposite of when the guys bummed a room, and his body was having the opposite reaction.

He placed her on the bed, tugged off her shoes, and shifted the comforter so she was covered. There. He put the phone near her pillow so she'd find it when she awakened and would not worry.

Ronan left with one last look and shut the door.

※

Whirr. Whirr. Clip. Whirr. Whirr. Clip. The soothing mechanical rotation was broken by a catch.

Calista blinked her eyes open. Dim morning light filtered through the blinds. Awareness as to where she was hit her in the next minute. She had stayed over in Ronan's guest room. The seams of her jeans rubbed against her legs, and her jersey was bunched at her waist.

Calista checked her phone, but the battery was dead. Someone needed to invent a battery that worked on room temperature air or pollution. Not that anyone would be concerned about her. Her parents were on their cruise, and Piper mostly stayed at Mikah's house. After a lifetime of checking-in, she felt disconnected.

Whirr. Whirr. Clip. Whirr. Whirr. Clip. The whirring plea of the machine that needed a tune-up called to her. Calista ignored the sound and found the unfamiliar ensuite bathroom.

Bedhead couldn't be fixed without shampoo. Washing her face with hand soap wasn't great either, and she really wanted to change. Most people put on pajamas before bed. Her pet peeve, to sleep in dirty clothes and then have them on the next day, made her antsy. She had yoga clothes in her car. Yes, be right back shower.

Calista toed on her shoes and headed to the hall. The whirring noise was louder here, distracting her, and she followed the sound to the doorway of an exercise room.

Her heart almost stopped at the view.

Ronan was running on the treadmill. Basketball shorts revealed the strength of his legs, his tank top revealed his biceps. No one had bodies like hockey guys, incredible specimens, and Ronan's was the best, tall, sporty, and strong. The Snowers were so lucky to have him.

"Hey." Ronan gave her a nod and kept running.

"Mind if I take a shower?" Her voice came out sleep husky.

"Not at all." His own voice was clear and easy, as if he'd been up and about for hours.

Whereas she couldn't even get her sleep-wake cycle right. "Thanks." Calista tugged on the hem of her jersey. "Love this but hate to wear the same thing twice."

"I've only seen you in that." His voice deepened. "Almost only that."

Calista grinned. "I have more than one jersey."

Ronan pointed behind her. "My room's across the hall, help yourself."

Calista's interest perked up, and she nodded. She didn't tell him about her yoga gear and that her bag was full in the car. Normally, it would be empty by now, but with Mom on the cruise, Calista hadn't been to the yoga studio to refill her locker. She had three of her own clean t-shirts in there. She wasn't stupid enough to turn down Ronan's offer of rummaging through his closet though.

Calista wandered across the hall, through a bedroom decorated in masculine green and black tones. His room did need a makeover. The space would look great with a light blue Snowers comforter. She could imagine Ronan laying on top. Whew, she'd burn down her phone battery taking pictures of that. She smiled to herself and found his closet, foreign territory.

The space was large and cedar lined. The closet was the size of her bedroom at home but laid out like a high-end men's store with suits on one side and casualwear on the other. The stack of t-shirts was easy to spot. She walked to the back of the closet breathing in the masculine cologne that lingered in the air and snagged a light blue shirt and a green one. She left and dropped them in the guest room.

Whirr. Whirr. Clip. Whirr. Whirr. Clip.

The howls from the poor machine made Calista wince. She went back to Ronan's home gym.

Ronan wiped his sweat-dampened face with a towel and smiled at her as he kept running.

Calista pointed to the tracks. "I can fix that for you, the sound."

"Sure," Ronan said easily. "I'll be off in thirty."

Pleased to have his trust and a mechanical puzzle to solve, Calista nodded and went down to the foyer. The alarm panel was lit green so she went outside, grabbed her phone charger, full yoga bag, and her heavy toolkit.

Returning, she showered with her own toiletries from her yoga bag, dried off, and put on black yoga leggings and Ronan's green shirt over her white sports bra and pale blue cotton panties. She brushed her wet hair and clipped it up.

On the guest bath vanity, Calista found several packs of guest toiletries and made use of a new toothbrush and the white wintergreen toothpaste in the zipped bag. She preferred her own brand but getting a pharmacy delivery here might be weird for him. Then again, it might not. She plugged in her phone and typed what she wanted into the app, then she put on a cherry lip gloss. Powered by the electric cord, her texts populated. Vivien and Olivia had both messaged to ask about Ronan taking her to coffee. Calista typed in that he had team questions.

Vivien typed a big-eyed emoji. *"And he thinks you'll answer?"*

Olivia did a thumbs up. *"Make his agent go through me."*

When the whirring of the treadmill stopped, Calista took her toolkit to the exercise room and went to work.

Lunchtime came. Ronan had expected Calista to come down for food or a drink, but it was noon, and the mechanical clanks from upstairs continued unabated.

Would she descend the stairs and cook him something amazing? Most women would. What was he in the mood for?

Stop.

Calista wasn't most women, she owned the team. He needed to set a boundary with her, ask his teammate's questions, and get her home. Ronan made his own salad and a smoothie. He could face her disappointment at not getting to cook for him.

Two hours later, no Calista.

She'd eaten nothing. He was a shitty host.

Ronan blended another smoothie and grabbed a bottled water to take up to her. He found her in the gym and froze in the doorway.

CHAPTER 20

Ronan's treadmill was in pieces on the floor around Calista. He didn't know what he thought he'd find, but it wasn't this. He blinked and didn't know what to say. All his hours in the gym, and he'd never even seen a deconstructed treadmill.

Calista had her phone propped against a massive toolkit, and she was staring at a diagram of a treadmill which was put together.

Had she done this before? Did she know what she was doing? Ronan went to scratch his head, but realized he held her drinks. He'd deal with the practical until he figured out what was going on. "Thirsty? I brought you a water, and a smoothie. Today's drink is strawberry, spinach, yogurt, and protein powder."

Calista wrinkled her nose but nodded.

He moved forward and handed them over. When she reached up, his green t-shirt shifted, drawing attention to the shade of her pretty eyes. His heart revved, though he took a deep breath to calm himself. Seeing a woman in his shirt the morning after the night before was fueling a sexual reaction completely out of context. He tried to get his brain to explain that to his body.

Calista tried the smoothie, looked from left to right as if considering the taste and nodded her approval, then she chugged some water. "Thank you."

"I'll leave you to it."

Dinnertime came, and Ronan went back upstairs, carrying a small pharmacy bag that had been delivered for Calista. Everything looked the same as when he'd last seen it, destroyed. He placed the bag inside the door.

Calista was on her hands and knees, lifting the treadmill's screen from its casing. Her ass, though, firm and right there. He held in a groan. Women should only wear yoga pants all the time. She had great legs too. A skirt would look nice, also pajamas, nothing. He swallowed and resisted thinking about how much more of her he'd seen when they first met, and then again at the Mer-bar. Images flooded his mind anyway. Stop ogling the owner. Ronan focused on the parts that had once been his treadmill. "I do use that, you know."

Calista didn't look up. "I'm improving it for you." She set the screen aside.

Okay, he could always hit the Snowers' weight

room and use their equipment. Looks like he'd have to.

"Have at it." Ronan paused. "I wanted to check about dinner."

Calista reached for a wrench. She froze in that position and tilted her head toward him. "I could eat."

There it was. What guy didn't want the occasional home-cooked meal. No man he knew. No law against being well-fed. Ronan rubbed his stomach, suddenly much emptier than it had been a minute ago. He loved a woman who could cook. Why the hell was he still single? A woman at the stove, then in his bed every night, that was what he wanted. He needed to up his game and find a life partner. As soon as he was back in Seattle, he'd find the right woman, then he'd never have inappropriate thoughts about his former owner again.

Calista rose, and they went downstairs.

She headed straight to the sink and washed her hands. What was her specialty? He wasn't craving anything in particular, something creamy maybe. He eyed her arms.

All he could see of her was her fingertips to her elbows, and her neck under his V-neck tee. The shirt hung over her hips and her leggings covered her. Calista had on sneakers and a hint of pink low hang socks showed above them when she stretched. This was nothing like the day he'd met her, but he was reacting the same way. His body stiffened, and his brain melted. He'd seen so much creamy skin that day. He hadn't been able to go in the conference room since without indulging in the memory of lush curves, petal soft skin, and the fragrance of vanilla.

Stop.

Ronan took a seat at the table. "What are you in the mood for?"

Calista came and sat opposite him. "Whatever you like."

That answer from those pink lips undid him, though he could detect no flirtation in her gaze, just a question in that lush alto voice of hers. What would he like? Her in his bed, on his couch, this table, all of the above.

Geeze.

What was wrong with him? He'd been without a woman for months. Until now, he'd been nothing but happy to have a break from the drama. Hix ex, Bria, had never consumed his thoughts like this.

But with Calista, he was fixated. Hungry for forbidden fruit. Ah, his shoulders tensed as he identified his problem. He couldn't have her, so he wanted her. Hmm, not a particular affliction that had hit him before. He was a traditional guy who liked being in a relationship. He was only a man though. "I'm open."

Calista arched her eyebrows, "Italian, Mexican, Asian?"

Right, that was a diverse list, this woman was talented. He'd keep his mind on Seattle, not over-heated Austin. "Seafood?"

Calista nodded. She patted her pocket and groaned. "Phone is upstairs."

Ah, was she going to have some special ingredients delivered? Look up a complicated recipe? Nice. The frozen fish filets in his freezer could wait until he was home alone again. Ronan nudged his phone toward her. "Use mine."

Calista tapped on the screen, paged through the websites, then she handed the phone back. "I went with my favorite seafood restaurant, but we can fight it out if you want?"

A restaurant, hmm. And the teasing way she'd offered was like he was her friend, that was disconcerting, and not appealing. Though it should be, that wasn't a bad dynamic to have with the front office. No, it was way too involved. When Calista made an organizational decision Ronan didn't like, it would be like being mad at a buddy. He breathed out. He'd keep this business-like. Ronan checked the display. Restaurants weren't inherently romantic. Calista was being professional. Sort of. He was the one failing the keep-it-professional test. Ronan added his order to hers and hit send. He gave her a neutral smile. "Do you like wine? The rental came with a refrigerated wine room."

Calista hesitated.

Smart, liquor wasn't always great with business, but he wanted to keep this friendly so they could go over the guys' questions and make a plan to get his treadmill fixed.

"May I use the guest room another night?"

An hour ago, he'd have said *no*. Having the owner sleepover was not typical, however, having seen the state of his gym, her sticking around to reassemble his equipment made sense. "I would like my treadmill back in one piece, so I'm thinking that your being around is for the best."

Calista giggled. A womanly, surprised feminine sound that showed she relished his mild teasing.

She was too appealing. Ronan got up and went to the refrigerated wine room. Calista followed him through the glass door. He put on a social smile. "You have a favorite?"

"Nope, your pick." Calista checked the vents, the refrigeration unit, the temperature probe and got to her knees to touch the pins that held the racks to the walls.

Calista spent a lot of time on her knees. Ronan swallowed, forced his attention to the white wines, and grabbed a German bottle that would pair well with seafood. Trying not to look at her, he bent and tugged on her elbow to bring her up.

Calista followed him back to the kitchen. She rewashed her hands while he uncorked and poured the wine, and then they took their glasses back to the living room.

Okay, he'd get this business conversation on track. "The guys have questions."

Calista wrinkled her nose and looked away.

His direct approach didn't always fly with women. He knew that, and Calista seemed to spook more easily than others. If she bolted, he'd have to spend his evening shopping for a treadmill and forming an explanation for the guys about why he had no update for them. He changed course. "That said, I would like to get to know you a little better first, on a professional level." In the shallowest manner possible. "That way we'll know where we're both coming from, that okay?"

Calista nodded enthusiastically and took a drink of her wine. "Yes, let's do that."

Ronan smiled, ready to take charge.

Calista jumped in. "Tell me about where you grew up. Your favorite coach? What kind of program did he run? Off league? Does anyone else in your family play?" She eyed his body with an appreciative gleam, which made her light green irises sparkle. "Fitness regimen?"

All that was unexpected for a quiet woman, and that gleam rubbed his ego the right way. Ronan felt himself smiling even while heat flushed his face. He took a drink of the sweet, crisp wine, fighting how flattered he was, or was this stealth business questioning? Her questions were what he'd hear during a professional league interview.

At least she wasn't asking how soon he'd retire. That was the question that finally clued him into the nature of his ex. Bria had wanted a family life, but one that contained ample staff and jet setting, not home minding, kids raising, cooking, and caring for each other. Why was he comparing Calista with Bria? They were nothing alike.

Calista was the one being appropriate here. He was the one whose thoughts were racing outside his lane. Not his fault really, not with the mixed signals she'd sent when they'd first met. Had they been mixed? No, Calista had been naked save for his jersey, her interest had been clear.

Ronan flattened his palm on the smooth oak table and focused on her questions. "Seattle, played in school and college, love it."

"Ahh." Her voice sounded so sexual, relishing each word. "Would love to see that footage. My favorite part of your playing is your flexibility, there's nothing you can't do on the ice."

Her attention was intense, and Ronan had to let her go on.

She did, with stellar recall, starting from the first game she'd seen him in on TV when he'd played in Washington state, up until he started with the Snowers. Before she could finish describing her favorite highlights from each game, his phone pinged, announcing their delivery.

His flush had gone down to his chest at this point. They were on their second glass of wine, and he'd let her praise him and ask him hockey questions the whole time. What was wrong with him? He didn't know, but he felt fantastic when she gushed on about his awesomeness.

At least he'd learn one thing, one critically important thing, Calista straight up loved hockey. She wasn't lying about that. Dodo did also, but Dodo equally loved the lifestyle, the entertainment, the puck bunnies, and the powerful favors he could grant for executive fans. Still, Dodo would be the easier owner to back, because Calista came with complications, seriously, base, primal ones.

Calista eyed the phone and popped up. "Food's here, I'll get it." She jetted to the door and went outside.

Ronan put his hand behind his neck. Not like him to let the woman do the carrying, but he was trying hard not to view her as a woman. Five minutes passed. What was going on? The delivery guy should have handed over the bag and left. The hair on his arms prickled.

Calista was unassumingly gorgeous, not flashy. Guys often overlooked her type, but no mistake, she was as desirable as any woman he'd ever met. More. Ronan wouldn't be alone thinking that.

And he'd let her run out and greet a strange dude. Guy could have grabbed her and taken off. His muscles tensed. He was being stupid and had clearly watched too many nightly news and forensic shows.

He headed to the door anyway.

CHAPTER 21

The delivery driver had parked right in his driveway. The hood of his beater car was open, and Calista was staring at his engine.

Ronan's heart rate dropped back to a normal speed. "Problem?"

The delivery driver gave him a competitive look that had his shoulders tightening and his chin lifting. He read the guy loud and clear.

"I was just taking a peek." Calista pulled her gaze from the vehicle and lowered the hood. "This is Brandon, we do the work on his car."

"Hey," Ronan said in greeting. He couldn't help the dick note in his voice though that wasn't his usual style. Guys normally liked him, he was cool with everyone.

Brandon gave him a brief nod and went around to his trunk. He popped the lock and withdrew their food from a heated insulated bag.

"Brandon delivers seafood to us on Saturdays."

"I didn't know the order was for you," Brandon handed the bag off to Ronan without looking at him and spoke to Calista. "I'd have put in extra sourdough rolls."

"Yum." Calista smiled. "Next time. My parents will be back in two weeks. More rolls then, please."

Brandon nodded. If Brandon recognized him as a Snowers' player, it didn't show. All his attention was on Calista. He held up two fingers. "See you in two weeks."

Calista waved, and she headed back to the house.

Ronan stepped ahead and got the door. "What's wrong with his engine?"

Calista wiggled her fingers. "We just did a belt change last time. That should have fixed the problem. We'll try another." She sounded intrigued. "Could be something more though." Her interest was more about the mechanical problem than the dude.

Ronan found that oddly satisfying. "You're into cars." They went in, and he locked the door behind them.

"All mechanics. Dad's the one fixated on autos specifically." Calista grinned, and the flash of a dimple showed in her left cheek. "That's how Mom got Dad to go on the long cruise they're on. They're doing a Ferrari stop in Italy. After Mom suggested that tour, Dad's hemming and hawing about leaving for so long ended that night. They left a week ago." She sounded forlorn.

"You live at home?"

Calista nodded. "Piper and I both do, but she's been staying with Mikah."

"You're alone right now?"

"Temporarily." She looked a touch lost.

Ronan wanted to dig deeper, but this wasn't his business. "Keep that on the down low. Don't let weirdos know."

Calista tilted her head and assessed him. "You're not a weirdo."

Ronan placed the bag on the table and went for plates. "Not me. You can talk to me. Don't tell that to delivery people. As it is, they'll recognize your order is smaller than normal. Just saying be careful." Together they emptied the bag on the dining table, washed their hands, and got the food sorted as if they'd performed the ritual many times over.

Ronan pulled her seat out and then took his own. "You don't cook?"

"Nope." Calista winced and pointed at the crab. "I don't enjoy working with raw biological organisms. Too fragile, too gross. I do like eating cooked ones though." She smiled happily, pried the leg off, cracked the shell, wiggled the white meat out, and poured melted butter over the top. "Mom sorts out meals for the family."

"Nice." Ronan nodded. "I want to marry a woman who cooks."

"That's no woman in my family."

Ronan laughed, pleased Calista wasn't offended that he'd just let her know she lacked a key trait he was looking for in a wife. They dug into their meals in a companiable manner, and then he had to ask. "What are you studying at Sage Hill? Have to admit, I'm curious about your class."

"My degrees will be dual PhDs in mechanics and innovations."

Ronan whistled. "Impressive." He offered her the last sourdough roll. "These are good."

Calista grinned, reached out, and twisted it so they split the bread.

He liked her move. "Which interest bought you the Snowers?" He bit into the fluffy carbs.

"Innovations. I've made a few automobile tweaks over the years." Calista spun her finger. "Most flopped. A few took off. My money manager used the proceeds and snapped up Snowers stock along the way. Then a block came up, and I bought it."

Sounded like a fair deal to him. "Will Dodo overturn your purchase?"

Calista frowned. "I don't know." Her face grew dreamy. "If I get to keep the team, the benefits are amazing. Dahlia retains her job, I can watch practices, go to all the games, make improvements, and get my favorite seats. We'll both be upset if the sale doesn't go through."

"And if you don't get to keep the team, what will you do with your money if the funds revert back to you?" After drinking more than his usual single glass of wine, he was stepping in none-of-his-business territory with abandon.

"Same as now. Give most away, set up trusts for my family, and invest the rest."

Solid plan. It always stunned him how carelessly some of his colleagues dealt with their money given how short hockey careers were. Many went for the high life, some got spread thin because of extended families, others planned for the far future. Not his business though, people got to make their own decisions and map out their own lives. He was mostly socking his own money away in hopes of a wife, kids, and a boat. "No billionaire champagne lifestyle?

"No," Calista whispered. "That's why I kept the money secret so long. I didn't let Dahlia and Piper know that I had listened to them all the times they'd encouraged me to patent my ideas and sell my inventions." She stared at her wine glass. "I didn't want things to change at home because we have a great life, all of us together, supporting each other. Now, they're changing anyway. Piper is always at Mikah's. He could stay with us some, but I think he thinks that's odd when he has a place in town."

The urge to cuddle and reassure her pushed at his conscience, but that wasn't his place. Piper should reassure her younger sister about their relationship. "Mikah comes from a big family," Ronan said noncommittally. "I'm sure he enjoys time with you guys too."

"You're an only child?"

"Lonely only."

Calista snickered. "You can come over some time."

Aw, that was sweet. Ronan swallowed and didn't answer. He wouldn't be in Austin much longer to be able to go to her house and hang out. He'd be home in Seattle. He couldn't clue her into that, because discretion mattered, but he wanted to be open with her. Shame he couldn't.

They finished up with companionable chitchat, cleaned the table, and moved into the living room. He liked that she didn't shove him away and insist she clean up after him. A high energy guy, he didn't mind clearing, and honestly, when women did that, he always thought there was a touch of dishonesty there.

Sure, many were nurturing, and if that was her intent, grand, but when a woman babied him to snow him; the truth eventually came out. Besides, he was aiming for a full partner. Calista was not life partner material, but damn, he was enjoying this time with her, though he had no clue where tonight was going. Would she make a move? His body was more than a little alert.

Calista looked shy all the sudden as they took a seat on the couch and put their drinks down on the coffee table.

What was she thinking? Ronan braced for the proposal, the flirtation, or a request for something he couldn't give. He knew women. He stretched out his legs. His foot bumped into hers, accidently, because his legs were long. He wasn't flirting. "What are you thinking?"

Calista glanced back at the table. "I was wishing the dining room tabletop were thicker. We could put a dishwasher underneath. The tabletop could open up, the dishes would drop down inside for the wash cycle, then they would rise clean and dry, ready for tomorrow, no dishes to put away or carry to and from the kitchen. Wouldn't that be wonderful?"

She had an interesting, unexpected mind. Was she just as inventive and focused in the bedroom? Dang, this gal was turning him on. Should he make a move? Touch her? He lifted his hand.

Ronan's phone rang, and he altered course to check the screen. His old GM's name and number populated. Fate was intervening to get his head back on business. "I need to take this."

Calista nodded.

She'd already seen him step away once for a call. Doing so twice could make her suspicious. He could hide his secret in plain sight. Ronan stayed beside Calista and hit the video call button. He jumped in before GM Olson could say anything. "Hey, I'm here with the Snowers future owner." Ronan turned his phone in Calista's direction. "Meet Calista Amvehl." He wanted no freaking secrets between him and his old boss, and Olson hearing he was consulting with the new owner would keep Washington aware he was in demand.

Calista initially waved, then she blinked, and slid right up beside Ronan on the couch, clearly recognizing Olson. "That's Olson Urqhardt."

He felt her soft warmth and breathed in the delicious vanilla fragrance of her lotion. In another lifetime, his lips would be on her neck at this point. His arm dropped down behind her without his permission. Her enthusiastic face was tilted toward the phone. Olson had been a superstar player back in the day, and her adoration of another man caused a tinge of jealously to jolt through him. His finger tensed to hit the red end call button so she'd concentrate only on him.

Calista looked from Ronan to the video screen. "You're still in touch? Can't imagine how you left Olson Urqhardt, he must have taught you so much."

Yep, a fire sparked in his chest. He hadn't wanted to leave. His GM hadn't wanted him gone either, nor had his family. Now, Ronan was close to putting his career back straight.

Olson chuckled. "You flatter me. That kid there has got it all."

"I know." Calista nodded hard. "Ronan's exceptional. Did you see Saturday's game?"

She was better than his agent.

Ronan shifted his hand to the small of her back, and she relaxed against his touch.

Olson continued. "The front row had to feel the spray of that ice."

Calista nodded hard. "You work for Washington still?"

Olson nodded. "My son is negotiating my final GM contract. Ulric's the finance guru in the family. He's got them at the right ballpark, just need to get the four-year duration, so I won't have to move around as I run up on retirement."

Ronan glanced at Calista. "His son's a whiz

managing my finances too. He focuses on the long term."

Olson ran his hand over his graying hair. "Will be nice for the wife when we know where I'll ride out the rest of my career."

Calista nodded. "Our current GM walks if Dodo loses majority share." She frowned. "Maybe I shouldn't say that." She shrugged. "Can you recommend a new GM for us if we take ownership?"

Her conversation wouldn't have made much sense to most outsiders, but Olson was up on hockey news.

"I'm sure I can drop a name or two," Olson said easily. "You guys going to watch the Yotes tonight?"

Calista glanced at the clock and squeaked. "Yeah, nice to meet you." She jumped up and went to the stairs. "I'll get my computer." She paused, eyeing Ronan's big screen and arched her eyebrows at him. "You have all the sports channels?"

Ronan nodded. "I'll take this outside, you do your thing." He took the call out to the screened in patio.

After a satisfying conversation with Olson confirming he was moving forward with trade negotiations, Ronan returned.

Ronan and Calista watched the Yotes game together. Watching hockey with Calista was a unique experience. She was quiet and completely focused. If he asked a question or pointed out a move, she responded. Other than that, she was into the action and in her own head. Unique was a great word for her. After that, they hit the sack early.

The next morning Ronan found Calista in the gym working on his treadmill, and he brought her a breakfast sandwich. A suitable reward because his treadmill parts were coming together again. He left her to work and went to practice. After he returned, he went straight to his gym. "How's it going?"

Calista frowned at four small bolts in her palm. "Done this week for sure, probably."

"Good. If you like, you're welcome to stay over."

She nodded. "Care if I do laundry?"

"No problem."

Calista stretched. "Mom makes me go to yoga. Mechanical work is physical, but it can be a long time spent in one position." She curled her fingers over the bolts and stretched her body straight out on the floor. "I need to thank her."

Ronan watched as Calista went from lying flat to rolling up onto her tiptoes reaching for the ceiling. He admired her form until the alarm on the front door chirped, breaking his attention.

"Ronan." Bria's voice called out; the sound carried up the stairs sharp and clear.

"Bria." Ronan cursed softly. "My ex, she knows the entry code, didn't think to change it."

CHAPTER 22

Curious about his ex, Calista followed Ronan downstairs.

She'd describe Bria as tall, with dark hair, and deep tan skin. Bria wore a tight red dress with stilettos, and she was gorgeous. Wearing slinky red dresses took confidence and a more vivid coloring than Calista had. Calista felt weird about meeting Bria but couldn't put her finger on why.

Bria stared straight at Calista. "Who's this?" Her question came out like she had a right to know.

Ronan stood with his hands clasped behind his back. "Calista Amvehl, potentially the new owner... and friend."

Calista's heart warmed at the word *friend*, though the way Ronan said the word felt cursory rather than as a declaration of friendship.

To be friends with Ronan Stromkin, that would be something. Calista gave a small wave, but by the time she finished the gesture, Bria's focus had fully zeroed back in on Ronan.

Bria touched her index finger to the corner of her mouth, but her matte scarlet lipstick didn't smear. "I left my cashmere sweater here."

Calista got that. She left stuff places.

Ronan looked at Bria blankly. "I'm sure the housekeeper would have set it aside. I'll check the laundry room." He left the foyer and returned carrying a fluffy red sweater.

Calista stayed quiet, not knowing how she fit into the scenario. Going back upstairs would feel like running away but being the awkward third wheel didn't feel great either. Calista went and got her laptop from the end table and curled up on the window seat out of the way. She stared at the blank screen then peeked over at the former couple.

They were striking together with their opposite coloring as they stood there talking.

The tinge of jealousy she was feeling surprised her. Why did she care who Ronan liked? Was she getting possessive? Attracted? Sure, he was the most stunning man she'd ever been near, but all the players had great bodies, his was just better. His crooked smile and those intelligent blue eyes, his thick light brown hair, he was a handsome man.

She wasn't into Ronan, not like that. Her family teased her about her crush on him, but her fondness wasn't romantic. Her admiration was natural as a hockey fan, not hormonal. She simply had an awareness and appreciation of his skill. She also loved the interest in his eyes when he listened to her, how he put her at ease, and the way his hand felt when he touched her.

He was truly perfect. Her heart beat in a trippy rhythm. Even if she were a hint of a smidge drawn to him, her interest wouldn't matter. She was blond, quiet, and a lot for most people to take. A lot. A lot. Ronan's ex had walked in the door and cleared any delusion that Calista had that she was Ronan's type. He evidently liked loads of heavy dark perfume, black hair, and slinky women. Her brain tightened. Calista held in a groan. When had her admiration turned amorous?

Ugh, she hadn't even powered on her computer. She was being silly. Calista put the laptop down and went upstairs to gather her clothes. When Calista returned, Bria was gone, and Ronan was in the kitchen.

Calista found the laundry room and got her load started. After that, she took her laptop to her room until it was time for the switchover, and then she returned and tossed the wet clothes into the dryer. Calista hit the start button, and the familiar churn made a nice white noise. She sank against the floor, opened her laptop, and played on the internet until the dryer buzzed.

Calista scooted forward to pry open the warm door and used her gym bag for a hamper. Taking one item out at a time, she started with Ronan's shirts, the ones he'd loaned to her. Each was the right size and softness to be her new favorite sleep top. She folded them, reached into the hot drum, and scooped out her own stuff last.

Imagine having to do this chore for a ton of clothes, or a family's worth of clothes. The removal would be so much more efficient if the backend of the dryer tilted and dumped out in one go or if the dryer had a ramp. She could prop the ramp onto the opening so as she shoveled, the laundry would slide into a hamper. The ramp would be more work than a dryer that emptied for her, but it would be a cheap and efficient accessory. She'd try one out at home and give a copy to Ronan's housekeeper to get feedback. Her mind spun around the practical and impractical aspects. She'd long wanted a top washer that emptied itself into a top loading dryer. How would that alter with this idea?

She pulled out her blue cotton panties last. Those comfortable hi-cuts would set no guy's libido aflame. Piper was right, she should dress better.

Ronan stretched out his arms. Was Calista ever coming out of the laundry room? She wasn't his woman, and he wouldn't cater to her brooding. At least he understood the reason for her sulk. Jealousy. Bad luck that Bria stopped by, but that hadn't been his fault, though he should have changed the door code. He fixed that omission as soon as he shut the door on Bria.

At least Bria left with minimal fuss, and no shoe

throwing. Who acted so toxic and then thought they could pop by and be welcome? Ronan shook his head. Next woman he was with, he was going to schedule a ton of time with her so he could suss out all her crazy.

Calista emerged at last. She had her folded clothes in an open gym bag atop her computer. She slid her bag onto the end of the couch, shrugged on a number twenty-two jersey over her yellow exercise tee, and then she carried her laptop to the window seat.

The pretty blond hadn't gone off on him yet, but it was coming. May as well get her rant over with. Ronan moved to stand near her feet.

Calista said nothing. The sunlight hit her hair, turning the gold mass sparkly. She was gorgeous. Not that her looks mattered, her intentions for his team mattered. Better keep her on an even keel and head off any bad mood. He'd let Calista know he was open to talking about Bria, but only in a shallow co-worker bumped into his personal life way. "The new door code is 4212."

Calista said nothing.

The window seat was wide, but he was a big guy. Ronan nudged her feet toward the window to sit down with her.

Calista kept her eyes on her computer monitor. "Okay."

Huh, he bumped her feet, and she talked. That had happened before. Nice, he'd found a way to pull her attention. Now all he had to do was say something easy and final about Bria. If Calista pushed, he'd set her straight that she didn't get an opinion on his love life.

From here, her vanilla fragrance was overlaid by his fabric softener, which should not be attractive, but it was. They'd been having a pleasant enough time. Now he'd soothe her feelings, be the bigger person. "I know what you were thinking back in the laundry room."

Calista blinked her green eyes, and her gaze swiveled to her folded clothes. "You do?"

His shirts were there, two of them. They'd serve as an ice breaker. "You can keep the t-shirts, if you like."

Calista stayed quiet.

"You were in the laundry room a while," Ronan prompted lightly.

Calista folded her laptop down between her thigh and the window. She leaned back, and with a few sentences, described her ideas for a more efficient accessible dryer.

Her mechanically focused words blew away every preconceived notion he'd had that she was thinking of Bria and him. He didn't know Calista at all, and he found himself really wanting to. How could he reconcile his need for distance and his interest? He gripped his hands together, fighting her appeal, struggling to find a way to get them back on a clear, professional path.

Calista blushed, and the flush went from her face, down to her chest, and under the V-neck. "There's more to what I was thinking in there, to be honest."

Intrigued, Ronan smiled, because he wanted to know, had to know. Ronan shook her feet covered in pink socks. "Yeah?"

Calista grinned at his hand. "Piper kicks my feet when she wants me to talk."

He'd been right, not that he should know this about her. He couldn't help being pleased that he'd deciphered a piece of what made her tick, because he liked what he learned. That didn't always happen when layers were peeled back. "You have an innovative way of thinking." He wasn't a guy put off by smart women. He wanted a well-rounded family. Ronan shoved that thought down. He was thinking in the abstract, not about wanting kids with her in particular, little blond ones who destroyed the house.

Calista shrugged her shoulder. "I get wrapped up in my own head, Piper found a way to pull me out. Piper's right about most things."

"Is she?"

Calista moved her light green gaze to his. "Piper thinks I should get out more, be social in a different way. I've been mostly resisting." She opened her palms. "I love hockey, working on mechanical puzzles, my friends, and my family. That's enough, right?"

Sounded good to him, plus sex. Who didn't want sex? "Only you can answer that."

Calista flushed harder. "I need to improve my romantic life."

Whoa, Ronan was following and knew he should shut this topic down. They'd gone from zero to deeply personal within a heartbeat. Derailing this conversation would be easy. Rise and turn on the TV. Heck, show her to the door, tell her they'd speak at the office. He couldn't make himself move. "Do you need more?"

Calista looked at him helplessly and nodded. "I told her that when I met the right guy, I'd put in the effort. She pushes anyway. Now, I think she's right."

Don't ask. Shut this down. He was going three hundred miles an hour toward the wall. That wasn't how he played his game. "Why is she right?"

Calista shrugged.

"You can tell me."

Calista looked at him with big honest eyes, so open his chest hurt. "I was in the laundry room, and I had other thoughts too." She pointed to a pair of blue cotton panties atop her pile of clean clothes.

Snowers blue. He swallowed and rubbed his jaw. She was so sweetly consistent.

"Those are the type of undies in my gym bag." Calista opened her palm. "I know you're not a guy."

"I'm a guy." Ronan said that with absolute certainty. If he weren't, he would be able to rise and step away from her while she described her panties.

Calista looked out the window. "I know, I mean one who is into me. Guys aren't into me as a woman, they don't get me, they're into women like Bria." She pointed to her undies. "Not women who wear comfy blue cotton instead of lacy thongs."

Ronan said nothing, but his heart pounded harder. *Not going there. Not doing it.*

Calista tilted her chin. "I have been out with guys before."

Not going there. Not doing it. His lips tightened. He went there. Of course she dated, of course guys were interested. Look at her, enticing and gorgeous. Why had she brought that up? He wasn't tracking, or she wasn't speaking in a linear pattern. "Yeah?"

"My love relationships never work out. I can't get past a few dates." Calista tapped her temple. "I'm a lot."

A lot? Fair. Took a real man to handle a lot. Ronan shrugged. "You dated weak men. That's what dating is, weeding out the non-contenders." He played with talented guys who were a lot. Every one of them was a star. "Everyone on our team is a lot." Had he just compared her to a bunch of sweaty guys? Idiot.

Calista blinked, looking surprised. She smiled sweetly at him. "That's one of the nicest things anyone has ever said to me." Her voice was quiet despite the delight in her green eyes.

Damn, she needed more people in her life who appreciated her and her uniqueness. Ronan put his hand over her ankle and squeezed gently.

Calista swallowed hard. "Piper thinks I should dress better. Order nicer lingerie. I like comfy. But back in the laundry room, I wasn't only re-imagining the dryer." She wore a confessional expression. "I was thinking, if I had fancier undies, and this kind of sleepover happened with a real guy, I'd be excited to have silky tempting lingerie to wear, instead of dressing like I was casual and wouldn't put in any effort for him. That's fully what I was thinking about in the laundry room."

Who knew honesty could be such a freaking aphrodisiac? All he could think about was the clothes she wore against her skin. He had to stop. Focus on work. Hockey. *Calista in blue Snowers' panties.* Puck. *Nope, don't go there.* Rink. Ronan edged his fingers along her shin and under the hem of her yoga pant leg, then slid his thumb against her silky ankle.

Calista's pupils dilated.

Ah, she was attracted to him. This was not just hypothetical, nor was it professional, at all.

He'd never touched Dodo's ankle, never had any desire to, never would. But here he was with Calista, and he couldn't make his fingers drop away. His sheer inability to pull up even a speck of his mammoth discipline was throwing him off. He'd borrow some of her restraint. Open his mouth, say she was the owner, and they should disband and meet back at the stadium.

Ronan swallowed. "I was involved with a woman in the Washington office, an executive. When things went south, I was traded. The move was best for the team. I won't make that mistake again." He knew his fingers were still rubbing the back of her soft ankle, but he couldn't stop. Her skin was like petals in the sun, and by comparison her soft stretchy yoga pants felt rough. "You're lovely, but you see, our not getting together is not about you. My past has taught me better than to mix professional and personal."

Calista shifted against the cushion, and her arms

fell to her sides. "I didn't know I was attracted to you until today."

Her admission punched him in the chest.

"I mean, I adore you, you're my favorite player, but I didn't know I wanted..."

Ronan put his finger against her soft lips to keep her from finishing her sentence. His heart rate picked up. He knew what she wanted.

"You, that way," she whispered, and her warm breath set his nerve endings alight from his finger up his arm and to his chest. From there, every part of him went on alert. He was narrowed in on the answer to a deep want, a building desire, an unshakable pull. He tightened his grip on her ankle.

Calista nodded. "I understand what you're saying. Look what happened to Dodo and Dahlia. She had to leave her job. Who would want to work under their ex? If my stock purchase gets officially stamped, Dahlia will still be in an awkward position, but at least she'll be equal to Dodo. I can do that for her. She deserves it, and I'd love to help her."

Ronan didn't want to talk about her cousin or the front office. "You believe the sale will go through?" His voice came out raw.

Calista nodded. "I think within the month the paperwork will be sorted. Or, just over a week if our arbitration works."

"That gives us a week." What was he saying? Was he really inviting Calista into his bed for a week? Had his desire smashed all his discipline, and rationalized a timeframe to get what he wanted, what they both wanted?

Calista blinked rapidly.

Ronan shook his head. "I shouldn't have said that." He was right though. They had a brief window where they could be more than friends. "The idea was in my head, and the words popped out of my mouth." There were so many reasons they did not suit each other. "There's no point though, I'll hurt you. I want a homebody, cook and take care of me woman. You're..."

Calista finished his sentence. "A lot, I know."

Ronan shifted. He leaned forward, put his finger under her chin, and tilted her head up to his.

CHAPTER 23

Calista widened her eyes, and then, Ronan was kissing her. One minute they were ruminating on heating elements and dryer drums, and the next he was heating her. His kiss was firm and certain. Her lips parted at the touch of his tongue, and erotic tingles shimmered from her lips downwards. He was like a sorcerer who'd splashed her with a love potion.

Wow.

Ronan threaded his fingers into her hair and cupped the back of her head. He pulled back and dropped his forehead to hers, his chest rising and falling hard.

Her world and concept of what a kiss was were expanding, Calista put one hand on his hard thigh and the other on his shoulder, needing to anchor herself in this moment on this earth, to both hold on to the sensation and to understand.

She couldn't. This was beyond comprehension. Ronan Stromkin had kissed her. He'd been rubbing her ankle, making happy flutters dance with her nerve endings, all the while telling her why he couldn't be with her. That contradiction alone had knocked her socks off. He was speaking as if she had a shot with him. Then he explained why they wouldn't work. His reasoning was solid. And then the man kissed her.

Were men this confusing to all women? Or just her? She'd been on dates, she'd been kissed. How was his kiss so different? Chemistry? She'd never given that field the credit it deserved. This was no pleasant peck to end a night, this was a spark lighting a wick, a dive into the Mer-tank, a prelude to an explosion. Yes, that.

Her body hummed, and she wanted more of him.

She wanted an orgasm. How to word that after all he'd said? "What's happening?" Calista patted his arms and curled her fingers into his hard biceps. Even losing her mind, his body made an impression on her. His strength stunned her and drew her to him. Calista tapped her fingers, half on his short-sleeved shirt, half on his skin. Touching him was delightful, like living in a daydream and doing exactly as she wanted. She slid her fingers down and back up and under his sleeve. Yes, she traced small strokes against his muscular biceps.

"I'm not a casual one-week kind of guy." Ronan kissed her neck.

Electricity shot through her, nothing fleeting, a full, strong pulse. Calista sucked in a breath.

He licked her skin, and the feeling made her legs part.

Calista shifted causing her laptop to jostle against the window. "Oh."

"Are you?" His voice deepened and held a plea.

"Am I what?" She sounded out of breath.

"Into casual sex? Or are you a relationship-only person like me?" His voice was deep and alluring, like sex and hockey combined.

"I've never gotten far enough to find out. Again, I'm a lot, too much for most guys." The intimate sensations numbed her brain, letting her share her vulnerability, and the difficult truth came out without the usual reserve.

"I like simple." Ronan kissed her neck, again sending trippy throbs through her. "But I can't seem to stay away from you, though I need to."

Hmm, the compliment buzzed warm inside her, and she wasn't even put off by his truth. She understood. "I know you're not the problem, it's me." She giggled. "We both know it's me. That's okay."

Ronan cupped her head and looked into her eyes. "It's not you. It's the situation. You're damned interesting, and my fingers are dying to touch more of you, and have you put your hands on me." He looked dazed, his blue eyes glassy. "Your touching me is like having petals fall over my body."

Nice. She forced her brain to consider all he'd said, and not just all she was feeling, such as their intense mutual attraction, all his reasonable arguments, their complicated work situation, the sensible thing to do, the importance of discipline, and yep, even the purity pledge. She pressed her fingers into his biceps and flattened her palms against his hard muscles. Touching him was divine. She wanted more, and despite the complexities, that won. "Yes, let's do that, more touching."

Ronan stilled. "My cards are on the table. We only have a week, possibly a touch longer, and we have to keep our affair private. Why would you accept so little? Is this because you're a fan?"

Calista shook her head hard. Whatever this was, she didn't want him to think her feelings were one dimensional, because that reasoning had an element of using him. She wanted him to understand. "I adore how Liam plays. He's so frenetic, he'd make me crazy and comforted at the same time. And Saxon, when he's not in his head, whew, one day soon he'll be unstoppable. And Mikah, he's a blur, but when he stops, he's beautiful, a model on skates. And Kiernan, unpredictable but somehow reliable. He's exciting to watch."

"Okay, for my ego, you can stop now." He lightly, teasingly, bit down on her collarbone.

Calista didn't have the urge to giggle this time. That possessive grip was hot. "I admire how they play. I don't want their clothes off. They are extraordinary, you are so much more."

Ronan groaned.

She loved that her sincerity caused Ronan to make that sound.

"I think the same about you," his voice was deep and heartfelt.

That warmed her and helped her continue. "I don't know when my admiration changed. Maybe when you touched me in the conference room. I had quivers all over, from just your fingertips on my arm." Calista let her bewilderment show in her voice. "The sensations weren't like anything I've ever felt."

Ronan's blue eyes heated, but he made no romantic move. His chest rose and fell with his breaths. "This is temporary, though."

Temporary was a lifetime more than Calista thought she would get with him. "Okay, temporary." She held her breath, alert to the tension of his body, eager to see his next move, hear his next words, and feel his next touch.

Ronan pressed his lips together before speaking. "You're agreeing, but I want to make sure you understand. When the paperwork's done, our relationship changes. I won't have a front office romance."

Was she in control of this? She was, and being with him felt right. Calista reached up and cupped his face. "We have a very short window, maybe until Monday of next week, a few weeks at most. We'll never make it past February." She'd never said truer words. Even without the organization ownership issue. "A day, a week, a month, I'm on board, and I won't make this weird for you."

"It isn't you."

Calista nodded, and got that this time, it really wasn't. Being with her would cause him all kinds of grief and attention. Was she being selfish? Maybe. She looked down.

He placed his fingers on her chin and lifted until she met his gaze. "It isn't you," he repeated.

She nodded. "Where do we go from here?"

Ronan eased off the window seat and stood in front of her. "What do you want? Say it simply for me, so I understand."

Calista spun to face him, putting her back to the window. Verbal clarity was not her strength, but she knew what she wanted. Calista tilted her head back and looked up into his blue eyes. "An orgasm."

CHAPTER 24

Calista watched him closely for his reaction. Ronan's mouth dropped open, and a flush hit the top of his cheeks. "You always surprise me."

Calista looked down. Before the feelings of *not being normal* could swamp her, Ronan tilted her chin up with one finger. "I like it." He bent and brushed his lips over hers. "You surprise me in the best ways, and I love your request."

Pleasure sparkled through her, and a new surge of confidence made her run fingers up his arms to his shoulders. Calista grazed her nails lightly against his tan skin and tunneled her hands into his hair. She did not want to waste a moment of time with him.

Ronan slipped his hands under her jersey. They were warm and strong on her bare skin.

Sensations zoomed through her. "Mmm."

Ronan dropped his hands to her thighs and parted her knees so he could step between them, and he hooked her legs around his hips. The move was intense and exciting, like watching him on ice, but on a sexy level.

Ronan put his hands under her bum and lifted her.

Calista tightened her grip instinctively, though she had confidence in his strength. Being in his arms had cracked open an alternative universe to her, and she was happy to be carried through the portal.

Ronan bent to kiss her neck, licked the same spot, and then began walking, taking her upstairs and into his darkened bedroom.

Her mind was reeling. This was happening.

Sex.

With Ronan.

Unbelievable and perfect, at the same time. What would he look like without his clothes? What would he feel like?

Ronan placed her atop his fluffy comforter and bent to pull her shoes and socks off while he kicked off his own. He scooted her up toward the pillows then sat beside her. They were both still fully dressed, and he moved slowly, as if he wanted to take his time with her. He kissed her. His mouth was warm and sent flutters from her lips throughout her body, relaxing and thrilling.

The more they kissed, the more her clothes became restrictive, heavy, and she gripped his biceps hard, wanting more, needing all of him to touch all of her. She let go and tugged at her shirt.

Ronan followed the motion with his gaze. "I love

my jersey on you, but now all I want is for it to come off."

She felt the same. Calista lifted the top further.

Ronan groaned, and then helped clear the jersey and exercise top from her body. "You're gorgeous." He stripped off his own shirt.

Calista shivered. "You're stunning." Her mouth dried up. All that honed athletic perfection within touching distance. This sexual moment was more overwhelming than when he wore his uniform, and that had caused some crazy vivid flutters. This was different, erotic. She leaned forward and licked and sucked on his neck to show him how she was feeling. He needed to do something about her tight nipples and her aching core, to put his glorious body to carnal use. She wiggled her hips and shifted, rubbing against him, going with what felt good. "Mmm." The sensation eased one heartbeat and then intensified the throbbing between her legs in the next.

Ronan moved over her, pressing his knees between hers, wedging her legs open, and creating space to settle between her thighs.

Calista dropped her head back to the pillow. "Yes, like that." Being with him was amazing. His masculine hands and their connection were beyond enchanting.

He cupped her through her pants.

The sensation was shocking but enthralling and sent an explosion of lava through her. "Oh, I like that too."

Ronan chuckled in a husky, pleased way and met

her gaze. "Me too." His lips landed on hers, parting them with his tongue. He played with her lips with his teeth and explored her reactions.

More drugging kisses and her bra was gone. She rubbed her breasts against him, indulging in the sensations.

"You're even softer than I imagined, and your moves are killing me," Ronan said in a husky voice between kisses that trailed from her jaw to her breast. Then he took her left nipple in his mouth and sucked while caressing her other breast with one hand. "Tell me everything you like, and I'll give it to you."

Gah, she couldn't form a sentence. "Yes, me too." Did that even make sense? His weight was so satisfying, while contrarily his mouth was making her ache and writhe. "Please." Calista didn't recognize her own plea. Her need, and how right she felt with him emboldened her, and she moved her fingers from caressing his back to the button of his jeans.

Ronan rolled off and stripped. He reached over to the nightstand and grabbed a box of condoms. He struggled with the wrapping, as if he, the most highly coordinated man she knew, was having difficulty getting a box open. He ripped the end off and shook condoms out on the pillow before letting the box fall to the bed.

Ronan tugged her yoga pants lower, but not off. His gaze was caught on the pale blue of her panties. "So pretty." He slipped his fingers under the elastic and cotton. He touched her lightly, exploring and setting off trembly vibrations through her. "I don't care if you wear comfy, I love your reactions." He stroked her again.

Calista jerked, licked her lips, and her breasts rose and fell with her heavy breathing. She clenched her fingers against his hips. "Kiss me."

Ronan stretched up and kissed her, and zings spread from her lips downwards. At the same time, his fingers traced her skin under her panties and gently delved between her slick folds, creating even more powerful quivers. "You're so lovely." His words were a hushed, reverent whisper.

Calista arched her back, her yearning intensifying. She touched him everywhere she could reach, wanting him to feel the same delicious sensations. "You too, you're remarkable."

Ronan took his hand away and Calista panted out a breath. He had her on the edge.

Ronan's own breathing was just as ragged. He slid her panties and pants down her legs and off. Cool air touched her skin, then his warm body as he nestled back into position. She rubbed her smooth legs against his rougher ones, restless, and her passion heightened.

He gave a pleased murmur.

Calista squeezed his hard muscles and relished every caress he gave in kind.

The ache at her core was driving her mad, and she thought this part would feel foreign, but it didn't. Being close to him was natural and mind-blowingly exciting. She wanted to know more, feel more, and take this even further. Calista reached lower and cupped him lightly, searching his gaze to see if the move was okay.

Ronan squeezed her hand, encouraging her to go harder. She did, and he moaned. He moved his fingers to her core. The mutual touching was sexy and not unlike a synchronized puzzle. He stroked, sending wild flutters through her. She touched him with the same motion, and he made guttural appreciative sounds, then they repeated the same moves and changed them, amping and spiraling the sparkles inside her.

He kissed her throughout, nipping her bottom lip and licking it. Her center was tingling, aching and wet, her nipples pinpoint hard, her mind gone, and she wriggled against his erection with intensified need. "Please."

Ronan understood her gasped plea because he grabbed a foil packet, tore the end with his teeth, and fitted the protection to his body. He lifted her again, positioning her so he was at her core. He slowly pressed forward, sliding smoothly into her, filling her. "You feel like heaven, tight, silky." He gasped out the compliments. He moved in and out of her slowly, in a smooth, satisfying pace.

"You too." Calista searched for the words so he'd understand her delight and amazement. There were none. His power, command, and movements thrust her into an unexplored universe of sensation and then further. *Oh, yes, there.* There was one word. "Perfect, you're perfect."

Pleasure washed through her, cresting in starlit

waves that dissolved her from her body and made the world disappear, and then the blackness stopped and she returned to earth.

Ronan murmured praise against her ear. "Beautiful. Delicate. Incredible."

Calista found more words. "Like you filled a void, then the waves of pleasure destroyed every atom until I wasn't here anymore." The same sensation was filling her again. "Oh, like that."

Ronan smiled down at her. "I really love when you share your thoughts." He kissed her, his thrusts grew more rapid, and he pumped faster in and out of her.

More delightful sensations were building in her anew. Within seconds, she was crying out again, holding him tightly, pulling him closer.

Ronan groaned, and with one final thrust, he came inside her, a primal sound she echoed as she reached her second climax. Warm and complete, and marveling at the echoes of sensation, she wanted to be nowhere else.

Ronan carefully untangled himself from her arms and left her body. He pulled himself up to lean against the headboard. His expression was sated, happy, and a touch shocked.

She totally understood. Tonight was unbelievable. Lingering erotic ecstasy clung to her body. He'd given her what she'd asked for, orgasms which were more delicious than she could have dreamed. "Wow, thank you."

He kissed her forehead and slid down to embrace her. "That's what I was going to say."

Ronan was relaxed, satisfied, and kicking himself for waiting as long as he had. Being with Calista was wonderful. Giving in wasn't a demonstration of his lack of discipline, but a homage to how strong he'd been in resisting. He knew that now.

Calista looked at him with bright eyes and curled against his chest. He loved the feel of her soft curves. She shifted back and forth, re-energizing his body.

He groaned. "You're so damn soft." He moved his hand between them, and cupped a breast, giving it a gentle squeeze and thumbing her nipple.

Calista blinked. "People think I can't compromise. I can."

He had no idea where that came from, but was happy to follow the trail. "Can you?"

"I'm self-absorbed, I know that." She flushed. "Spoiled. My family, my school, my friends. People indulge me."

"I like how you are." Ronan tipped her chin up and kissed her. He meant every word. Even more were filling his chest, but he shoved them down. This was temporary, to get sidetracked by believing anything else would hurt them both. "You deserve to be indulged."

Calista cupped his jaw. "You're in a small

precious-to-me club." Her eyes looked at him wonderingly.

His heart was melting, and he pretended not to like the light in her eyes as much as he did and rolled until she was cuddling him.

This was the one day a week she had to go to class early. Feeling glowingly sated, Calista wanted to stay in Ronan's bed. She lay there warm and naked, with his strong arm around her waist. Relishing this moment was something she could do for a whole lot longer. She found her phone and checked her email, hoping for an excuse to stay in.

A notice popped up from Dodo. Calista wrinkled her nose. Olivia said she'd emailed Dodo again, reminding him communications had to go through her. Guess Dodo didn't care.

"Dear Calista. Glad you're trying to take a hand in things, and not just fangirling at the stadium. In that vein, I'm putting you in charge of the January birthday celebration for this weekend. You can handle a b-day BBQ without dumping more on Dahlia's shoulders, right?"

Grr, that woke her up. One week was minimal notice. Mom would be great for this task. She was on a cruise. Piper could arrange this in under an hour. Piper needed to stay neutral. And the email itself implied Calista couldn't do this without Dahlia's help. Dodo wasn't as stupid as he looked. Calista would have to be in charge of a social event. She had no clue where to start. Calista clicked the screen off and shoved the phone under her pillow.

"What is it?" Ronan murmured, his eyes still shut, his arm tightened at her waist, snuggling her closer.

She'd never bother him with this. She'd take the problem to the special project's room. "Just class."

"Hmm," he murmured, his chest rising with a slow just out of sleep motion. "You want me to comment on that as a captain or as your lover?"

Lover? Ooh, the word sent a heady thrill through her. Captain? Her heart pulsed, that term was great too.

"You still thinking?" A hint of amusement entered his voice, and he opened his blue eyes.

Calista leaned against his chest and propped her chin on her folded hands. Underneath the sensitive skin of her palms and fingers, his heart beat a steady rhythm.

She wanted to slide on top of him and speed the pace up. Her body lit up at the thought, her nipples hardening while her core melted. She'd love to stay right here with him. He'd asked her a question. The answer wasn't either or for her, she wanted to know all sides of him. "Both." Her voice came out morning husky.

Ronan lifted his hand and stroked her back from her shoulder to her bum. "Stay in bed with me."

Her mind lit and eager tingles shot through her like magic heated ice tapping along her nerve endings. She bit hard on her lower lip to stifle a whimper and shifted her breasts against the warm muscles of his chest, rubbing to ease the ache.

Ronan caught his breath. He moved his hands to her hips and clenched his fingers against her. "As captain," his voice sounded deeper, and he relaxed his hold. "I want all your dreams to come true. You should go meet your commitments." He stroked her back, up and down. "You decide who to listen to."

The pull to stay instead was so strong that if he had any idea of the intensity coursing through her body, she'd overwhelm him, that was for certain. That consuming need was the persuading factor. Bottling up her wishes, she eased away. "I have a morning and a late afternoon session." She pressed her lips to the side of his jaw, stunned that she had even that freedom. "So I suppose it's dream now and desire later." She went to hop in the shower.

Relaxed and crazy happy, but also preoccupied with her new Snowers task, Calista got to class before her classmates, though she was barely on time. Her friends must be sick of the restrictions on their schedules also.

The assignment on the board suggested they work on explaining their team project and delegating tasks. Independent group study was weird, but she was glad the professor wasn't hovering over them each day. She sank onto her desk chair, though she was tired of sitting upright in this student desk. A professional office would be nice, at the stadium.

Ronan could drop by and say hello. As captain, he might like an office. All the players could use one, to meet with their agents and to simply have a professional space away from home. They'd never fit comfortably in one of these chair-desk combos, though. They needed big chairs. Her email pinged, delivering the previously requested stadium blueprints. Nice, timely. Calista dug in, ignored when the others arrived, and did a combination of studying and reminiscing about last night until her phone buzzed, letting her know class was almost over. She looked up.

Her classmates were involved with their own work: Vivien staring hard at her laptop; Olivia writing in a legal pad; and Artie, running his weird robot arm in circles around their chairs. The robot wrist was bent backwards, and a red sensor beamed from its fingertips.

Calista bit her tongue to stop from muttering how eerie the toy was. The professor would likely consider that unsupportive. See? She had restraint. "Dodo emailed. He wants me to arrange the January team birthday party for this weekend. I don't even know who all has a birthday in January."

"Hang on. I'll check the HR database." Vivien tapped on her laptop.

Olivia frowned. "Dodo's emails are supposed to go through me."

"I know." They shared a look about how annoying Dodo was.

Olivia made a note to herself, then looked at Calista. "It's a simple request, he has my email address." Olivia sounded put out. "At least he could copy me. He's setting you up."

"I can handle a party." Calista's voice wavered.

Vivien pulled her llama hoodie back and arched her dark eyebrow in doubt.

Olivia's gaze shot to the window as if something fascinating were outside.

Whatever, she could handle a party.

Vivien clicked her mouse. "Liam Velhausen, your goaltender. He's the only player who has a January birthday. What do you know about Liam?"

Calista opened her mouth.

"That's not about hockey," Olivia said before Calista could speak.

Calista closed her mouth.

Artie said nothing.

Dude could participate. He was a guy, they knew what men wanted for birthdays.

"Liam likes Scotch. He's Canadian." Calista racked her brain, but that was all she had. And the last Scotch they'd shared had gotten them banned from Dodo's office.

Olivia wrote on her legal pad. "Great, branch out from there. What do Canadians like?"

Vivien did a quick internet search. "They like hockey."

Calista opened her palms. "See."

"You're not giving him hockey." Vivien scrolled through multiple websites in quick succession. "They like other stuff." She expanded her search. "Not much else though; snowshoeing, moose hunting..."

They had none of that in Austin, and Calista wanted to stay in town. Their jetting off to the Merbar had been a risk, and she didn't need an unexpected absence messing up her diploma. Calista wrinkled her nose. "I don't want to do those."

"Fair." Olivia bounced up and down in her chair and pointed to Vivien as a fresh idea came to her. "You're the computer guru, do a dating red flag search on Liam."

Vivien typed faster. "I'll take a quick peek at his emails."

"Don't tell me how you do it," Olivia's voice squeaked. "Though, if you're accessing his work email, there's no problem. At least, there won't be when Calista is granted her seventy percent ownership. Then we'll have full privileges to have a look, nay, a corporate responsibility." Her tone calmed.

"Sure, that's where I'm searching." Vivien's tone convinced none of them.

Olivia looked up at the ceiling. "Good."

"This analysis could take a few minutes, depending on the complexity and diversity of his likes." Vivien's laptop speaker chimed. "Nope, his profile is loading now. He whines about his ex. His family is all up in his business asking for money, he gives it. And he likes maple syrup and hockey." She nodded. "That's about it."

Didn't leave Calista much to choose from. "Should I send his family money?"

Both Vivien and Olivia looked at her like she was an idiot.

Calista shoved her hair back and twisted the length into a braid. Hey, people needed what they needed.

"That's not a typical birthday gift," Olivia explained.

True. "Okay, but you said no hockey." They were boxing her in here. "Maple syrup it is."

"Yeah, great." Olivia didn't sound enthused. She gathered her stuff. "We'll firm up our ideas this afternoon."

"No syrup around my robot." Artie said, as if he had more than an arm going. An arm that could be washed.

"Whatever," Vivien said. "You shouldn't try and restrict us. Do we try and restrict you?"

Artie snorted. He eyed Calista's hair and drew a hairbrush from his toolkit. "Want me to smooth your braid?"

Calista scrunched back in her chair. "No thank you."

Leaving her row of seats after practice, Calista was on a high. Her body was relaxed and her mood buoyed by activities she couldn't think about in polite company. Plus, during the last hour, she'd come up with a killer birthday idea for Liam, and no one had bothered her as she hung out and placed the order for the gift. Take that, doubting Dodo who thought she couldn't party plan.

Ping. A text from Dodo appeared as if he'd heard her thoughts.

Her shoulders tightened. Well, she had told him not to email, not that he couldn't text.

His text read, *"Come down to the conference room, I want to run an idea by you."*

CHAPTER 25

Calista shook her head at her phone. Nope, no grade depended on brainstorming with Dodo. Dodo could email the idea, and she'd consider it. Then again, he'd said, 'down' and that meant the conference room by the lockers. She may run into Ronan, then she could skip afternoon class, and go with him back to his place before he had to leave for his away game. Her lips curved up, and her heart did a happy patter.

What was she thinking? She didn't even know if Ronan wanted her to stay over again. Being together didn't necessarily mean under the same roof. She was presuming, but she did need to finish his tread-mill. She couldn't help a little skip as she shifted her feet in the direction of the tunnel. Calista reached the conference room adjacent to the team locker room, opened the door, and slipped in.

Fluorescent lights glowed, and deep-voiced chatter met her. Her feet stumbled to a stop.

Dodo stood at the front of the room below the overhead screen. That wasn't what stopped her.

The room was packed full of players chugging blue sports drinks and talking all at once. Each side of the table held eleven seats with additional spots on the end. Normally, the room felt large, now it was cramped.

Calista backed up a step.

The room quieted as all the players' eyes caught sight of her.

"There she is, knew she'd get here eventually," Dodo said to Willow, as if Calista were late.

Was she late? Calista resisted the urge to check her schedule on her phone. She would have remembered an all-team meeting.

Willow sat at the head of the table in a red tank dress, her lips pouting. "I can handle the party. January's almost over, and we've scheduled it for this weekend. We need to move on the planning." She turned to Calista. "I got this, you can go back to... you know, your stuff."

Calista simply didn't have it in her to give Willow anything she wanted. Not when Willow had hurt both her sister and her cousin. At first, Calista had only blamed Warren. When he had been dating her sister, he was the one who had cheated. Willow hadn't been the one to make promises. But after Willow had gotten together with Dodo. Well, Willow had been actual friends with Dahlia at the time. And Dodo and Dahlia had been publicly engaged. There had been no excuse. The combined factors hardened her against Willow.

Calista shook her head. "I have plans for the January birthday bash." Ooh, she should tone down her language and their expectations.

"Elaborate," Dodo said.

Her throat dried up. Okay, she didn't exactly have plans. Yet. But she had thoughts. One thing she'd done was order the guys overstuffed, wide, leather massage chairs for in here. Who didn't like a big comfy chair? They were all looking at her. She had to say something. Embarrassed heat flushed through her.

She could delay explaining by darting out to find Dahlia, that would work. She tilted her head and eased back a step.

Calista caught Ronan's encouraging gaze. He wanted to hear what she had to say. That was nice. The embarrassed heat inside her shifted to a fluttery warmth. Truth was, she didn't want to run out and look unprofessional in front of him. Ronan needed to know she could handle herself. Which she could, couldn't she? Calista took a breath and tilted her chin up the way Dahlia did when confronting Dodo.

She also reached for her inner Olivia to throw logic at the thirty percent owner. "You want me to say what Liam's birthday plans are? Won't that spoil the surprise?" Her stomach flipped as the eyes in the room stayed on her.

"We just want to make sure you're on top of it," Dodo said in a condescending manner.

He had only just given her the task. Did he want a diorama? Her annoyance eased some of her nerves.

Dodo winked and made a finger gun at Liam. "Liam is one of my starters."

She knew that.

"Give us something," Willow said, speaking slowly as if Calista had an IQ functioning problem.

Calista stared her down. Fighting with her in the Mer-bar aquarium had been easier.

Jerry rolled his chair back and the base squeaked. "Do I have to be here for this?"

Calista's gaze lit on the wheels. She could fix that noise, and she would before they donated these old chairs.

Dodo nodded.

Why was Dodo pressuring her? Did Dodo want to take the planning away and give all special events to Willow? If he'd simply emailed that Willow was handling the party in the first place, Calista wouldn't have thought anything of it. But now that the event was assigned to her, she wasn't giving control back. Was he nuts? Did he not understand how women worked at all? "I can tell you, I've decided on new chairs for in here, big recliners, in honor of Liam."

Eyes blinked at her.

Why weren't they clapping? They were always on about their muscle aches. "Leather massage chairs, a gift for everyone to commemorate Liam's birthday."

"Heck, yeah." Liam nodded, his expression eager. "I want that."

She knew he'd get it. That chairback could be

kneading his shoulders right now. Liam's enthusiasm was making her feel okay, and some of her tension eased.

Jerry scooted his chair over, making the armrest bump against Willow's. Her chair slid half a foot, and Willow yelped. "It's too crowded in here already."

Not wrong, but the new chairs would be worth re-doing the room. She'd measured. After her changes, they'd fit. Plus, they had footrests that raised. No one would be fidgeting around like Jerry and bumping into his neighbor. Their feet would be elevated. This was why she needed Dahlia to present. She wasn't the best at articulating her ideas. Calista didn't know which part of that they'd want to hear. She focused on Liam. "The leg rests have kneading, rolling, and tapping settings."

Liam's face took on more enthusiasm.

More than half of the other players were now nodding.

Making an electric whirring noise with his mouth, Kiernan pretended to push an imaginary recliner button and slid down in his conference room chair. "I love that. I'll be kicked back, relaxing while Coach screams at me."

Jerry pointed to the sky with his middle finger. "If we're laying down, how are we going to see the overhead?"

Calista had thought of that. "I've ordered a screen for the ceiling." If the blueprints allowed, she'd dome it like an observatory.

Kiernan nodded. "Oh, yeah, like a mirror above a hotel bed, knead me."

Mikah thumped him on the arm. "Watch it."

Kiernan rubbed the spot, but he nodded, accepting he'd deserved the rebuke. What would Mikah think of Artie? She really didn't have to ask that, they'd last five minutes in a room together before Mikah left or punched him.

"Facility changes need to be run by the GM," Dodo said, for no reason she could think of. He had not indicated that previously.

Mikah gave Dodo an impatient look. "I'm out." He rose, looking like he had bit back what he really wanted to say, and he squeezed Calista's shoulder on his way to the door, a gesture that made her feel valued.

Ten guys followed him and slipped from the room, but most gave her a nod on the way out.

Willow shrugged. "I don't know, sounds crowded and expensive to the organization. Wouldn't the men rather have that money as a bonus instead?"

That earned Willow a few grumbled agreements which made Calista's words catch in her throat.

Jerry rose to his feet. "Whatever Dodo decides has my vote." He headed to the door.

"Ignore him, Cal-chair," Kiernan said. "He's always a whiny puck."

Jerry flipped him the bird. "I pay attention, that's the difference between me and you Kelchier."

Kiernan's teal eyes lit, but Jerry left before Kiernan reacted further.

Calista tilted her head, this was on her, for not presenting well. "I'll keep the rest a surprise." She wanted to leave and should have taken her chance when Mikah had walked out. She could have bounced in a graceful move. Now, she was standing here hanging, hands clammy, with nothing more to add. Did she want to meet with the GM about the chairs she'd already ordered? Nope. Did she want to cancel the order? Nope.

Dodo tossed his phone on the table and hit speaker. "Buddy, Calista's got this idea of twenty-five ginormous chairs for the conference room. We've told her they won't fit, but you know women and re-decorating."

The GM chuckled.

"I've told her it's a no go, want to add anything?"

"No, you've got this, Applebaum." The voice came through the speaker. The guy offered no push back.

She could measure. If Dodo shut her idea down, what was she going to do with twenty-five massage chairs? Calista gave in and looked at Ronan, hoping he'd help her out. He looked so handsome today, his blue eyes were bright, his wide shoulders broad against the upright backrest. Her insides melted.

Ronan gave a small shake of his head, keeping neutral.

Her mood sagged, but she knew better. What had she expected, a disruptive vow of loyalty? Dang, her heart leapt at the thought. Maybe she had. Disappointed, but embarrassed by her own needy reaction,

Calista focused on Ronan so she could speak. "I should have explained the dimensions better." She pointed to the wall behind the overhead. "We'll have plenty of room after we demolish that wall and build out." Now they'd understand.

Dodo's certain expression wavered, and ran his hand through his hair. "I need to talk to the GM in person." He headed to the door.

Willow hurried after him. "Yeah, me too."

Everyone left except Ronan and Liam.

That Ronan was staying behind gave her heart hope. As for Liam, this failure of a meeting had been about his party. Calista crossed to his side. "I do have more of a birthday surprise in mind. I wasn't just saying that."

Liam gave her a friendly wink. "I believe you."

Liam's certainty warmed her, but she was known for plowing ahead and wanted to take a pause here to better consider his wishes. "Did you have something you wanted? A trip home?" How did she ask if his family needed money? Was there a socially acceptable way to phrase that?

Liam waved off that idea of flying up to Canada. "Nah, whatever you got planned is cool."

"You like the massage chair idea?" Calista was sure he did, but she needed a little reassurance, and she wanted the strength of his certain backing before she went head-to-head with Dodo again over the gift, which seemed highly probable.

"Heck yeah," Liam pointed to his shoulder and

groaned. "Fat ass Jerry rammed me into the boards at practice, feel the knot."

Calista pressed on the large muscle of his massive shoulder. She couldn't tell much except that he was huge. No one with a body that bulked up enjoyed a small conference chair for long. The wider chair would suit him well. Maybe he was delaying because he wanted to talk about his family situation. "Want me to fly your family over?" Calista patted his shoulder.

Liam groaned. "Nah, love them, but they always want me to do shit. Your family like that?"

The dancers' new costumes flashed through Calista's mind. She had not enjoyed wearing the puck bikini. "Sometimes," Calista whispered. She lowered her voice even further. "Do you like pancakes?"

Liam nodded with enthusiasm. "Love them."

Ronan was up and over, his gaze dark and intent. He removed her hand from Liam. "Liam was on his way out."

Liam blinked and rose. He looked from Calista to Ronan holding Calista's arm and shook his head as if dislodging a crazy thought. "Yeah, later guys."

As soon as the conference room door clicked shut on Liam's exit, Ronan lifted Calista to the tabletop. "I'm freaking jealous of that thick Canadian." He moved between her knees.

CHAPTER 26

Loving Ronan's attention, though he had no reason to be concerned. Calista leaned back on her palms to meet his gaze. "Don't say that."

Ronan kissed her lightly. "Say you prefer me."

"You know I do." Calista didn't have the experience to know what his possessiveness meant. He only wanted temporary, right? She didn't have the nerve to ask for more. If she could channel her sister, she'd tease him about limited time, but that wasn't her.

"Tell me to go." Ronan nudged her knees wider and moved straight between them, pressing himself against her core.

Calista's eyes flared at the sexy move. The feel of his hips on her inner thighs, his sex against hers, warmed and sent sparkling sensations from her core outwards, and then they spiraled and double-backed. He had to be feeling this. She tightened her muscles and crossed her legs around him. "I'll never tell you to go."

Ronan groaned. "Time for desire then?" He leaned forward, licked her neck, and sucked. "Come back to my place." His demand was draped in a request. "Keep me company, while I pack for our away game."

His words and actions tumbled a thousand thrills through her body like he'd wrapped an enchanted lasso around her. Calista wanted him as tied up in these sensations as she was. At this angle though, she couldn't get closer unless he lowered against her again. Or could she? She shifted her weight on her hands and raised her hips. Marvelous sizzles flashed through her. The position felt amazing. She arched her back higher, reaching for another pulse of sensation. "Yes."

Ronan's eyes flared and flashed electric blue. He moved his palms to her bum and squeezed. "You feel great. Do that again."

His words and the encouraging press made her rotate her hips against him again, then she rubbed, and he gave her more pressure. Heady fuzziness filled her brain, and her body hummed with an unending buzz. Calista licked her lips.

Ronan's breathing grew heavier. "Yes."

The rolling clatter of a heavy four-wheeled cart sounded from the locker room. The laundry crew were making their post practice rounds.

She wanted to stay right where she was. In this position, but with less clothing and more privacy.

Calista hopped up, and the proximity made her body flush against Ronan. Heat shot through her at more angles. So much to explore.

Ronan stood still. "I can't move. You'll have to step away, or my hands will be on you again." His voice was low and husky. "But go slowly, or fast." He threaded his hand through his hair. "I don't know, both?"

Calista loved his tortured expression. She ducked under his arm and headed to the door. "Coming?"

Ronan followed her.

The door swung inwards, and Calista jumped back.

Saxon tucked his head in. His gaze searched out Ronan. "You're still here, good. I need to talk to you about what to get Liam for his birthday."

That could in no way be more fun than what they'd been doing. This birthday bash was giving her all kinds of grief. Calista looked over her shoulder and up at Ronan.

Ronan's expression went neutral. He backed up. "Yeah." His eyes shut her out. He took a seat and rolled up to the table. "I'm here for you."

Saxon came in and gave her a nod. "Hey, Calista." He paused. "Sure, you're not busy, Captain?"

"Nope."

Ouch. Calista left.

※

Instead of going straight back to Ronan's, Calista went to class like she was supposed to. Stupid two session class day. If pressed, she'd have to admit that she'd given Project Genius no thought when Ronan had been between her legs. Sigh.

Real world hit Calista as soon as she walked in. All three of her classmates were in position, and the dry erase board was filled with mathematical notations in a heavy masculine scrawl, making the room smell like dry erase marker in addition to the usual beef jerky. Why couldn't Artie use the smart board and restrict smelly snacks to his home? She got the vibe that he'd been there since this morning without leaving. Calista shoved open the window and fresh crisp air wafted through the room, clearing the stink.

"It's cold," Artie said.

Calista ignored him. She took her seat and vented to Olivia and Vivien about the Dodo ambush.

Olivia frowned and her mouth tightened. "You shouldn't meet Dodo without legal counsel present."

"True." With her annoyance lessened, Calista was able to shake her impatience with Dodo off and roll to a decision. He'd told Calista to plan the party. She'd be the one to plan the party. Office chairs were a part of her gift. She was not consulting the GM about them, not unless the GM was required to vet all of Liam's birthday presents. "Liam deserves a special day."

"Oh yeah, hot guy party planning continues, now that's a class project." Vivien shifted to face them and wiggled her colorful energy drink can in the air.

"We're going to be pros at social events before the year is out."

Yikes, she hoped this was the only event she'd have to throw. This would definitely go on her agenda with Dahlia when the ownership paperwork was final. They could offer the party planning job to Piper. Piper could whip up a great bash easily, like Mom. If Piper wasn't interested, they'd post the position.

"Let's consider the title, Hot Guy Party." Olivia had her lawyer-look on. "We can't use that when describing our activities to the professor. We have to think this through. We're not just free-wheeling coeds. We're after our diplomas here."

Vivien looked mulish. "There's no shame in calling a hot guy hot. The professors here aren't as prudish as you would think. You wouldn't believe what half of them are into." Vivien side-eyed her laptop indicating where she'd gotten her intel.

"Spare me," Olivia said.

At the same time, Calista asked, "Like what?"

Olivia held up her palm. "We need to work out the festivities. Let's face it, we don't have a stadium ton of experience speaking to professional athletes, much less catering to their needs. We need time to research, but we're on a tight schedule."

"True," Vivien said.

Artie revved up his wheeled arm and lapped the room. The motor roared. He had a dual battery pack strapped to the forearm, that gave more speed, but the noise level had also increased. For every gain there was a drawback.

"That's loud," Olivia said.

Artie nodded enthusiastically, as if torturing their eardrums was a positive outcome.

What did he drive? Before now, Calista would have guessed a wagon with an elongated hatchback to hold his gear. Now, she was thinking jacked up truck with oversized speakers.

"Calista," Olivia prompted.

Right, party planning, Liam. "My idea is a pancake brunch. I'll call a local restaurant to handle the cooking, everyone can sleep in, and then arrive at a catered feast." Calista made the motion of flipping hot cakes on a griddle. Her stomach danced. That actually sounded good right now. She'd skipped lunch and was hungry.

Vivien twisted her lips, and Olivia tilted her head as if waiting to hear the rest.

Oh, she had more. "All the guys are invited, and they can bring dates. Full waitstaff will serve, I'll import a variety of maple syrup. We can have a big coffee, tea, and juice bar." Their faces were still unimpressed. Calista's voice died off, that was what she had.

Vivien arched her dark eyebrows. "So, breakfast? For twenty-three athletes. Okay for an initial idea."

"It's brunch, that way they can sleep in." Calista crossed her arms over her chest. "I also ordered big recliner massage chairs for the conference room." Though the placement of those might have to wait until she knocked out the wall to expand the space. How were her friends not high fiving her? Everyone wanted pancakes in a big chair. She wanted a fluffy buttermilk pancake right now with melted butter and, yeah, maple syrup. The more she pictured the golden round pancake, the more her stomach grumbled.

"It's a fine idea," Olivia said carefully, "It's just not…exciting."

"Meh." Vivien contributed.

Calista's shoulders sagged. Though, their mediocre resistance was better than Dodo and the GM's outright rejection. If Dodo and the GM had their way, the big chairs wouldn't happen, and that left her with pancakes. Was there anything else Liam liked maple syrup on? Waffles? Or was that only in the French part of Canada? No, that would be crepes. Where did waffles come from? Why was this so complicated?

When could Piper help her again? Surely, Liam's party crossed the ownership divide. No, if she called and begged Piper, it would be like Dodo winning. No one wanted that. Jerry did. Willow did. The GM did. Calista had to get out of her head before she tanked her own idea. "What are you guys thinking?"

"Bigger." Vivien pumped her palms in the air. "Like the Mer-bar, but full of syrup."

Olivia tilted her head. "The fish…"

"The only fish will be people."

Interesting, like diving inside a tree, though that didn't sound scientifically possible. Calista arched her brows. "Have O2 tanks been tested in those conditions?"

"Veto." Olivia said. "You know I can't swim."

Vivien frowned. "After we decided on the maple syrup theme, I used a bit of discretionary cyber funds, and ordered tubs full of Vermont's finest. We are on a deadline, so I was being proactive."

"Bathtubs will work." Olivia nodded as if seeing her vision. "Like in Vegas, where waiters lounge in tubs holding up cocktail trays, but guests will need to volunteer to lay in the stuff. Voluntary consent. No paperwork needed, just a sign with an open invitation to sit in the syrup at their own risk."

"Yes, yes." Vivien nodded. "But make it communal fun, one big vat, come one, come all."

Frankly, Calista still liked her own idea best. Not that the two were mutually exclusive. Still, their lack of enthusiasm for her fancy brunch stung. Maybe only guys thought with their stomachs. The workers at Dad's shop would have been stoked to have a pancake brunch. "Artie? Any input?"

Artie made slurping sounds with his mouth. "Girls could wrestle in the syrup."

Olivia held up her palm. "Clean it up, Artie. Your next contribution had better be something you could say in front of the teacher, your mother, and your priest, or you won't like the consequences."

Artie held up his phone so the microphone was nearer to Olivia. "Say that again, but in a sharper voice."

Olivia gathered her things. "I'm out."

Calista left too.

Without thinking too much about her destination, Calista went back to Ronan's house. When she walked in, Ronan was headed out, a travel bag over his shoulder. Calista put her keys on the table. "Any interest in food before you go?"

"They want us at the stadium early. I didn't pick the best day to start us." He closed his eyes.

She didn't want him to go, but she totally understood. "Have a good game," she said quietly.

Ronan met her gaze and brushed her lips with his. Their lips parted, and he lingered, sending echoes of the sensations she'd felt last night through her. He lifted his head, gave her another quick kiss, and backed to the door. "I have to go." He slipped away.

The door clicked shut, and she sighed. Should she have suggested meeting him at his away hotel? Would that be welcome or too much? Some other women would likely know instinctively. She did not, and she was missing him already.

Hunger tightened her stomach. That she could address. Calista went to the kitchen and stared into his fridge full of fresh fruits and vegetables, then ate an apple and drank a glass of milk for dinner. While dining, she thought long and hard about people being in maple syrup, and how that applied to an adult brunch, and she couldn't reconcile it.

She texted her friends. *"The syrup will make a cool visual, but no humans inside. Beyond that, you're free to take the event up any notch you like. I'll contact the caterer. Olivia, will you arrange the venue? Vivien, will you sort the decor and party favors?"*

Olivia texted back right away. *"On it."*

See, she could delegate. Day-to-day operations weren't beyond her reach. Calista emailed her favorite breakfast restaurant, put her glass in the dishwasher, and headed upstairs. She had nothing to worry about, she'd leave the rest of the planning to her buddies.

The next two days went quickly, though Calista only got to see Ronan on TV. On screen, he remained her favorite hockey player, but her fan feelings were mixed with new knowledge and complex layers. She texted him after their win, and he replied right away.

Despite his not being back until today, she was still staying in one of Ronan's guest rooms. She reasoned that she still had work to do on his treadmill; once she left, it would be weird just to show up again; plus, home was big and empty with her family away.

The party planning kept her distracted and was on track. Olivia had chosen the parking lot of the men's favorite bar as a venue. Everyone knew how to get there, they'd use heat lamps to keep the area cozy, and there was ample parking across the street. As soon as Calista got out of her SUV and felt the stellar Austin sunshine and sixty-degree temperature, she knew her brunch would go off perfectly. She focused on that, instead of the overwhelming fact that she was about to see Ronan again.

The décor was breakfast all the way. There was a giant blown-up slide the width of a minivan that looked like a strip of wavy bacon. The end landed in a bowl of syrup covered by a clear heavy-duty plastic. The bowl itself was the size of two round king beds. Calista couldn't resist reaching her arm over the top and pressing down. The wobbly sensation was the same as a gel filled toy she'd had as a kid. Would make a nice landing.

She wandered over to the seating area. Ten tables had been set up. Most had five chairs, some had booth seating, and the one in the middle had a throne. Her lips twitched, she could see this event actually working out nicely.

"Hey, Calista." Liam weaved through the tables to reach her.

Calista placed his final present from her in front of the throne. "Welcome back."

"All this for me?" Liam wore a big grin, casual jeans, and a green polo shirt the shade of his eyes.

His getting there early worked for Calista because she did better with small groups. She nodded. "Happy Birthday."

Liam placed his hand over his heart. "Dude, wow, thank you."

Calista pointed to Olivia, who was stacking oranges in baskets by the juice bar while the caterer threw up her hands as if Olivia had implied she'd piled them incorrectly to start with. "Olivia picked the venue, and Vivien did the décor."

"Epic." Liam did a double take. His gaze was glued to the slide and king-sized bowl.

Vivien was carrying a stack of human-sized pancake cushions. She piled them by the stairs leading to the top of the slide.

"We ride down on a pancake cushion?" Liam got it right away. He grinned even bigger.

Calista nodded. "Looks like it."

He stared at the bowl. "What's in there?"

"Come see." Calista moved in that direction.

Liam quickly caught up and passed her, his stride easy and athletic, his bright green eyes fascinated. He patted the side of the bowl. "Looks like syrup. Great color. Looks real."

Calista reached up and over the rim to pat the brown sun-warmed top. "It is," she whispered.

"No, freaking way." Liam copied her moves with both hands, an easier reach for him because of his height. The wind ruffled his hair, which was a cooler brown than the amber liquid.

Vivien saw them and waved. She raised her voice so they could hear her from the pancake stack. "What do you think?"

"This is amazing." Liam waved. "Thanks, Vivien."

Vivien blushed and adjusted the stack of pancakes. "You're welcome."

"This is making me so hungry." Liam had his

gaze glued to the bowl, but he dropped his hand to his stomach.

"You don't have to wait, the pancake part is my doing." Calista led him back to the throne. "You get the king's chair."

"Hell yeah." Liam slid in place and eyed the menu, which had different flavors of pancakes, juices, coffees, and teas. In the center of the table was a glass container of maple syrup atop a heating element. "Amazing, I'm the maple syrup king." He drew the title out, and his emerald eyes gleamed. "Thank you, Calista."

"You are super welcome." His delight was making her get why Mom and Piper made time for party planning.

Calista slid her final gift over so it landed right in front of him. "Open mine early."

Liam tilted the blue paper to the sunlight, admiring the Snowers wrapping, and then he tore off the paper.

CHAPTER 27

Inside the birthday gift was a circular maple box, cut like a hockey puck. Liam smelled the box, and then lifted the hinged lid to reveal an array of glass bottles. Each held syrup from different maple-producing regions in Canada and the U.S.A.

"I love this so much." Liam pulled her to him in a side hug. "Best owner ever."

Calista giggled.

More voices came from the area where people were parking.

Liam carefully closed the lid and put the box beside him. He put his hand on the top, started to read the menu, then shook his head, and rose. "This isn't for sharing. I'll put this in my truck." He took the gift and jogged back to the parking area, holding his treasure tight to his side.

His happy reaction sent perfect, warm fuzzies through her. Maybe she'd volunteer to do the February birthdays too. But probably not.

Piper and Mikah pulled up.

Calista's heart lifted higher.

Her sister had her elbow hooked with Mikah's, and they were walking in now. They looked like a superstar couple in their casual day clothes, cashmere sweaters, jeans, and sunglasses.

Calista waved, and they came straight to her.

Piper hugged her. "We thought we'd come early to help out, but everything looks handled."

Mikah gave her a fist bump while nodding. "You nailed the Canadian."

Calista giggled.

Piper tightened her warm grip. "This is great. You know these guys can't sit still, and you gave them a distraction to go with their treat."

Calista nodded, her elevated mood bubbly. "I'm the pancake part. The rest was Vivien and Olivia." Her two friends were currently over by the juicers, setting out glasses.

"They outdid themselves." Piper waved at the two women and gave them a thumbs up. The music started through the speakers, fun popular tunes, and Piper and Mikah grabbed a booth with her. More guests arrived and snagged Liam who was returning.

"How's your class going?" Piper asked.

"Professor Terrence says hi. Olivia says we need an angle to pass. Got any intel?"

Piper nodded. "Sounds like a great conversation to have over pancakes."

Mikah lifted the menus. He gave Calista a nod of

approval, and after quick selections, the three of them had breakfast together.

Ronan came with the second wave of arrivals. Her enthusiasm simmered, but Calista kept her emotions on the inside and her stares discreet.

Ronan took a chair at an outer table with some of the newer players.

Calista couldn't help how much she wanted to hear his thoughts, but she resisted going over. Everyone already knew he was her favorite from her jersey-wearing choices. She had no problem with that truth, but because she and Ronan had taken their relationship to a different sphere, she didn't know quite how to act or contain herself.

"Want to circulate?" Piper asked.

"Nope." Best to stay neutral and greet people as she ran into them.

Mikah chuckled. "We'll see if anyone needs anything." He rose and joined Piper, putting an arm around her back.

"I'll check the equipment." Calista went to examine the coffee station. Not much to see, giant grinder, big bag of imported beans. The grinder's blades spun cheerily, giving the booth the aroma of the best coffee shops. The electrical cords were taped down to the asphalt, and the caterer had everything covered. Hmm, that rotation was a touch sluggish. With a minor adjustment, they could grind coffee beans twice as fast. Calista took a step toward the grinder.

"Hey." Ronan's deep voice came from her left.

His one word triggered a yummy shiver. Calista turned to him. Wow, his height, his build, and she knew what he looked like without the navy t-shirt and dark jeans. She was so lucky. She quivered as delighted electrical sparks bounced through her.

"I've been trying to keep some distance, stop obsessing over you, and maintain perspective." Ronan turned so he stood beside her, facing the crowd. "Staying away has been torture." He put his hand on the small of her back. The warm solid weight was affectionately reassuring, and the small taps he was making charmingly flirty. He put his mouth to her ear. "Don't look at me like that, or I'll blow all my good work and sneak you out of here before the griddle cools."

Calista giggled. "I'm the host, I can't leave yet." Could she?

Ronan shifted her hair so the length fell behind her shoulder, and he toyed with the strands which felt heavenly. "You did an amazing job." He sounded sincere.

The over-the-top event hadn't thrown him off. Dang, that made him even more attractive. Not that she couldn't handle good-natured ribbing, she could. Calista smiled up at him, relishing his appreciation on a deeply feminine level. Yep, she was into him.

What was it about this guy beyond his surface attributes? Some instinctive recognition that he was a good guy, or that they'd be compatible in bed? She'd gotten both right. Heat rose in her cheeks, and she shifted her attention to the crowd, most of whom were wishing Liam happy birthday.

With Liam, his appreciation for her efforts on his behalf had made her happy in a developing friendship kind of way. With Ronan, the idea of hanging out with him today was as tempting as a mechanical puzzle, a pull almost impossible for her to resist. If she weren't the team owner and in public, with all the complex issues that came with that combo, she'd love to take his hand, hear him speak with his team, and simply learn more about him. What flavor pancakes had he eaten? Did he prefer pulp free or high pulp juice? What made him laugh?

Ronan lowered his head to speak into her ear. "The way you look at me is such a turn on."

His breath brushing her skin made her tremble. If she left with him, she could be with him right now. His eyes gleaming and enthralled, his hands on her body, masculine, and in constant motion. Her chest rose and fell, and her bra became too tight, while her core warmed and ached. She pivoted toward him. Wherever he wanted to go, she was in. She braced her palm on his taut abs. "Okay."

Ronan's eyes flared.

"Yo, Captain." The masculine voice came from a few feet away.

Calista dropped her hand from Ronan's shirt.

York walked up, Minnesotan, tallest player on the team at 6'8" which gave him incredible reach and the ability to hit out-of-range pucks. He waved at Ronan, and when he spotted Calista, the motion extended to include her. "Hey, Ms. Amvehl." York nodded to the barista. "Espresso, please."

Ronan reached out, and York bumped his knuckles. "What did you think of the Rangers' third period defensive move?"

The question was fascinating, but Calista was still reeling from her powerful reaction to Ronan's nearness and his suggestion that they take off. She eased away, leaving Ronan to speak with York, and joined Olivia and Vivien.

Her friends were carrying discarded pancake cushions back to the pile at the base of the stairs. Calista joined in and helped.

"We're killing it." Vivien released her armful revealing her custom t-shirt, a llama eating a pancake.

Cute.

Olivia had gone with one of her preferred Peter Pan collared blouses paired with wide-legged, high waist trousers.

Coming over here was a good idea. Calista could use some female advice.

"I'm getting great feedback and even better photos." Olivia grinned, a clever glint in her eyes. "We can definitely present this as a group project for class." She tilted her head. "We'll be careful with how we phrase Artie's participation."

"He didn't veto anything," Calista suggested.

"That's true." Olivia brightened. "And he made adequate warnings, about the risks of robotics and liquids."

"Team genius." Vivien held out her fist, and though the words were cocky it was fun bumping to them.

School work aside, Calista had a romantic problem she could use advice on. How to word her dilemma? She wanted to leave with Ronan, but have the two of them not be noticed, and why hadn't Ronan pulled her to him in front of York? Sigh. She knew why. People noticed Ronan. He was the captain. He had charisma and a genuine interest in his players which made them come to him. Next guy she fell for needed to be less popular and have nothing to do with hockey. Her body shuddered. Ha, that guy held no appeal for her. Had Ronan ruined her ability to fantasize about other men? Maybe so because she couldn't even imagine a man who was more than him. He was the whole package.

"Who you staring at?" Vivien chuckled and elbowed Olivia.

Ugh, she wasn't going to ask them for man advice, not when she had yet to update her sister and cousin with what was going on. "I'm going to say hi to Dahlia." Dahlia had arrived about ten minutes ago and was sitting with Piper. Calista raised her chin and headed over. She slid into the end of their booth and exchanged greetings.

Dahlia sipped her tea and looked at her with bright green eyes. "This brunch is so fun."

Heat hit Calista's cheeks. "The décor was all Olivia and Vivien."

"But you chose those two, sweetie, that's brilliant." Piper snapped her fingers as if she'd just thought of something and pointed at Calista. "I went by the house yesterday. You're clearly not staying there." She exchanged a big sister look with Dahlia. "The house was super clean."

Oh, an opening for lady talk. Piper and Dahlia would understand her overwhelmed feelings and give her loving guidance. She leaned in and whispered, "I'm staying with Ronan."

They said nothing.

"Ronan Stromkin," Calista clarified.

There was silence.

Then laughter.

Dahlia wiped at a tear from the corner of her eye. "Stop stalking our Captain. If you're really at his house, get out before he discovers you there and has you arrested for trespassing."

Calista flushed hard, the kind that felt the way she had when the Bunsen burners had exploded.

"You are so cute," Piper said. "Really, text me later which friend you're staying with, we can get lunch."

Calista looked down.

Mikah came up and stood behind Piper. He leaned against the half booth and cupped Piper's shoulders, not saying anything, looking content to be there with her.

Piper tilted her head back to meet his eyes. "Any luck booking tickets to see the twins?"

Mikah nodded. "If we can get approval to do the extra day in Wisconsin, it'll work." He looked at

Calista and arched his dark eyebrow. "If you get control, what would you say to that request?"

It would embarrass her that he'd even ask.

Dahlia jumped in. "You know she'd say yes."

Calista squirmed. "You'd never have to ask me, of course you could go." The twins were Mikah's brothers, he should see them play whenever he could.

Mikah leaned over Piper and gave Piper a quick upside-down kiss, then he canted his head toward her and Dahlia. "Piper, pancakes, and now this? The arbitration judge wants player feedback, and you three are swaying me in the Amvehl direction." Mikah touched Piper's cheek with the tips of his fingers in a quick caress so it was clear to all of them Piper was the most important factor in that teasing list.

Despite his tone, hearing he was leaning in their favor, and not angry about her purchase of the team which mixed his professional and personal life weakened Calista's knees in a definite relief. Calista honestly hadn't known who Mikah would prefer owner-wise. Most people didn't like change. Now, he'd let her know, without saying the words, that he'd choose them over Dodo. Calista wiggled her shoulders and *seventy percent* rolled through her mind. At ease, she made herself a cup of tea from Dahlia's carafe and sipped the warm brew as she listened to them round out their plans to see his brothers.

Dahlia peppered in comments easily.

Calista would love to see the twins play too but

didn't want to be a third wheel. Also, she had to stay geographically close to Austin, given her class requirements. She'd check the twins' schedule and pick a different game closer to home.

The brunch had thirty minutes left when Willow and Dodo arrived.

As a couple, they made her uneasy, and because of their history with her family, they made her feel protective of Piper and Dahlia. Calista couldn't say she was sorry they hadn't been here for the duration. On the other hand, no one liked a slight. The couple headed straight in her direction. To save Dahlia from the impending encounter, Calista slipped from the booth. She moved away and stopped under a pancake-shaped umbrella that shielded mimosas from the sun. Calista took one and let the pulpy sweetness brace her mood.

The duo grew closer. Dodo wore a Snowers polo with khaki trousers. Petite Willow wore a red, one-sleeved sweater dress with a slit on the side. She walked double-time in high stilettos to keep up with Dodo. Her heavy strawberry perfume reached Calista a second before the couple did. They snagged mimosas and greeted her. After that, Calista didn't know what more to say to them, so she stood there quietly.

Willow tilted her scarlet framed sunglasses up to look around. She shrugged her bare shoulder. "A bit amusement park, right?" She drew in a long sip of her adult beverage and stirred the ice with the clear straw. "But as long as the guys can go into the bar after, they'll have fun."

They could do as they liked. Slide, plus beer and velocity would be a super mashup. Calista didn't plan on being here at that point.

Liam strode over with an easy grin and shook Dodo and Willow's hands. "Thanks again." He included all three of them in his gratitude. "It feels like you all really thought of me when putting this together."

"Of course," Willow said. "You're a starter."

"Here you go, Liam." Dodo handed Liam a round wrapped birthday package with shiny red birthday paper and ribbons.

"Thanks." Liam unwrapped his gift, revealing a gold puck paper weight. "Cool, thanks." He pocketed the puck, and his trousers dragged on that side. He sounded sincerely appreciative.

Hmm, he could melt that down, sell it, and give the proceeds to his family. Dodo had mastered a subtle way of giving money, clever. Social events were teaching her stuff, and she was learning. Calista nodded at Dodo and Willow. "Nice gift."

Liam balled the wrapping and did an overhand toss, making the shot in the bin.

Next holiday, she could have diamonds cut like tiny pucks and let Liam know he could sell them. Happiness flitted through her at the subtle solution to his familial money dilemma.

Willow touched her scarlet fingertips to her neckline. "I picked the gold puck out." She went on for a few minutes, describing where and how she'd made the purchase. Willow drank the last of her drink, put the empty glass on a discard tray, and adjusted the knitted waistband on her dress, pulling the cleavage down half an inch. "Why don't we go on inside the bar now? Why should the men have to wait?"

Liam looked between the pancake grill station and the neon lit double door. "There's still thirty minutes left on brunch."

Willow turned her impatient dark eyes to Calista. "Surely you won't hold Liam to an exact departure time?"

Calista tightened her lips. Why not? Sage Hill held her to a strict window for class.

Kiernan walked up, catching the end of Willow's question. "Bar drinks will taste better if Liam has to wait." He cuffed Liam's shoulder. "Hold the birthday boy here, I'll keep his barstool warm." He cocked his square chin. "I am always here to help."

Liam shoved Kiernan's hand off. "Can I go?" he asked Calista.

Okay, Calista was admittedly no party expert, but having the guest of honor leave early had to be a bad sign. Doubts fluttered through her, and she tasked her brain for a solution. Got it. "Of course." Calista gave a dramatic pause the way Olivia did when she was making one of her legal points. "*If* you want to miss the grand finale."

Kiernan's teal eyes brightened. "Shit no, finale us."

Liam nodded in agreement. "I'm not missing

that."

Vivien had been right all along. These high stakes players wanted high drama. Calista pivoted on her earlier decision. "This way."

Kiernan and Liam followed her over to the base of the slide. Calista signaled an "M" for maple syrup with her fingers toward Vivien. It took a moment, but when Vivien got the message, she did rally arms over head.

"What happens next?" Liam asked in a loud whisper.

Ignoring the immediate consequences for the end result was one of Calista's strengths. "You have to go to the top to see." Calista moved to the steps.

Liam and Kiernan followed her.

Ronan jogged over and caught up to them as they began climbing. "What's up?"

"Grand finale, Captain," Kiernan said with confident enthusiasm.

"Okay." Ronan continued up the flight of stairs with them.

They reached the platform. Olivia was the only person up there. She had her camera out and was taking shots of the crowd. From up here they had a great view of the tables with people still finishing up. Olivia backed up to the rail to make room for them. "Vivien texted. I've got the camera ready." She paused with a still expression on her face. "If you're sure about this?"

"Hells yeah," Kiernan said, as if Olivia had asked him. Kiernan put his hand in the middle of

Liam's back and shoved him forward. "He wants it."

Liam punched one of his large fists into his other palm. "Yeah, I want it." He turned to Calista. "What is it?"

Calista pointed downwards.

Below, Vivien and the workers retracted the see-through plastic tarp. At first, the bowl contents looked the same, burnt amber with a sunlit shine, then the wind wafted over the top and the aroma of maple syrup became unmistakable.

Liam dropped to his knees. "No way."

"Holy vat of tree sap." Kiernan whistled. "I did not see that coming." He looked at Calista with admiring eyes. "You really get him."

Calista giggled.

Kiernan stepped closer to the edge. "The only way this could be better is if we involve a nubile-syrup-loving woman." Kiernan eyed Calista up and down, reached out, and clasped her elbow. "Hey, you're a woman."

Calista smiled bigger.

"Kelchier." Ronan's voice held a friendly warning. He took Calista's hand and tugged her away from Kiernan and closer to him.

The moment was kind of perfect. The stunning weather, the happy teasing hockey players, her family below eating pancakes, and most of all, Ronan, here, keeping her close.

Ronan ran his fingers in a circle on her palm, making her insides shimmer like the amber syrup in sunlight. Calista tilted her head up to Ronan. She knew she was beaming and couldn't stop.

Kiernan looked between Liam and the giant bowl of maple syrup. "I get you now, man, in a way I never did before." He spoke solemnly.

Liam laughed. "I'm not that complicated."

Saxon bounded up the stairs carrying a pancake cushion. "What's going on?" His sneakers screeched as he slowed to a stop and took in the scenery. "No way."

"Oh yeah." Liam got to his feet. "This is happening."

Kiernan nodded. "Calista's quite the planner." He stepped between her and Ronan. "And Ronan is the best Captain." He broke their clasped hands and took Calista's arm. "But it's my bro Liam's birthday, so Ronan will have to wait his turn." Kiernan handed her arm over to Liam. "Liam's taking Cal-cake down with him."

"That's not happening." Ronan gently clasped her elbow.

More guys shoved onto the platform, making them shift into a tighter group.

"Oh, it's happening." Liam gently tugged Calista in his direction, he was chuckling. "My birthday, Captain."

Two guys, Havard and York, carrying pancake cushions, barreled past Saxon to get to Liam, making everyone adjust their footing to make room.

York slapped Liam's back. "Happy birthday, bro."

"Gratulerer med dagen," Havard echoed the senti-

ment in Norwegian. He stared at the bowl of maple syrup. "Eagle's view of Liam's dream come true. Good day."

Liam dropped her arm to hug his well-wishing teammates. "Thanks, bros." He sounded sincerely touched by their attention. The big guys made a festive huddle.

The mass of large athletic bodies had Calista stepping backward to give the men room. She was too close to the edge. One foot hovered over thin maple-scented air.

CHAPTER 28

Calista fell backwards. There was nothing, a weightlessness, her only anchor Ronan's arm, and then her butt hit the bouncy slide. "Oomph."

Ronan landed beside her, but he lost his grip on her.

Pop music played, and shouts came from above, followed by heavy laughter. Calista and Ronan were sliding fast. The first bump in the crispy bacon shaped surface slowed her enough to dig the heels of her sneakers into the plastic to try and stop her descent. The rubber skidded, squealed, but her feet wouldn't grab purchase. Her body was zooming toward the vat of syrup.

Liam jabbed the sky with his arm. "Go, Captain. Go, Calista."

The smell of breakfast increased with every foot, and she couldn't stop gravity. Swoosh. Calista reached the end and sank into the viscous syrup. She shoved her feet down and was covered up to her chest in an instant. Beside her, Ronan spread his arms. He pushed against the surface, but his hands sank into the goo. His surprised, bewildered expression was adorable.

Their gazes caught, and they laughed. A worker pointed up at the platform. "Incoming, clear the vat."

Calista looked up.

Liam was in dive position with his arms straight out over head, knees bent.

Oh, wow, Liam should not go down face first. Oh well, she was not his keeper. Calista waded through the syrup toward the side.

Every move called for a conscious shove against the liquid's thick resistance. Now, this was a workout. Yogi Murharwi should add this to the yoga studio floor. She snickered at the image.

Ronan smiled and took her hand, tugging her with him. He reached the side first. He let go, grasped the top of the bowl with his wide arms and half vaulted, half slid over and out. Once he righted his feet, he leaned in to scoop her free.

His move was reminiscent of their time at the Mer-bar, but this go around had a unique sticky clinging pull. The other difference was that last time she had wanted to avoid the crowd and sneak out. Now, she wanted to escape with him.

Calista gained her feet.

Ronan released her. He arched his eyebrow. "You, okay?"

Calista nodded.

A worker hurried over with white terrycloth

robes with crown emblems and the date embroidered on the front. She hadn't known about the robes, but they were clever brunch souvenirs. The worker held the robe by the shoulders and got behind her.

Calista shrugged her goo-sticky arms through the sleeves. The terrycloth instantly adhered to her skin.

The worker let go, then stepped carefully around the pool of syrup at her feet to raise the second robe up for Ronan. "You're a wild man, Captain." The worker held out his knuckles for a fist bump, glanced again at the puddle, and jerked his hand back. He nodded at Calista next. "If you go in the bar after going in that syrup, someone's losing their deposit." He shook his head and then jogged over to the stairs where partiers had lined up. "Bring more robes," he shouted to one of the other workers.

There was laughing reluctance from some of the people in line and eager faces on others.

Above them, Liam and Kiernan still hadn't gone. They were making elaborate diving motions, playing up to the crowd.

"Go Liam," the partiers in line cheered. "Go Kiernan," they continued.

In the end, Liam and Kiernan chose the classic slide position of feet first and hands high. With a whoosh, the two men raced down the ramp. They landed one after the other into the syrup and high fived each other.

Liam's expression was as blissed out as she could imagine.

Vivien and Olivia came to her side. "That was something." Vivien whistled. "How was it?"

Calista gave a thumbs up though her review was really mixed. The slide adrenaline had been a rush, and the ooey-gooey had been fun. Now she felt the way she did after a day at the beach. Though, instead of sandy covered and hot, she was sticky chilled. She tapped her fingers together and watched the strands of syrup web between them. "I need a shower."

"You're getting in your car like that?" Olivia's hazel eyes got big. "Even with the robes, you're still covered in syrup."

Calista shrugged. "Got to get home somehow." She chewed on her bottom lip. "We should have brought in portable showers."

Vivien nodded. "Next time."

"Someone else should drive. If you sit really still, you might not make a total mess." Olivia jerked back and held up her palms realizing her words could be taken as an invitation. "Don't look at me," Olivia said. "I don't even let people eat in my car, this is next level." Olivia looked at Vivien, then they both eyed the bowl of shimmering maple syrup, and back at each other. "I've never seen anything like this."

"And you never will again." Vivien knotted her llama t-shirt at her waist. "Let's do it."

Both women chuckled and ran for the stairs.

Ronan bent to Calista's ear. "Let's get out of here."

Like before, Calista had no desire to resist the

suggestion made in his deep, appealing voice. She licked her lips and nodded.

"We're making a mess," Calista giggled. She and Ronan stood in Ronan's double-person shower about to get clean. Maple syrup was smeared on the forest green tiles everywhere they touched. Could the plumbing handle this much gunk? The sparkling silver drain was about to be tested. "Your house-keeper is going to think you ate breakfast in here."

"I'll use extra soap." Ronan hit the electronic controls on the shower, typing in preferences for the jets. "On you." Ronan leaned down and nibbled on her neck. "You're so damn sweet."

No one ever called her that. With each nip of his teeth, a heady languor took over her body, while warm water jetted out from multiple angles. Calista held her arms high, enjoying the pulsing spray. "I've never been in a shower like this." She let the clean water run over her fingers and down the opening of her robe sleeves. The terry cloth became heavier and dragged her arm down. "I like it."

Ronan linked his hand with hers. "I like sharing firsts with you." His voice was low. He looped his other arm around her waist.

Calista met his gaze. His blue eyes heated. He released her and slipped his hands inside her robe. He cupped her maple-syrup and jersey-covered waist, then he ran his flattened palms from there, up to her breasts. He pressed gently against the curve of the twenty-twos, tracing until his thumbs found her nipples. Her heart rate doubled while her mind slowed.

"Mmm." Ronan lingered, relishing the feel of her, before gliding his hands to her shoulders, pushing aside the thick white fabric, and drawing the weight off. The oversized wet terry fell to her feet.

Before she lost her head completely, Calista wanted to thank him for sacrificing the front seat of his truck to their desire to clean up. Calista toed her shoes off. "I'll take your SUV to my dad's auto shop, get the inside detailed for you." She kissed his pecs, tasting syrup. "No charge."

"I knew there were perks to dating you." Ronan clasped her jean-covered hips and lowered his lips to her neck again. He edged his teeth against her skin and licked. "Despite all the maple, I still taste the hint of vanilla." He traced his fingers up and down her back and met her gaze with heated blue eyes. "How is that possible?" He didn't wait for an answer. His mouth met hers. His lips were certain and slow as he parted hers with his tongue, causing a sensual rush inside her body. He touched the tip of her tongue, then kissed her bottom lip. Kissing under the water was wow. Sensations waved through her, from the warm wet spray of the water cleansing her sticky skin, to the press of his hard solid body, to the hot sensual stroke of his tongue. All the stimulation encouraged her to want more.

Calista grabbed his terrycloth covered arms and rubbed up against his hard body.

Ronan groaned and shrugged out of his robe. The mess of fabric landed on the drain, and Calista nudged it aside with her toe covered in a water-soaked sock. "I know a lot about plumbing now, we can't block the channel."

Ronan laughed and dropped to his knees. "I'm not doing my job if you're thinking about the bath fixtures, and I pride myself on how I do my job." He unfastened the button on the waistband of her jeans.

CHAPTER 29

With that one practical flip, the button of her jeans loosened, and Ronan kissed his way down as he lowered her zipper. All of Calista's thoughts short-circuited, all of them. "Oooh." Thrills, amber, and sparkling consumed her as the shower spray pulsed over her.

Ronan ran his hands over her body as if tracing her reactions, and he murmured appreciation all the while. All of his touching was happening over her Snowers blue cotton panties. Even with that barrier, the sensations overwhelmed, and her knees lost the ability to hold her up.

Calista kneeled, threw her arms around Ronan's neck, and kissed him slow and long. The push, the pull, the taste of him was heady and delicious, maple-tinted, but masculine. She lowered her arms, sliding them down the front of his t-shirt covered chest, and up under the soaked fabric. The navy t-shirt hung heavy on her arms, and she caressed his wonderful, warm skin.

Ronan reached back and yanked his t-shirt over his head, giving her a visual to go with her sense of touch. The overwhelming power of his physique was stunning and admirable. Water droplets raced atop her fingers and over his cut abs. The view was sensual and captivating, she'd seen nothing like it. He was giving her an amazing mental screensaver.

Now, there was a billion-dollar idea, video abs. She traced her fingers up his back and down over his chest, relishing the sensations against her palms. She paused to brush her thumbs over his nipples and caused him to moan before tracking the path of the water droplets.

Ronan squeezed her bum. "I'm losing it, and I don't even have your shirt off." Ronan's voice was husky and intimate, the way he sounded in bed. "Arms up."

Calista didn't want to stop the patterns she was making and bit her lip to gain control. She raised her arms, her body in a kneeling yoga mountain pose.

Ronan made quick work of her jersey, and the garment fell to the tiles, landing in an intimate tangle with his t-shirt. If she had her phone, she'd take a picture and frame it for her bedroom wall. Did their phones still work? They were a few feet away on the bathroom counter with his keys. Calista shifted in that direction and started to lower her arms.

"Nuh uh." Ronan clasped her wrists in one of his

hands. "You're not leaving me." He draped her arms around his neck and tugged her closer.

Calista giggled.

"I swear, tell me, you want to create electronic sliding doors for my shower? Add a fifth body jet? Fire up a heated towel chute? What?"

"Heated towel chute." Calista snickered. "Stay right there." She got to her feet, not recognizing her own suggestive voice, as she padded over to the vanity. She took a moment to brace against the granite and yank her socks off, grabbed her cell, and returned. Aiming the lens, she took a photo of the shirts.

Ronan chucked. "Not where I thought you were going with that."

She looked at him. Water darkened hair, handsome face, ultimate body, and then because she couldn't resist, she took a photo of him in the water flow.

Ronan linked his arm around her waist, pulling her to him. "Selfie?"

Calista held the camera high, put her face against his, and snapped the shot.

Ronan took the phone from her and set it outside the shower stall. "I want a copy, please."

Calista nodded.

"I like it when you agree." His voice grew huskier.

Did she ever disagree with him? Thus far, she relished all his moves. Calista reached for the front closure of her bra.

Ronan shook his head. "Let me." He pressed his thumbs to her nipples as if that was how to unhook a bra.

The shock of sensation swept straight through her. Calista dropped her head back and groaned. "Wow."

Ronan pinched gently and liquid heat rushed to her core. He removed her bra and licked her breasts.

The water flowed over her in rushing contrast to the slow pull and suction of his mouth. Calista closed her eyes and reached for him.

Ronan caressed her back and drew her syrup-saturated jeans and panties down. He got to his feet and helped her up so she could get them off. "Is no condom, okay? Guessing you've seen my medical records. I'm healthy."

He'd just made HR charts interesting. "Me too, and I'm on the pill for my cycle," she said, loving how the conversation was natural, not awkward.

"I'll make this worth your effort." Ronan grabbed a spongy ball instead of reaching for her and dispensed twice the normal amount from the soap dispenser. A spring water fragrance joined the steam of the shower. He circled the sponge around her neck, following the path with his free hand as if his fingers were jealous of the sponge.

Calista's chest rose and fell with deep breaths that only deepened. As he washed her back, the contrast of the foamy suds and his warm hands had her center throbbing with an ache that made her want to grab him and copy the motions. A syrupy strand of her hair stuck to her cheek deciding for her. She grabbed his shampoo and conditioner combo and filled her palm with the liquid. She washed his hair as he thoroughly washed her body; the dual movements were entangling her with him in a new intimacy.

Ronan stuck his head under the rainfall showerhead to get the shampoo out. Calista shampooed her own hair twice, and then she took the sponge from him, and re-soaped the surface. She turned the sponge on him and took care to cover every visible inch of his upper body in the opalescent bubbles. The freedom to touch him like this, and the pleasure on his face were heady. She hooked the ribbon hook on the sponge over her pinkie and reached for the closure on his waistband.

Ronan took over and stripped. He kicked his clothes to the corner.

Calista soaped up the rest of him, luxuriating in every moment, and he pulled her close in his arms under the rainfall to remove all the lather. The sponge fell from her hand, and she clutched him, delighting in all the sensory pleasures.

Ronan caressed the back of her thighs, and then lifted her. Her back was to the steamed-up tiles, and she wrapped her legs around his waist. The pressure was twisty amazing. He shifted so he was right at her throbbing empty entrance, and he held her there, letting the anticipation build.

"Yes," Calista gasped out the needy plea.

Ronan kissed her, a slow wet kiss, hotter than the

warm water pulsing over them. He squeezed her bum and lowered her onto his length.

They both pulled their heads back and gasped in a breath. Then he moved his hands to her folds and traced her bundle of nerves as he pumped into her. Minutes and two rotations of the earth later, Calista fell over the edge losing touch with her body and then crashed back to it as another rush of pleasure consumed her.

Ronan groaned. "Calista." He dropped his head to her shoulder as he came. A moment passed, and then he carefully lowered her and led her back under the water while cradling her against him.

Later that night, Ronan drove her back to her car, holding her hand. She wore one of his shirts over a stretchy loose pair of shorts. He parked beside her SUV, and Calista reached for the door handle.

Ronan tightened his grip on her fingers. "Don't get out yet."

CHAPTER 30

"Okay." Calista sat still.

Ronan released his seatbelt. The night was dark except for streetlights and the neon glow from the bar across the street. The music from the radio played a love ballad.

What was he going to do? Would she get a good-night kiss? Calista parted her lips.

Ronan leaned over, caressed her cheek and kissed her, a slow, sexy kiss she was helpless to do anything but respond to and enjoy. And relaxed languor overcame her muscles. When he gripped her thigh, her energy flipped from tranquil and satisfied to needy. Calista leaned into him, but the seatbelt restricted her.

Ronan looked into her eyes, his blue ones dark, sexy, and sincere. "I couldn't stop thinking of touching you on the drive over. Have to feel you." He traced his finger over the center seam of her shorts.

Electricity flashed through her. "Oh." Calista made a strangled sound and bit her lip at the startling sexy power he had over her body.

Ronan made a pleased murmur. He traced his hand down to her knee, up over her thigh and into the loose stretch leg of her shorts, and under her panties.

Calista squirmed.

Using two fingers, Ronan nudged his way inside her, adding a satisfying pressure.

Calista dropped her head back, lips parting, and grabbed his biceps, squeezing encouragingly. With his free hand, he reached under her shirt and palmed her breast.

Fingers pumping, palm circling, breath coming faster. Calista sought his mouth, and he gave her what she wanted. The fairy lights blew up inside her in white flashes, and she pulled her head back to gasp as she came. "Magic."

Ronan slowly withdrew his fingers, damp against the skin of her thigh. "Look at me."

Calista forced her eyes open.

"We can't keep doing this, us, you get that, right?"

What? Stop? Where'd that come from? Calista stared at him. Vulnerable, hot and cold flashed over her skin. She disagreed on a thousand levels but didn't know how to put her objections into words. If she opened her mouth, it would be to tell him to unbutton his jeans, slide the zipper down and pull her onto his lap, that's what she wanted. His skilled fingers had rocked her, he moved her. Didn't he feel the same? She touched her tongue to her lower lip. He couldn't yank her from one realm to another and expect her to be coherent, and if he wanted her to choose between cold practicality or golden flickering delight, well, she knew where she'd land.

"The way you look at me." Ronan moaned, leaned down, and kissed her with a long, hot, wet kiss. He drew back. "I need you to say it."

Say it? Her brain was fuzzy. Calista couldn't even get the seat belt off or the melted muscles in her legs to work. Say it? "I want on your lap, you inside me."

Ronan's jaw dropped open. He froze, but his chest rose and fell as if he'd circled the rink for hours. Then he moved. He unclicked her seatbelt. The soft pop was oddly erotic in the quiet of the night. He cupped the back of her thigh with his big strong hand and curved her leg toward him.

The side of a fist banged on the driver's window. Ronan let go as if she were volcanic, and Calista fell back into her seat.

A player in a Snowers ballcap stood outside.

Saxon.

The rookie held up a beer and stumbled sideways. Syrup dripped from the brim of his cap to the ground, he was covered in the goo.

Ronan turned off the radio and rolled down his window.

Saxon pointed to the building behind them. "Kiernan paid that bar a shit ton to turn the slide into a beer funnel. It's happening."

In time with his words, floodlights lit the parking lot and strobed on, highlighting the slide. Saxon blinked and wobbled. "Join in." Workers wheeled kegs toward the slide. "I told them I can lift the keg to the top. Give me a hand, man."

Ronan gave him a thumbs up. "Give me a minute, buddy."

Saxon nodded, but the motion made him stumble. He reached out to brace his palm on the vehicle, every move from this star athlete a concerted effort.

Calista rubbed her temple, her brain working again, though her body hadn't quit throbbing. Why had Ronan said they had to stop? He wanted her.

This was spinning out of control for him too. Why not choose her and damn the consequences? Her heart thrummed as wildly as her thoughts.

He was saying nothing.

She'd have to ask to get her answer. Her chest tightened. His response could break her heart. That truth had her pause. She parted her lips but couldn't force the words out. She had to act normal, like a grown-up who could handle an adult end-of-the-evening goodnight. "Guessing you need to handle him." She reached for the lock and unclicked it, then the door handle. She got out slowly enough for Ronan to call her back.

He didn't.

Her heart cracked an inch. Calista spun back to the cab. She couldn't ask the questions she wanted to ask, but … "Your guest room…"

"Yours while you need it."

Puck back on her side of the ice.

❄

Calista went back to Ronan's that night but barely saw him over the next two days. They co-existed like two friendly roommates, and she didn't know how to change their relationship, or if it was even fair to him to try, because on a business level, she knew he was right. On a romance level, his choice of distance was cracking her heart.

Thursday, in class, Vivien held up Dahlia's email about the dancers' costume contest at the team's favorite local bar. "Dahlia's event is tonight. We going?"

Calista couldn't help her nod, and later that night she found herself in the back corner booth, alone. Vivien was on the dancefloor in a short llama dress. The puffed fur did resemble snow, but other than that, there was no connection to the Snowers. Other customers wore costumes that ranged from literal hockey sticks to suggestive barely there bits of fabric. Calista wore her usual, jeans and a jersey. She was here for support not to compete.

The bar noise, loud conversations, and pop rock buzzed outside her bubble. Yep, this was her, on a Thursday night hanging at a bar. And people thought she wasn't social, hah. She wasn't even bored. Calista pinched the screen on her tablet and widened the image on an MIT article. Interesting, the curvature of the design was unique. After she finished the article, she sent off emails to the crew she had working on the stadium shower situation. She was starting with the visiting team's locker room first to make sure she got it right before doing the Snowers side. She'd love to hand off the day-to-day project management, but she also wanted the locker room to be exactly as she envisioned. The Snowers deserved nothing but perfection.

Her friends came and went, as did various players who stopped to say "Hi." She greeted each without fail and returned to her reading and emails.

The only time her attention jolted was when Ronan joined her, sliding into her booth, his masculine presence unignorable.

Calista kept her breath slow and even, liking the warm and solidness of him. She gave him a quick look from under her eyelashes.

His blue shirt set off his eyes. His attention was on the room, his expression convivial. He had a mostly full beer bottle in one hand, and his jean-clad legs sprawled under the table. A faint hint of his cologne was refreshing in a room that smelled mostly of freshly poured beer, and under his cologne was a hint of his clean shower wash. Her body perked up, and images of their shower threatened to take over.

But Ronan wasn't here for her, he'd made his intentions clear by his absences. The reason for his sitting beside her, now? Well, she'd take that as a friendly gesture. A beautiful intention. Who wouldn't want to be friends with this handsome, talented, amazing man? Her mind calmed and warmed.

Taking a deep breath, she put the tablet face up on the table to reach for her glass. The ice clanked against the side. She hadn't realized she'd drained her drink. Whatever.

Ronan took a sip of his beer.

This was companionship, nice. Her gaze went back to the MIT website. She read through the future speculation section and swiped the page. The fascinating info was only half holding her attention now. Friends did not distract friends from their scholarly pursuits. She didn't wish him away though.

The weight of Ronan's free hand landed on her thigh, warm and heavy. Her nerve endings jumped in a rush. *Yes, please.* The position of his fingers was fine, friendly even. Calista kept reading. The reference list held a few surprises. She clicked the link on an accompanying article.

Ronan flexed his fingers back and forth, moved them an inch higher, and then another inch.

The words blurred, Calista's breath grew heavier, and she lifted her head.

"Your glass is empty." Ronan's blue gaze met hers. "May I buy you a drink?"

Calista nodded. "A malty one, please." She mentally shuffled through the options she'd read on the menu earlier. "A White Snowers." Cream, vodka, and coffee liquor made up the concoction.

Ronan placed the order on his phone.

Calista, rather than stare at him as if he was more fascinating than a scientific discovery, focused back on her tablet. This article was on a compound MIT developed using a novel polymerization process, two-dimensional polymer sheets. Fascinating. Though she really wanted to read this, she needed to ensure the tile guy was set on the install date. Waiting until summer would be a better time to renovate the stadium, but she wanted to do the improvement while she had the opportunity.

The waiter dropped off the drink and refilled her water, then he left the two of them alone.

Calista took a sip of the creamy sweet liquor while reading. This was lovely, chilling here with Ronan, getting a project refined, being social, but on her own terms.

Ronan edged his hand to the top of her thigh, cupped his fingers, and pressed on the inner seam of her jeans. His pinkie could go no further without bumping into intimate proximity with her...

His fingers shifted higher.

CHAPTER 31

Sensations blossomed from her core and outwards, eager for more action. Calista froze. The tablet fell from her loose grip to the table, and the bar dropped away, reality ceasing to exist. Her whole universe narrowed and consisted of his cologne, his hand, and its potential for movement, and the promise of pleasure. She held her breath.

Ronan nudged the glass into her fingers. "Don't you like it?"

Calista took a drink of the cold shake-tasting beverage. The sweetness on her tongue was yum and satisfying. In contrast, the warm proximity of his fingers had hardened her nipples into aching points of neglect. She wanted him to drop his drink so he could use two hands on her. One at the inner junction seam of her jeans, no, the button, the zipper, slip inside her new lace panties.

She shifted on the booth. He could slide his other hand under the hem of her jersey. Up, pinch her nipples, caress her breasts, say nice things to her, then use his mouth to follow the path of his hands. Her own palms ached to touch him. She could do for him what he was doing for her. She moved her palm to his thigh.

The workouts he did had given him the most wondrous body. She wanted them to move to obtain some privacy, in a room with better lighting. She dropped her head back against the booth and met his gaze helplessly. Her lips parted.

"Damn," Ronan murmured.

"Hey guys." Kiernan popped in front of them. He leaned his back against the edge of their table, his phone in one hand, his beer in the other, and his gaze on the costume contest.

Ronan dropped his hand from Calista, and he chugged some of his beer.

The host called out number twenty-three, and a woman in a fire costume climbed the few steps to the small, raised stage. Customers cheered and clapped.

Kiernan raised his beer bottle in tribute, before turning to Calista. "I've never been turned on by arts and crafts before, but daaammmn." He pivoted back to the stage where the fire-themed costume wearer was flapping her flames. Kiernan waved his cell phone. "You've got my vote number twenty-three, you melt me."

The host waved for the next woman to take the spotlight.

Kiernan whistled. "Check out the snowflakes on

number twenty-four." He typed in the app. "She's got my vote too."

The snowflake costume in question had strategic sequins, which would stay on during a routine. A contender, for sure, but high maintenance.

"Who are you voting for?" Kiernan asked Calista.

Calista opened her palms.

Kiernan winked. "I'll vote enough for both of us." He turned back to face the stage.

"Do you care about the dancers' costumes?" Ronan asked, a note of curiosity in his voice.

"Of course." Dahlia cared, and the dancers deserved something wonderful. Hockey fans should get the whole entertainment package as long as everyone was happy with the parameters, a certain level of modesty, another layer of fun, and above all fabrics which were structurally sound. "I didn't at first, but then I tried one on, and that changed my perspective."

Ronan gave a cut off groan. "I remember that." He put his lips to her ear. "I want you to come home with me and try one on tonight."

And men thought women were contradictory? She was game though. Calista wiggled. "You'd have to do something for me too."

The host continued the rotation of contenders. Kiernan shouted his enthusiasm.

"Anything." Ronan's voice came out resolute, and as soon as his own unshakable word left his mouth, his face blanked, and he shifted to the edge of the booth. His blue gaze looked alarmed. "I have to join the guys." He slid out, rose with his perfect balance, and touched Kiernan's shoulder. He pointed to the stage, and the men strode away.

What just happened?

Humans were inexplicable and intriguing. Machines were also fascinating, but she could figure mechanics out, not Ronan. She dropped her gaze to her tablet. Polymer sheeting. Ronan. Polymer sheeting. Ronan. Dang…the material didn't hold her focus the same way now that he had sparked her hormones to life. Why had Ronan left?

Did a player need him? Someone need a ride? Nope. They had the ride app on the purity website. Ronan hadn't signed a purity pledge, had he? Like her? She knew who would know. She searched the room for Dahlia. Her gaze jumped over Willow, who wore the strappy black puck costume and a pouty expression. There, just beyond, were a group of dancers wearing their own individual costumes. Aww, Dahlia looked pretty. She wore a skin-colored mesh overlayed with swirls of white silk and icy crystals. The tiniest of fairy lights lit the short hem and the center snowflakes. Her high-end design hit the right notes she was trying to achieve.

As if feeling her gaze, Dahlia smiled her way and waved. She wound up her conversation and headed over. When she reached Calista's booth, Dahlia leaned in and hugged her. The familiarity of her floral perfume contrasted with her exotic makeup. She'd used crystals to highlight her eyes and a shimmering blush atop her cheekbones, perfect for a winter princess.

"I'm voting for your costume." Calista grabbed her phone and made her first vote of the night. "The mesh will hold in place through their routines, your makeup is super pretty, and you know I love the twinkles."

"Thanks. When we dim the stadium, imagine the drama." Dahlia beamed and adjusted the number three on her placard. "I'm getting top votes." She rolled her eyes, and her mouth turned down. "So is Willow." She pointed to Calista's phone. "Hit refresh and check the summary ratings."

Calista hit refresh and angled the screen so her cousin could also see the readout. The top four contenders were fire, puck, light up, and llama.

They shared a look. "Vivien's llama costume is riding surprisingly high in the ranks." Dahlia's voice was ironic.

"Hmm." Calista said noncommittally. They both knew the odds of that were improved by Vivien's computer skills.

How could she segue this into asking about Ronan's purity status? She shouldn't have to, but he was so confusing. Lady talk shouldn't be this difficult. But straight up inquiring didn't feel right because this seemed like Ronan's own private business. Having Vivien hack the list would provide an answer, but also felt wrong. Calista wet her lips. "What percentage of the guys signed purity pledges?"

Dahlia shrugged, making her sparkling straps twinkle. "Exact percentages can be difficult when the subject is people. I mean, when you go into decimals, that's just dehumanizing, right? What's half a person?"

"I'm pretty good with math. Give me a number. Twenty-three guys and..." From there she could narrow down the names, or maybe Dahlia would reveal the names when listing the players, then she wouldn't have to ask about Ronan specifically.

"Well, none, exactly."

"None?" That stumped her and crushed her theory. Calista took a drink of her sweet icy drink. How was that hard to calculate? "Zero?"

"Right, zero." Dahlia sounded a touch defensive and shifted her gaze to the front where the host was up to number thirty, a man in a barrel with hockey sticks glued to the outside. "Several players have indicated interest." Her voice picked up. "Kiernan vowed he'd sign. You were there, I just haven't gotten his signature or verbal recitation." She huffed out a sigh. "Pinning him down has been impossible."

"The guys may be expressing the behaviors without formally pledging?"

Dahlia turned back to her. "Exactly."

"Men are confusing."

"I hear you." Dahlia took a sip of Calista's drink. "Yum."

Calista looked away, then forced herself to be braver. "I'm at a bar, how am I not interesting..." she wanted to say to Ronan, but this wasn't the time or place to expose the secrets of her heart. "To any guy here?"

Dahlia's chipper social expression shifted to a loving familial one. "Oh, sweetie, it's not you. The women out there are half-dressed. Men are simple visual creatures, like deer in headlights."

That didn't help.

Dahlia must have seen that on her face. Instead of softening, she put her hands on her hips. "Calista," she said in a firm voice Artie would love. "You're wearing the captain's jersey, stating your clear preference, and your head is in your computer. It would take a special kind of guy to push past that."

"Interesting." Calista slipped the tablet into her bag to signal she was eligible.

A devious smile curved on Dahlia's lips. "I know it's inappropriate, but I was thinking about your Mer-bar drama that you described for me. It was unlike you to participate like that."

It had been fun. Calista shrugged.

"You enjoyed it, I could hear that in your voice," Dahlia said.

Dahlia was like Piper, she knew her. Calista nodded.

"If you're really ready to put your computer down and come play, I brought an extra costume inspired by your Mer-bar story."

Calista tilted her head.

"I know," Dahlia said. "I wasn't going to force you unless you expressed interest."

OMG, social class was working, because the urge

to dress up and re-capture Ronan's interest was pushing through her. "I'm interested."

Dahlia did a dance move, hooked Calista's arm, and pulled her from the booth almost before she could grab her bag. They went to the back of the bar and into a keg storage room. Dahlia went behind a row and lifted a tote from a low bench. "The manager said I could store my stuff back here." She unzipped the heavy-duty zipper to reveal the costume.

CHAPTER 32

Dahlia drew the swathe of fabric from her tote.

She'd brought Calista a mermaid costume. Turquoise silk shaped like clam shells made up the bra top. The skirt was fitted to below the knees in a skin-colored mesh with waves of sequins in the same turquoise color. From there, tulle sprinkled with crystal gemstones flared out to the floor. There was no way the dancers could do their acrobatic moves in a gown this long and tight, but the mermaid costume was so thoughtful, Calista could only beam at her cousin.

Her cousin hadn't once chastised her for her Canadian adventure, though the social media from the Mer-bar could have gone so wrong. So cute of her to think of this. Plus, Ronan had to find a mermaid costume intriguing. If anything could remind Ronan of how interested he'd been in the beginning, this was it. Calista's heart pattered and she wiggled her shoulders. If she was underwater in the Mer-bar tank right now, she'd make a mermaid emoji pose.

She was in. Calista lifted her jersey over her head.

"OMG, you wore a sports bra to a sports bar." Dahlia shook her head. "We've taught you nothing."

Calista rolled her eyes. "Turn around." She did a quick change and placed her clothes in the tote. She shoved all her stuff under the bench. "I'm ready."

Dahlia spun back. "Gorgeous." She gave her a thumbs up. "You'll get all the attention you want in that." Her phone buzzed. She checked the screen and pumped her fists out in front of her chest. "I'm up two votes. Re-do your lipstick, I'll see you out there." Dahlia jetted, leaving Calista to primp.

Calista got out her compact. She lined her lips in a pretty mauve, filled them in, and then did a top layer of cherry gloss. Ready, she put her cosmetics in her bag's outer pocket and stepped out into the corridor. Taking a deep breath, she moved toward the bar, taking mincing steps that swayed her hips because that's all the costume permitted.

Ronan stood not two steps away. He met her gaze, moved to check out her body and did a double take. He opened his mouth and then closed it. "You changed."

Calista chewed on her bottom lip, tasting the cherry flavor. "It's like the Mer-bar."

Ronan swallowed. Behind him, the crowd roared as the next contestant moved into place, but Calista couldn't see them over his head. Ronan clenched and unclenched his fists. "I wish we were alone."

Calista tilted her head. She crooked her finger and backed up slowly, mostly because of the tight cut of the skirt, and the pace worked the same as the gradual reeling of a fishing line. Ronan followed her without question.

She led him back to the storage room and closed the door, muting the sounds of the party.

Ronan crushed her to him and kissed her with a fast, turn-her-on rhythm. He filled his hands with her sequined bum, traced her bared abs, and slipped his fingers under her bra top, caressing her. "You're so pretty, like dreams I've had, but here."

Calista roamed her hands over his hard arms and around his back, and under his shirt, showing her appreciation with her touch instead of words.

Ronan breathed heavily. He scooped her into his arms, looked around at the stack of kegs, and then headed toward the bench. He sat down with her on his lap and resumed the lusty kisses.

The chemistry twining around them zapped Calista's spine, and all she wanted was the feel of him against her. She wiggled until she was off his lap, and on the hard bench, from there, she lay back and held her arms up for him to come to her.

Ronan followed her down. His kisses slowed, matching the glide of his hands, and in a rhythm opposite of the pop rock music banging from the speakers.

He traced the shells of her bra, and then the center where they connected, and around to the back of the band. The costume bra had no hooks. He returned his attention to her nipples. He pulsed his fingers. Up, down. Stroke, light pinch. He kissed his way down her neck and replaced his fingers with the hot wet suction of his mouth right atop the silk. He lifted his lips to blow, chilling her already hard nipples, and then he repeated his movements, fingers, tongue, blow.

Her lacy panties dampened, and Calista moaned. "Ronan." She arched her back and rubbed her hips against the fabric of his trousers, finding his masculine hardness.

Ronan gasped and thrust against her in response. The friction eased her ache for a second and then racked her tension and need higher.

Calista breathed harder, tunneled her hands into his hair and kissed him firmly with a drugging, wet, open-mouth kiss to show him what she wanted.

Ronan felt at her waist and back, then along her abdomen, and to her hips. He pulled his head up and gasped in a breath. "Zipper?" His question came out rushed and husky.

"None."

"How?"

He didn't understand the theme? "I'm a mermaid, their legs don't part." Her friends' Mer-Maid virgin theory popped into her mind, but it wasn't the time to share stories from class.

Ronan opened and closed his mouth and stared down at her with a helpless tortured look.

A slow grin crossed Calista's lips, though her

mood was more languorous and her eyes wanted to close while she held on for the ride.

Ronan reached behind her to the back of her skirt. "I'll replace it." The fabric tightened at her waist and then loosened with a rip sound, exposing her lacy panties to his wondering gaze. He groaned like he'd uncovered a treasure.

"I don't know," a masculine drunken voice said from out in the hallway, an unwelcome interruption. "They think as captain, he should crown the winner, but he's not into it. Where is he, man?"

Calista and Ronan froze.

"Check the toilets," a Canadian male voice answered.

With the disturbance, Calista's need and urgency fell away. She calmed, and both she and Ronan remained still. They were simply two bar-goers hanging in the storage room.

The players moved on.

Ronan dropped his hand down to her shoulder. "Hockey. Puck. Rink." He said as if the words had the power to clear his head, and he lifted off of her. "I have to go."

The players finished their session with Coach and headed to the locker room. Ronan couldn't focus with Calista down at the half wall as if waiting for him like a siren. She'd been killing him in every feasible way. He couldn't sleep for the erotic dreams featuring Calista in a mermaid costume. He pushed himself at practice to impress her. He should be doing anything but moving in front of her right now, but here he was. He skated up to her. "Hey, Calista."

Calista chewed on her bottom lip. "You know the purity pledge has layers, depending on your goals."

What was she talking about? He straightened his shoulders. "Does it?"

She nodded. "Yes, like Dahlia wanted a wedding ring, so she was abstaining from sex until after the ceremony."

"I didn't know that." Nor should he know it now. Where was she going with this? Did Calista want a ring? Ronan's body tensed as if his skates had slid out from under him. Would she like a traditional icy diamond? No, a Snowers blue rock would be her choice.

She twined a strand of her glossy hair around her finger, and her clever green eyes seemed conflicted. "Did you take the purity pledge?" Her voice was low, though it was only the two of them there.

Heat touched his cheeks, and he didn't know what to say. Of course he hadn't, and obviously, neither had she judging by the hours they'd spent in bed...and in his shower. Vanilla-scented memories rushed through him. He touched the tip of his tongue to his lower lip as if to catch a memory of maple syrup.

Calista propped her arms on the edge of the wall, bending forward, making her closer to his height.

"What level were you thinking of following? Because it doesn't have to be all out abstinence."

His body shot hard, as if they were talking about sexual topics rather than the opposite. "I did not take a purity pledge."

"Then why?" Calista pressed her lips together. Then she tapped her cheek in front of her ear and pointed at him. She wanted to speak privately.

Heaven help him, he wanted to know more. If she were close enough, her lips could touch his skin. Ronan flattened himself right against the wall as if a three-hundred-pound enforcer had shoved into him.

Calista leaned over. Ronan stripped off his glove, and he braced her with his hand on her arm. He breathed in her delicate scent. He wanted to gather her to him, a ridiculous thought to have at the arena. He stilled his nerves. Nothing wrong with having a private conversation with the front office while in clear view of anyone who cared to look. He was the captain. He circled his fingertips against the petal soft skin of her inner arm.

Calista's cheeks flushed a pretty pink, and her eyes shined a pale green. Not glossy, like when he really made her lose her head, but with an inquisitive interest. She put her lips to his ear, and he held back a shudder. "Back when we were at the bar," she whispered, "in the booth. I wanted more, and in the back room, I needed more of you."

Damn, his body heated from simply that small touch. She was sweetly calling him out for turning her on and leaving her hanging, fair point. He swallowed and could not have moved if the whole Geels starting lineup came at him. He had no answer, so he delayed offering his reasoning like a weak rookie. "Let's talk about this back at my place." Was that leadership? Taking the front office home with him? He still didn't take back the words.

"Hmm," Calista murmured without agreeing.

She was hesitating? That made him want to tug her to him, flush against his body above the ice, and speak right here. Why was she resisting his offer? "Do you have class?"

"I have a flight. I'm going to see Mikah's brothers play in Ft. Worth."

He hadn't known that. "Alone? Tonight?"

She nodded. "I'll be back tomorrow."

Ronan tossed his own schedule over in his mind, and he couldn't resist the urge to go with her. "Text me your flight info, I'll join you."

CHAPTER 33

Observing Calista watch hockey live was something. She was quiet and still and deep into every play. When the end came, the Czerski twins' team edged ahead to claim victory. Fans wearing the dark green team colors were screaming. She eased back in her seat in quiet pleasure.

Ronan wanted to get her feedback on the game as much as he wanted to strip the college jersey she'd worn from her body. Seeing the green color as they left for the plane had jolted him. He'd gotten inappropriately fond of seeing his number on her chest. Now, this other jersey made his fingers twitch and his muscles tense, though in every possible way, he knew he shouldn't be possessive over her. They couldn't keep their clandestine relationship up, and the longer they did, the more in over his head he felt. Someone was going to get hurt. Unless…What were her thoughts on long-distance relationships? Would she consider seeing him after he moved to Washington? Was there a league-related conflict there? Even inquiring could start rumors flying and mess up his transfer.

The crowd began shifting to the aisles to exit. As they rose, a security guard stopped at the end of their row. "Mr. Stromkin?"

Ronan nodded.

"The camera caught you, and Coach sent me up. The players would love to meet you."

Ronan gave an easy smile. He enjoyed the fans and had been exactly where these guys were once. "Of course." He looked to Calista. "That okay?"

Calista nodded.

"Great." The security guard made a downward motion with his hand in Calista's direction. "Sit comfortably there, Miss, and we'll have him back to you before the parking lot's cleared out."

Yeah, like he'd leave his date alone in the stands. Ronan shook his head. "She comes with me."

"No girlfriends on the ice." The guard shrugged. "Policy, sorry."

Calista giggled.

Calista appeared delighted to be labeled his. Her pleased expression made Ronan's heart ache, and a stinging heat touched his cheeks. He'd been shitty with the lack of roses and candlelight. In no way did he deserve her expression. They had to end, and he had to stop the risky advances he couldn't seem to quit making. But tonight, this moment wasn't the place.

Out on the ice in front of them, both teams did the

postgame handshake, and then lined up in a single formation.

The guard waved for Ronan to proceed him.

"She stays with me," Ronan said again, his tone final, his expression the stern one he used to great effect on opposing enforcers.

The guard gave a nod to Ronan and backed up a step, as if making room for him and Calista. They moved down the aisle to the front row at the gated wall.

"The players are thrilled to meet you," the coach called up to Ronan.

The guard opened his palms. "I explained about no girlfriends on the ice, but it's a dealbreaker." Behind the coach, two assistants were spreading out a runner so Ronan could step out onto the rink.

The coach looked at Calista with a polite smile. He narrowed his eyes on the team jersey she wore and canted his head. He snapped his fingers and his face brightened. "Czerski twins. Got it." He looked at the security guard with critical brown eyes. "You need to keep up with hockey news. She's not his girlfriend. That's the woman who bought all those Snowers shares." His tone grew impatient. "Always let professional team owners down to meet the guys, that's every player's dream."

The guard flushed.

Calista touched the guard's arm. "You're protective, that's the right way to be for the team."

The guard's tense face eased, and he looked a

little infatuated. Ronan put his hand on the small of Calista's back.

The coach held the gate, and they stepped down a steep temporary set of stairs. The coach turned to Calista. "We hope you'll say something to the players?"

Calista shook her head. "Ronan is who they want to hear from." She waved to the Czerski twins who kept their places in formation but wore pleased grins on their faces. Ronan also gave a nod to the two guys who he'd met at the Snowers family functions. The duo looked not only identical to each other, but also a lot like Mikah. Had he not met them before, he would have guessed they were members of Mikah's family.

The coach held out his palm, inviting Ronan to speak.

Knowing the players were exhausted, he kept his speech short but thoughtful. He made a point to recognize their stellar highlights and teamwork. He was going to finish by shaking each guy's hand, but he turned to Calista first. "Anything you want to add, before I meet the players and Coach dismisses them?"

Calista shook her head. "You said it perfectly."

One of the guys, the cocky star from the home team, but not the clapper he thought he was, pointed at Calista. "Who would you pick for the entry draft?"

Minefield.

"You don't have to answer that," Ronan said.

Calista didn't hesitate. She pivoted to the Czerski twins. "Conrad and Jakob Czerski, of course."

The guys chuckled. Everyone knew these two were headed to the top. The twins' grins grew though, how could they not? Calista was a combination of sincerity, beauty, and passion. He'd never met anyone like her.

"Which twin?" the outspoken dude on the home team pushed.

Calista tilted her head, making her hair swing over her shoulder, long, fair with golden highlights. Several guys watched the motion and straightened on their skates, now interested in more than her opinion, and they had no idea of how incredible the strands felt tangled in his fingers. "They're equal. Certain positions don't get recognized that way, but they are. I'd love them both for the Snowers."

The team shuffled, but by the buzz in the air, Ronan could tell they liked her answer.

One of them said, "You're the first owner who's come to see us."

Calista's face softened. She tilted toward the coach. "I'm not officially owner yet, and I'm the worst at public speaking. May I speak with the players individually?"

The coach held out his arm in a gesture that encouraged her to go ahead. "Of course."

Ronan followed behind her.

Calista praised each player, and Ronan shook their hands after her, moving down the line. She had specific, unique words for each man. She told a clumsy skater she loved how he was where he was supposed to be at all times. She told another who'd been taken out in the second period that she'd loved how he'd touched the ice with his fingertips, and that the audience had held their breath at the athletic feat of pulling himself up after almost going down. Another, that although his final point was the star moment for the crowd, she'd liked when he'd fallen in the first period, had gotten up, and charged back even harder, that perseverance would get him far. And on and on she went, praising each one for something small but exact, with a stellar precise memory as if her brain had recorded the entire game.

Her thoughtfulness made his heart swell, and as much as he was ready to take her out of there, he could listen to her go on even longer, and he knew the men could too.

They reached the Czerski twins who hugged her and greeted him with a fist bump. "Did you mean what you said?" Conrad asked quietly, his arm still around her.

"Yes." Her one word was solid and sincere.

One word, and Ronan ached at her kindness, her ability to see beyond the obvious, and he needed to pull her into his own arms. If he'd had a girlfriend like her back in the day, he'd have never let her go. The rink spun around him, noise stopped, and the press of his heart expanding became all consuming. In that spinning moment, he knew he'd fallen for Calista. Ronan shoved that truth away before he did something stupid like fall to his knees in front of her.

He had to concentrate on the players, not himself, and keep his turmoil on the inside.

All the guys had remained until they reached the end of the line, both from enjoying seeing him there and from her compliments. Their delighted faces took him back another step and nudged him to make more time for the fans.

Calista reached the final player who stood by the away coach. He wasn't the best on the ice, but there was raw talent there. "If the Snowers sale goes my way, I hope you'll consider us."

The guy blinked rapidly, gaped, and nodded as fast as he was blinking.

His coach slapped him on his back. "Told you."

They went back to their hotel suite. Ronan's heart was still thumping hard against his chest. His own feelings were swamping him, and he was replaying her words in his mind like a melody. She'd been so sweet. How had he ever thought she was manipulative? He needed distance as much as he wanted her in his arms. He could do this, pull back, and give them both room, make decisions before being careless with her heart. "I'm going to shower and hit the sack."

Calista nodded and went toward the second bedroom without protest. Conversely, he was a little jealous by the ease of her agreement. Was she going to disassemble something? Was she not as rocked by the impossibility of them coupled with the over-whelming desire for them at the same time? Was he twisting off the ice by himself?

The heat of the shower helped him unwind but did nothing to calm his desire. Ronan padded out to the living room in pajama bottoms. Calista sat on the couch with her laptop. She had showered too. Her pink sleep shirt ended at her thighs, and she had pinned her wet hair atop her head. Her vanilla-scented lotion accosted his senses in a torturous here-I-am, taste-me lure.

"Did you want to go out?" They should have discussed after-game plans on the flight over, instead they'd talked hockey. He could suggest dancing, her body close to his, while they swayed to the music, and his hands on her hips directed her moves. The gray fabric of the couch sank down as he sat beside her.

Calista didn't look up. "I'm more of a homebody." She smiled a small smile. "If Piper marries Mikah, I'll have four brothers who play hockey. Can you imagine? I can go to so many games, I promise I'll be the best support."

Yeah, she would. Her compelling enthusiasm for hockey was unmistakable. "You're close to your family?" He'd gotten that impression more than once. He put his arm along the back of the couch, resisting the urge to release the damp strands of her hair.

She nodded.

"Me too." Which was only one of the reasons he

was going back to Washington. Ronan dropped his arm and clasped his hands between his knees. He needed to tell her that. He took a breath, taking in more of her fragrance. As if he had no control of his body, he scooped her legs over his, and ran his palm up her silky thigh. He wanted another night with her. They weren't in town, or in public, there was no risk. Did she want the same?

Calista froze, then looked intrigued.

Ronan smoothed his palm to the inside of her thigh.

Her hand shook as she stretched to put the laptop on the coffee table and turned to embrace him.

The shift of her stellar attention to focus only on him, shoved through his barriers, and the eagerness mixed with adoration in her gaze caused a visceral reaction in his body. "Calista." Empowered and powerless, he dropped his lips to hers.

Calista stood at the wall on the visitor's side of the rink and waved in Ronan's direction.

She could not be doing this now, not here. Ronan stood huddled with his men, trying to focus on Coach's insights about the upcoming Geels game and not his lover. His shoulders tensed, and he told himself the scent of vanilla was not filling his lungs, and he could not taste maple syrup on his tongue.

"Someone's calling their favorite over." Kiernan used his sing-song voice which had earned him more than one punch on the ice. "But I'm not exactly sure who she's looking for?" He pointed to his chest. "Could it be me?"

"Or me?" Liam asked in a voice that couldn't carry a tune.

Ronan kept his face neutral, not letting them know they were getting to him. Did they suspect? He'd been really careful not to draw notice to him and Calista. Well, not that careful.

Coach glanced over his shoulder and back at his men. "Owners." He shook his head. "Have yet to meet one who can wait. We've got twenty minutes left before the Geels take the ice for their practice, but something's more critical than our number one rival." He stared straight at Ronan. "Who's going to handle this interruption?"

Damn.

Ronan gave a short nod, though he didn't really want to go over to her. Washington was looking secure to the point where his agent was touching base with Dodo, and though Dodo was the official owner, negotiating with him seemed unfair to Calista, like he was going behind her back, which he wasn't, not professionally, no one should know until they needed to know. Signatures on dotted lines and packing boxes would hopefully happen before the Amvehls and Applebaums settled their ownership decisions. Until then, he needed to determine what he was going to say and ask from Calista on a personal level. Long distance had never appealed to him, but the thought of letting her go wasn't working for him. At minimum, he owed her the truth that he was moving. So damn complicated.

"What are you waiting for, Stromkin?" Coach clapped. "The rest of you, take a lap," he said to the men.

Ronan skated over to Calista.

Her cheeks were flushed and excited, the way she looked when he kissed her. His groin tightened, and he clenched his fists to keep from reaching for her. He needed distance, bad. He had discipline, he could do this.

Calista leaned against the wall and motioned for him to come closer. "I want to show you something. Can you come with me?"

Yes, his energy shot fully below his belt. Alone time with her was exactly what he needed. And continue what was becoming a lie by omission? No. He was a stronger man than that. He stiffened his resolve. "You can't call me over during practice, Calista. It puts me in an awkward position. It's not discreet, it's saying to the team I'm ..." Important, your love, have seen you laying naked against my pillow. His heart thumped hard in his chest. "...your favorite," he said instead.

"Everyone knows you are." Her eagerness remained undimmed. She fluttered her fingers over the twenty-two on her jersey. "I'm not surprising anyone."

"You know what I mean." His tone was gruff, but his mood wasn't really about her, it was about what he needed to tell her, about the decisions they'd have to make. About the expression he didn't want to see on her face when she learned he was leaving the Snowers. His chest rose and fell harder than this conversation warranted. What would she even wear for a top once his jersey was obsolete? "Does it have to be now? Dahlia should have warned you; Coach hates when people interrupt his practices."

Calista nodded. "Yes. Now. Yes."

He had no idea what she wanted to show him, but there was an intriguing sparkle in her clever green eyes. Not the sexual shine he put in them when he touched her, but a mischievous ingenious light. Damned if he wouldn't give his right skate to know what was behind that glow. All the freaking more reason to resist. But how? Every coach he'd ever had had screamed that women would mess up their games, to slam love lives and professional lives in separate boxes and lock them up. With Calista and her ties to shares and ownership, he needed that division most of all, but where Calista was concerned, he had less sense than a first-year rookie. He flattened his palm over the upper left shoulder of his practice jersey, feeling the embossed letter C, reminding himself he was the team captain. He had to man up and act like a leader who knew what play to call next.

They weren't even alone. The men skated laps behind him, no doubt watching their discussion. A flash of movement on the stairs reminded him they were in the stadium on a workday. Right now, Dodo was descending the stadium steps, heading their way, as if one owner at practice wasn't enough to tumble Coach's temper.

He'd tried to give Dodo the benefit of the doubt, but every time they'd had a meeting, his undercutting Calista had been clear. The dude wasn't trying to work within the proposed new structure. Ronan gave Calista a warning look and slid his gaze toward Dodo. Damn. Dodo could mention his negotiations with his agent before he got a chance to speak with Calista about his move. Ronan's hands grew sweaty inside his gloves.

Calista's expression smoothed and went neutral. Whatever she was excited about, she didn't want Dodo to know. That made her offer even more interesting.

Dodo reached them. He hooked his hands in his belt loops and nodded at Ronan, but his focus was on Calista. Ronan relaxed, this wasn't about him. Dodo got within two feet of her. "Look, Calista, I know you don't know how things work, but we have a rivalry with the Geels." He spoke to her like her IQ wasn't twice his.

Ronan tensed back up. He'd heard Dodo use the disrespectful tone with her before, had never cared for it, and was hating it in a new way now. To add to the tension, Liam and Kiernan skated over. Kiernan slid to a stop and angled his blade to spray ice. "Two owners walked into a bar," Kiernan said.

Liam snickered.

"Men," Dodo greeted them, not put off by the

teasing. "I was just informing Ms. Amvehl about the nuances of our relationship with the Geels."

Liam bulked his arms out. "They pretty much hate us."

"No," Kiernan corrected, "They envy us." He tilted his head. "Ah, no, you're right, after you dated Beast's sister, they definitely hate you."

Liam nodded, owning it.

Dodo smoothed down his starched shirtfront. "Anyway, you can't give those little pigeons, pardon my French, any excuse to complain." Dodo pointed toward the tunnel that led to the visiting team's locker room. "Keeping the Geels out of their changing room and shortening their practice gives them an excuse to lodge a complaint with the league and will lead to payback when we're in their stadium, and that's the best-case scenario." His voice was a level too loud. Either Dodo was either compensating for the swish of blades taking laps, or he wanted the players to hear there was conflict between the two shareholders.

"I'll handle it," Calista said, not looking at Dodo.

Was this what Calista had wanted his help with? What was the hold up with the Geels? Had she decimated their treadmills?

"Straight up you will." Dodo remained standing there. He held out his palm. "We don't own the stadium. We have a contract to manage it for the city. Not only does this cause a problem with the Geels, but the city could get involved."

She said she'd handle it. He really hadn't known

Dodo to be such a whiner. Had he missed it? Was Calista making him intolerant? Why was he in the thick of front office issues? No good could come of this.

Liam shuffled his skates. "Dude, uh, Dodo. You're sending her to the enemy camp? What about GM Hollis? Can't he deal with the Geels?"

"Calista's a big girl." Dodo kept a firm tone. "This is a small example of the fallout if I'm not in charge."

Calista rubbed her arms. "I'll handle the Geels."

Son of a bitch. Absolutely not. "We'll meet you over there, Calista." Ronan skated to the players' bench and grabbed skate guards. Liam and Kiernan followed him.

They caught up to Calista at the visiting team's tunnel to go with her.

Calista was running an hour behind schedule, a pivotal, critical hour. That truth was confirmed by the Geels congregating in the hallway outside of the visiting team's locker room. "Sorry." She hurried forward.

Ronan, Liam, and Kiernan were behind her, tall and imposing. She'd wanted to show Ronan and the Snowers the locker room renovation before anyone else. Now, that wouldn't be happening. Sometimes project timing didn't go as planned, but they'd accomplished so much, and she'd almost nailed the timeframe.

Her steps slowed as twenty-three Geels with put-out faces plus coaches and assistants stared at her.

She froze. Then individual stats ran through her mind, which helped. Tonight would be a great show-down. If she found the words, she could share that excitement. She had a million things to say and none. She huffed out a breath, impatient with herself. What did she want? For Ronan to speak in her place? No. Liam or Kiernan? Heck no. She'd show them she could handle this.

So many players, tall, imposing, staring at her, waiting for her to explain why they'd been held up, delayed, composing letters to the league, complaints to the city. She shook her head and stepped back a step. She couldn't handle this.

Men moved to the side, making way as Zee shoved to the front of his team. Zenon Czerski, 6'5", number ninety-nine, nicknamed 'The End All' for his name being the last letter of the alphabet and how many games he put away by unleashing the final winning shot. Remarkable player, handsome like his younger brother Mikah, but harder edged, and more chiseled. Also, one day, he might be Piper's future brother-in-law. That would be so amazing, plus she'd met him before. She moved over to him and tipped her head back. "Hi."

Zee Czerski shifted forward, and he dropped his frown. "Hey, Calista." He put his hand on her shoulder in greeting. "Guys are getting antsy."

CHAPTER 34

Ronan resisted the urge to ball his fists. Calista had to know Zee through Mikah. Look at him put his hand right on her as if he had the right. Ronan tightened his jaw and paced his breathing as if he were preparing for a long game. Nope, he stepped forward.

Kiernan and Liam got shoulder-to-shoulder with him, backing him up. Together, they moved behind Calista and gave nods to the other team.

Their two teams meeting up like this was highly frowned on. Fights before games happened, but his men needed to save their hostile energy for on the ice. Ronan pulled his gaze from Calista and Zee to check out the Geels. Twenty-three players, assistants, coaches, they just wanted to move forward and get past the hold up. Only a few guys at the front had focused intent, like the way Beast was eyeing Liam. A fight could be imminent. Good thing the Canadian had restraint, but he could throw down with the worst of them. At least Kiernan's cousin had his mouth shut. Was that a conciliatory expression on Kellan Kelchier's face? Good, because Kiernan wasn't over the prank his cousin had played on him on his last birthday. As captain, the best thing Ronan could do was back his two men out of here. As Calista's man, he was going nowhere.

"I'm sorry," Calista said to Zee, waving her arm to include his team. "We just finished renovating, and Vivien's putting your names up on the lockers. They should be ready now. You'll have powerful water pressure, and the hot water never ends, I promise." She took hold of the doorknob.

Ronan reached around her and held the door for her to go through.

He gaped. The floorspace had shrunk to half its former size and smelled of new paint and construction.

"We re-did the whole locker room," Calista explained.

The room was horseshoe shaped with a number of long slim benches in the middle lit from underneath with a glow strip in the Geels' yellow color. Although the floorspace was minimal, the lockers were larger, and they now had full-sized teak doors. Electronic screens had been mounted five feet up on each front panel.

"This way." Calista led them down to where her friend Vivien stood typing into a keyboard inset into the wall.

The big guys shuffled down the row until they were all in the room, dwarfing the space further.

Calista wore an expectant expression, as if they'd like the new cramped quarters. Aw, sweetheart, no.

"Pretty tight," one of the visiting players whined.

Babies. He'd seen worse. Well, maybe not, but he wouldn't be caught pouting about it.

"Wait for it," Vivien said enthusiastically, typing faster on the keys.

Calista bounced from her heels to her toes, her light green eyes bright.

She wasn't going to get a positive rave over this misstep. Someone screwed up the measurements. Damn, he should have come with her when she'd asked. Then he could have tempered her expectations. She asked so little of him, he should have given in the second she'd made the request. He was too tied up in his own head with his own issues.

Zee shouldered his way back over to Calista. A move he only allowed because Zee was Mikah's brother.

"Got it." Vivien hit enter.

The screens on the front of each locker lit up. Zee's populated on the screen two feet away. "Solid improvement," Zee lied. He moved down and slapped his hand on the panel under his name.

Vivien grinned at his praise.

Zee's name dissolved and a group of dancing llamas took its place.

Fitting.

The Beast laughed and moved over to the screen

with his own name, *Arturo Bezio*. "Look at them, I like llamas." Beast imitated the llama's dance move by pulsing his arm out. That, plus his laugh released the tension in the room. A llama populated on Beast's screen and reared like a stallion. "Yes," Beast said. He lifted the hem of his shirt, showing off a solid eight-pack and kept tugging upwards and doing his dance.

The llama image pawed the ground as if in encouragement and tossed its head like a frisky mount. Calista leaned down and slammed the panel over the computer controls, ending Vivien's llama-expressed flirting. "Open your lockers, guys, we've kept you waiting too long already." Enthused about her remodel, her voice was loud enough for the men to hear her at the end. "I'll show Zee, and he'll answer your questions, but go ahead, look in."

Calista touched Zee's elbow and squeezed in front of him to open his locker and slip through. Ronan got right there behind them.

Inside was a small bench with a laundry bag on a hook. The room was the size of a corner dressing room at a mall department store. The privacy was a nice touch.

Ronan stood at the doorway watching, not wanting to crowd Calista into Zee. Whether Zee was a good guy or not, there was no way he was letting Calista alone with a hyped up Geels player. He didn't turn around to see where Liam and Kiernan were but could hear the visiting players' comments like "whoa man" and "nice." Any trouble behind him seemed contained for now.

Calista pointed to the laundry bag. "Your clothes will be cleaned by the time the game or practice is over."

"Clever," Zee said.

Calista clapped her hands and pointed to an interior door. Zee opened it, revealing a deep blue tiled shower, and a half wall obscuring a toilet. The shower insets held large dispensers of toiletries. "Private bath." She chewed on her bottom lip. "We had plans for tubs so guys could soak, but we couldn't get the order in time." She tipped up her gaze to Zee. "Would you like that?"

"Oh yeah."

Ronan's eyebrows arched. Guests were being treated like kings. He was torn between amazement at her work, and the urge crawling up his spine to get her away from Zee. He had to be freaking civilized and focus on the renovation. The shower stall was huge with multiple shower jets. Steamy images of Calista and maple syrup swept into his mind. He wanted that again, every night.

Zee looked at him. "I've got this, you check on your men."

They were big boys. "I'm good."

Zee frowned.

Yeah, Ronan had his number. Zee wanted time alone with Calista. Ronan's shoulders tightened. Not on his watch, and not with his mermaid. Ronan gave Zee an immovable expression.

"One more." Calista opened the next door, revealing a smaller third room. She skipped through.

Her concept was amazing, and her enthusiasm adorable.

The small room held a large massage chair recliner centered before a wall-mounted TV over a mini-refrigerator. Calista touched the high-end armrest control panel. "After a hard game, you can unwind, or, before the game, some guys might need quiet and solitude." She opened an exit door that led out to a conference room bigger than theirs. The room had a narrow table and recliner seating, enough for the full team, and an overhead and a wall screen. "Or if the player prefers, he can gather with his buddies."

"This is amazing, Calista." Zee sounded impressed, and the way he said her name was familiar, as if he knew her. He didn't know her like Ronan knew her. He might be the end all for his team, but not for Calista. This room wasn't for him either.

Calista turned her beaming face on Ronan, looking for his response. That's how it should be.

Ronan strode around Zee and stepped into the conference room ready for Calista to join him and leave Zee to change. "Spectacular job, Calista," Ronan said, and he was being utterly sincere. He'd seen nothing like it at any of the visiting team locker rooms at any time during his career. After today, Ronan was taking this locker room for the Snowers. They'd work out the logistics. He needed to apologize for not coming the first time she'd asked, and praise her clever layout further, steal a kiss, turn her energy on him.

Zee reached over and shut the door in his face. The lock clicked, sealing Zee and Calista together inside the locker room, and Ronan alone in the conference room.

Son of a bitch.

Calista giggled as the door snicked closed on Ronan. Who knew serious Zee was a prankster? She looked up at him. "Not nice," she said, though her voice still held humor. The men's appreciation had buoyed her confidence. Being an hour late was turning out okay. "I'll go out the other way so you can explain if the guys have questions."

"They can figure it out." Zee took a seat in the big chair and wiggled to get comfortable. He nodded and relaxed into the Italian leather. "These are something."

Calista loved his easy acceptance. The last time she'd proposed better chairs, the topic had sparked a cringe-worthy battle and Dodo veto. She'd had the install team do as much build out as they could off site, and then had a huge crew complete the work while the team was away. She almost couldn't believe she'd gotten it done.

Zee looked up at her. "I heard you went to see the twins."

Calista's lips quirked up, remembering the duos enmeshed dynamic. Jakob would shoot forward, fast like Mikah, and Conrad would hang back, controlling the puck, then Conrad would shoot it to his brother seemingly without looking at him. "They're fun to watch."

"They said you'd acquire both of them if you owned the team, that true?"

Why was he even asking? "Of course." Zee must be blinded by a big brother lens. Calista looked at him indulgently and reassured him, "We'd be lucky to get them, both of them, either of them."

"Have you considered me?"

"For what?" Her question came out lively, her mood having gone from anticipatory out at the rink, sinking lower because of Dodo, and then lifted by showing off the men's locker room. Imagine when she did the Snowers side, they'd love her. And at school, the plumbing improvements and new layout would sway the professor to hand over her diplomas early. *Team Genius* bubbled to her lips, but she held in the words because her friends weren't nearby, and praising herself in front of others, even future family, could be taken as odd.

"You're scouting the twins. What about me? Can you imagine the four Czerski brothers playing together for your Snowers?"

Calista arched her eyebrows. Zee. *The End All.* The top player in the league switching from the Geels to the Snowers? Calista leaned against the wall, sank to the floor, and wrapped her arms around her bent knees. Zee and his brothers, all over 6'5", combined they'd have the tallest team in the league, and the best reach. With their looks, Dahlia would sell a shed ton of merchandise. The plays they'd make, they'd be so in sync, four players, one brain. Fans would shove at the gates to get in and see them play. She tilted her head up to him. "You'd consider that?" Her voice came out hushed and reverent. Not in a joking way either. The whole idea was beyond anything she'd imagined for the Snowers.

Zee's icy blue gaze was steady. "If things go your way, yeah, my contract is up, and I want to be here, so you've got me."

Her brain spun in a replay of images of all the times she'd seen him play. There were so many words to describe what a thrill having him on board would be. He'd be amazing in a Snowers jersey, number ninety-nine. Calista opened and closed her mouth. Words stolen, she simply nodded.

A grin settled on Zee's serious face. "If the owner-ship goes your way, my agent will be in touch."

Beyond blown away, Calista left him to change, on feet that floated an inch above the floor.

Calista went back out to the rink. Up ahead, Ronan, Kiernan, and Liam stood talking to Dodo. Her brain felt twice the normal size with the news in her head, but she couldn't share Zee's business, especially not with Dodo standing there.

Dodo turned to her, his face bright red. "Why in the ever-loving hell would you give those boys five-star locker rooms?"

Dodo was the pin to her balloon. How had Dahlia lasted a week with him? Her cousin deserved the world, this guy deserved the boot.

"Watch your language," Ronan snapped.

Dodo looked surprised but nodded. Kiernan looked like he was holding back a laugh, and Liam simply widened his bright green eyes to take them all in.

Calista clasped her hands together. She had to get a handle on speaking up in hostile situations, and crowds...and one-on-one. She spared Ronan a quick, greedy glance. Where did they stand? She couldn't go there now. She'd concentrate on the easier piece of the puzzle. Frankly, she was getting straight up tired of Dodo questioning her, doubting her, bringing her sunny days down. The ownership decision needed to be over with. She'd ask Olivia to poke the arbitration hearing with the judge and move the date up.

Her heart caught, but the decision felt right. The limbo phase they were in was worse, well, possibly worse, than losing the team. She needed to move forward without Dodo ragging on her every decision. She stood straighter. "Our guests deserve solid accommodations. We want to play all teams at the top of their game."

"No." Dodo shook his head and popped his knuckles. "We don't."

He did not love hockey like she did. There was no reasoning with him. Why bother? Calista turned away.

"What about my guys?" Dodo asked, as if at any

point he'd given her free rein to make changes, and she'd overlooked the Snowers. Did he not remember the recliner fuss?

Calista hesitated and turned back. This was clearly an opportunity. Dodo had now seen, or at least heard, firsthand what she could produce. There was a possibility they could move forward for the best interests of the Snowers. She was giving him one more shot. "Beta testing."

The men looked blank, as if she hadn't provided a concise explanation for the visiting team's locker room renovation. "The visitors will test out the new layout, give feedback, and from there, we'll build out for the Snowers, giving them the larger, more improved version they deserve."

"Hell yeah." Kiernan puffed out his chest and pointed in the direction of the locker room. "I want an extra body jet, one more than they get."

"Women." Dodo shook his head. "You don't get the game. These men need it rough. Gives them war stories to talk about, and conditions to bond over."

Private showers seemed basic to her.

"Eh?" Liam shook his head hard. "I want a mini fridge."

"And what's with llamas humping the players' legs?" Dodo frowned and asked the ridiculous question, as if it warranted her attention.

Kiernan snickered. He and Liam did a synchronized air hump.

They were having fun, and she shouldn't have to explain Vivien's computer glitch. Calista lost her patience with Dodo's picking. "Go look for yourself, then we can talk." She paused. "Through my attorney." She stalked off and pretended not to hear Kiernan's, "Whoop."

The game with the Geels went amazingly well, and the final score separated the teams by one point, with the Snowers on top. Calista glowed to see her team popping to the top of the national rankings. The team had it all, she knew they could hold their place. The current players were exactly right to win under the perfect leadership of Ronan Stromkin.

If a future acquisition brought on the twins, and Zee... Whew, the Snowers would exceed heights beyond what any fan could envision. As Calista watched the practice the next day, her mind spun with images of four Czerski brothers playing hockey here at this stadium. Amazing. If that didn't happen, these guys would shine on their own. Look at them, the win the night before had exhausted the players, but they brought their all to practice not one day later.

A flash of movement to her right and a delicate floral perfume clued her into the fact that she wasn't alone. Dahlia took the seat next to her, on the row where they'd come to countless games since they were little. "The Snowers have cleaning crews tidying the visitor's locker rooms and moving their stuff over. They're claiming the space until you renovate their own. I can't believe how amazing that space is. I would have helped, you know."

"Next bit, we'll do together." Calista gentled her tone to explain, "I didn't want to make it worse for you with Dodo."

Dahlia smirked. "Dodo is put out, like it's a big deal to change an electronic nameplate on a door." She rolled her eyes. "You know how superstitious he can be."

Yes, she'd heard about Dodo's lucky puck. His sensibilities didn't matter, the Snowers did, and they were so taken by her efforts that they wanted to switch spaces. That felt good. "Vivien's not here, I'll go program in the Snowers names." Calista hopped up and went down to the new locker room. "Want to go?"

"Nah, I'll get in your way with that. I'm working on social media, getting highlights from last night out there."

Fun. "I'll watch for those." Calista moved down the aisle, and around the rink to the visiting locker rooms. A rewarding happiness floated through her as she slipped inside. She could give back a small bit to a team that had meant so much to her. Imagine how great the stadium and the players' experience as a Snower could be if she had free control and could get their input without being shot down by Dodo.

She went to the control panel and typed in the Snowers' names, assigning their lockers.

The sound of skate guards clanking outside in the corridor had her type faster. The players must have finished up. She needed to get their lockers assigned. She made sure to give Ronan the locker which had slightly more room than the others. He deserved the best.

The door opened and skate guards made their distinctive footsteps inside the locker room.

"Almost done, and I'll get out of your way." Calista spoke loud enough so the players would be sure to keep their clothes on until she was out of there. She clicked so snowballs rained over the names, the LED light changed from yellow to blue, and she closed the panel.

Ronan reached her. He had an exercise-flushed face, and a playful expression. "Come quick." He took her hand and pulled her into the changing room with his name on the front and closed the door behind them.

Calista giggled. "Laundry goes in the bag." She pointed at his sweaty jersey. "Rest is self-explanatory."

"Wait for me on the recliner." Ronan's voice was low and full of promise.

Her teasing mood tumbled into a sexier one, and she nodded.

Calista went through and paced to burn her giddy energy.

There was the distant masculine chatter, and the opening of doors, mostly drowned out by the heavy spray noise from Ronan's shower, then he strolled into the cozy space to join her.

Wearing only a towel.

CHAPTER 35

Calista stood staring at Ronan's fit, hard muscled body. Her breathing slowed and mouth dried. Ronan took her hand and led her to the chair. He sank down, wrapped only in a towel, and hit the controls. The chair made a soft whirr as the motors powered into motion. He tugged her closer and scooped her onto his lap. He was so freaking strong.

"What do you want done differently for your new locker rooms?" Calista kicked her sneakers off and spun to brace her feet on the other armrest so her body formed a bridge over his. He was so cute, wanting her in here to cuddle. She put her arm around his shoulders and vibrations from the chair tapped against her skin.

"I like exactly what you did." Ronan scooped her closer and nuzzled her neck.

The move made her giggle.

"Shh," he whispered. "I don't want anyone to hear you."

"Why not?" Calista whispered back. "We're simply discussing your confiscated locker room."

He hooked his finger in the waistband of her yoga pants. "Q&A is not what I had in mind."

Fun. Calista's nerve endings sparkled, and he'd barely touched her. She took his other hand and flattened his palm over her breast.

"Umm." He murmured as her nipple tightened, and her body revealed her reaction to his touch.

Calista put her lips to his ear, and a finger over his lips. "Shh," she whispered softly.

Ronan cupped her head and gave her a wet, open-mouthed kiss. He pulled back. "Strip for me. Fast." He kept his voice low.

Calista wasn't worried about sound. She knew the solid structure of the walls and the insulated pipes between the spaces would dull the noise. Also, the other showers were blasting at full strength. No one would hear them.

Calista got up and removed her clothes slowly. Returning, she straddled his lap. His towel had ridden up and crisp masculine hair brushed her inner thighs and bum. Her breathing increased at the feel of him, the look of him, and his clear reaction to her closeness.

"Yes." Ronan squeezed her bottom and ran his hands from her hips to her knees and back. "Exactly what I had in mind."

Ronan put his hand between her thighs and traced lazy infinity symbols against her inner thigh, and then higher, up, around, over, down, and again.

Calista bit her lip and shifted. She squeezed his shoulders and kissed his neck. His skin was warm and fragranced by luxury shower soap. She ran her hands up and into his short hair, using her nails and tugging.

Ronan rewarded her by leaning up, licking and sucking on her nipples. He slowly rotated his thumb directly over her clit. He didn't move any other fingers. Just the pad of his thumb in one slow rotation, then another, then he slid two fingers over her damp folds and circled her entrance, making her ache and throb.

Calista gasped. She cupped his cheeks and kissed him, showing her need with the wet pulse of her tongue as she reached for the knot on his towel.

Ronan grasped her hand, stalling her. "I want the barrier, or I'll lose control too soon." His voice was gruff, and he dipped his finger inside her, one, then another. He made erotic motions, testing to see what she liked and encouraging her reactions, but slowing when she got close, keeping her needy.

Her mind sparkled and blurred, her body heightened to an unreal sensitivity. She put her lips to his ear. "Ronan, please."

Ronan's chest rose and fell. "Wish we were home, I could do this for hours."

Calista flattened her palm over the towel against his hardness. "I'm into that." Her voice was hushed and sexy. "I want to explore you too, know what makes you wild."

Ronan groaned and removed his fingers from her core to cup her hip. "You. You make me wild."

Calista moved her hand up, tugged his towel aside, and lowered onto him, the sensation full and satisfying. She controlled the motions of her hips, and he encouraged her pace with his caressing grip. He moved his free hand to her clit, stimulating the nerves, and driving her higher. All the while, the chair vibrated their bodies, creating an extra humming sensation to their vigorous movements. The erotic release flashed through her, quickly followed by his.

Ronan cupped the back of her head, pulling her lips to his in a carnal kiss, capturing her gasps of pleasure, and shielding their lovemaking from the outside world.

Leaving class the next day, Calista picked up a coffee and strolled toward the parking lot, while mentally replaying her time in the locker room with Ronan. He made her want on a personal level. To be around him now was about more than watching him play ice hockey. Not that she didn't still have a dream of owning the Snowers, she did. She'd make the stadium everything Ronan could dream of, if she had control, and Dodo got out of her way.

All Dodo's gamesmanship had done was make her even more invested and push her to be more strategic. She wished Dodo would lose, even if it meant they lost Jerry and the current GM too. A phone number flashed in her mind for Olson Urqhardt, the Washington GM. She hadn't consciously memorized his number when it had flashed on Ronan's screen, but she was good with recall.

Having a GM card to play could help her case, plus, Ronan clearly respected Olson to no end. Making Ronan happy by giving him a nice surprise like being able to work with his old GM would be wonderful. Like giving Liam maple syrup. That day, and how the night ended, had imprinted happy sparkles in her heart.

Calista wanted to be fair here. Was she making her decisions only for Ronan? Because that wouldn't be good for the organization. She wanted to make business decisions with her head, not her heart. She also wanted the big ones to be democratic. Get the players' buy-in along with Piper's and Dahlia's. But not yet, because having others help circumvent Dodo put them in an awful position should she lose her stake in the team. She didn't want that, and honestly, the call she was about to make was a no-brainer. Hockey lovers knew the name Olson Urqhardt. This would be like acquiring Zee. Getting him was a miraculous win. Missing an opportunity to make Olson Urqhardt a job offer would be a mistake.

Confident with her decision, Calista got off the sidewalk, leaned against an old oak tree and video-dialed the number.

Olson showed up on the screen. "Calista, this is a surprise."

Calista jumped right in. "Did you sign with Washington yet? Do you want to be Snowers GM if I keep the team? Work with Ronan again? I don't even know what to offer you except that I'd increase your salary and give you the four years you want."

Olson blinked.

She got that reaction a lot from people. Sometimes it meant good, sometimes bad. She held her breath. Birds chirped around her and leaves blew. The easy nature of the world still spinning calmed her down.

Olson rubbed his jaw. "You've knocked me back."

"That's not a no." Calista paused. "Do you want to discuss the offer with your family?" That was something she needed to do better. She knew her family indulged her, and after some point, she'd begun plowing ahead with whatever she wanted to work on despite the inconvenience to anyone else. She could work on that.

A younger man popped onto the screen, a handsome man with brown hair who had to be related to Olson, given their resemblance. "Dad, money's not everything." The man waved at her. "Sorry, you laid out your offer before I had a chance to leave the room. I'm Ulric, son and financial advisor."

A financial advisor should say money *is* everything. Calista processed what she knew, and it boiled down to the fact that she knew Ulric was also Ronan's advisor. She trusted Ronan's judgement, and a financial advisor would benefit the team. "Family matters to me, so the offer is the same for you, Ulric. A four-year contract, salary increase, and move package. You'd be offering financial advice to the players, dancers, and staff." Olson had mentioned his wife, so his family was at least the three of them. "My mom can talk to your mom about Austin if you like." Her voice grew easier, Mom was persuasive. Ugh, maybe he'd think that was unprofessional. She didn't care, the offer was authentic.

Ulric looked straight up shocked. "You don't know anything about me, or what I make." He rattled off his degrees and background, giving her a sales pitch and career snapshot which was both clear and convincing, though she didn't need persuading.

"Ronan trusts you, that's enough for me." Calista went with honesty. Not everyone could get a degree. That didn't mean they weren't capable. Look at her with no seal on her PhDs, and the class her friends liked to call Project Genius, but she knew it was project *prove you're not too much to handle.* "Think about the offer and let me know what else we can put in the contract."

Olson and his son exchanged a look and a nod. "We're not slow to make decisions. You get your position solidified this month, and you have a deal."

Wow. Power player had never been her goal, but this felt so good. Like the locker rooms, like she was helping her Snowers succeed. Calista smiled as she nodded, and then rang off.

She wanted to run to Ronan and tell him the news, but she couldn't. She shoved down her excitement. He'd know soon enough, if the arbitration went her way. If not, she'd share the news after, showing him she had the restraint to keep him out of an awkward position. Decisions settled, Calista went back to Ronan's, and upstairs to his gym. She got to work on his treadmill, adding the final touches that included a better WIFI connection for his screen.

Wait until he used it. The balanced track, the hi-def video, and the new speakers would turn the old whirring chirping machine into a bad memory from pre-Calista times. Her hands fell to her sides, and she stared at the functional treadmill. Fixing the machine ended her excuse to stay. Lingering at his place any longer because she didn't want to be at her overly quiet house and because she wanted to be near him were reasons based on emotions she'd have to voice if she wanted to stay. Calista went downstairs to find him. "Ronan?"

Ronan emerged from the kitchen holding a bag of spinach. Calista was coming down the stairs. His heart flipped at her prettiness, and he met her at the landing. "Heard you upstairs, and I thought I'd lure you into a meal. Where do you land on veggie juice with dinner?"

Calista put her hand on his waist and stretched up on her tiptoes. She looked like she wanted to offer her own suggestions about what interested her but hesitated and dropped back down without saying anything. Her face flushed.

He was game. Ronan put his hand on her hip and leaned down. "Hmm?"

"I finished your treadmill." She chewed on her bottom lip. "I should leave, right?"

Ronan hated every word of that, though she was making a prudent decision. They needed distance, not to be tangled together naked in his sheets. His hand slid around her waist and tightened. Let her go. Vanilla met his nostrils, and he nuzzled her neck.

A rattling knock jarred his intent. "We see you." His parents' voices came from beyond the glass inset in the front door. "Let us in, we want to meet your lady friend."

Holy hell.

CHAPTER 36

He'd been caught with Calista by his parents. Ronan jolted backwards, dropping his hands from her waist as if the world press was outside. Heart thumping, he processed the implications, and then his mind shifted, and his posture eased. His parents wouldn't know her name, and when he explained who she was, they'd be all over setting him straight. Mixing a relationship with business, that was what had gotten him tossed from Washington. This was what he needed, perspective. He touched her cheek. "Can you stay another night?"

"Sure." Calista beamed up at him with hope in her eyes.

His heart pounded. He needed to tell her he was leaving, but to do so, he had to be able to let her go.

Calista turned her head to the door, her eyebrows arched. "Who's out there?"

"My parents."

"Aw, I want to meet your family." Calista hesitated. "Wait, we're supposed to be—" she gestured from his chest to hers, "a secret."

"My parents won't be a problem." He needed this. He needed the reminder of home and his goal. He needed his parents take on Calista. His parents always met his girlfriends with open hearts but clear eyes. Their viewpoint aided his, and they would know to smash a front office relationship. He was his own man, but when the people who he respected most in the world spoke, he listened. This would likely sting, but he needed a helping hand out of the chemistry and fascination lake he was swimming in.

Flashes of times past shuttled through his mind. *Sure, son, you think Bria wants to stay home with you, but she's never in town.* His mom's probing questions to his third girlfriend had her admitting she hated hockey. He'd had no clue. With his fourth, he'd learned that she would hate to travel and never come to his games. His fifth didn't want kids. None of the things had been deal breakers. He'd even stayed longer with two of them, but once one truth came out, others had followed. Those combined lingered in his head, saying *they were not right together.* Ronan needed that now.

Because on a very real level, Ronan knew, clear as the Texas sun shined, that Calista was no ideal hockey wife. He just needed his parents to tease out the one critical flaw that would topple his fascination. The one that would erase her vanilla scent from his mind and creamy skin from his tongue, because his body and his common sense were warring.

Normal for a man, but his future, his life picture – that was the stuff on the line here, that's what he was risking.

"Are you going to let them in?" Calista whispered.

Ronan hurried to the door and let his parents inside. Dad carried two overnight bags that Ronan took from him and set on the stairs.

After the hugs and introductions were over, Mom turned to Calista. "You must think we're the worst, showing up as a surprise like this, but we had a longing to see our boy. And it's just an overnight. We'll watch the game and be home for bridge tomorrow evening."

Calista nodded. "Of course, you're family."

"Have you had dinner?" Mom headed to the kitchen. "No, of course not." She answered her own question. "Ronan looks like he's starving." Mom went to the fridge and waved to Calista. "My boy loves a home-cooked meal. Come help me."

Calista's eyes went wide.

This was good, very good. They all headed to the kitchen, and Dad sank down into the dining room chair with easy familiarity. Ronan leaned against the peninsula.

Calista trailed Mom. After digging through the fridge, Mom said, "I'm thinking turkey Dijon casserole." Mom set out ingredients for the dish she had in mind on the dark quartz countertop. "Healthy, but a tad indulgent." Mom held out the carton of eggs to Calista. "We'll need four in the small mixing bowl."

Calista got a bowl from the cupboard and centered it on the counter in front of her. She freed an egg from the Styrofoam carton and balanced the end in her palm. She tilted her head, and Ronan knew she was feeling the wobble, but from here, he couldn't see what she was looking at. He leaned against the edge of the counter. A tiny white feather stuck to the brown surface.

Calista stared at it, transfixed. "There's a feather on the shell." She sounded appalled.

His mom plucked the egg from her, ran it under the running water, and cracked the shell with one hand, and then quickly added the other three to the bowl. Mom nodded to the measuring cup. "Fill that with almond milk." Mom's every comment was a test, though Calista didn't know it. Would Calista argue about the type of milk or praise the healthy choice to suck up?

Calista measured the milk into a clear glass measuring cup. "To the line, even with the middle, or above?"

Mom shook her head, took it from Calista, splashed the milk in, and then poured the liquid into the bowl. "Why don't you set the table, dear?" Her voice said it all. Setting the table was men's work, in her opinion.

Ronan breathed easier. Calista hadn't morphed into a five-star chef in front of his eyes, his adolescent dream woman. She'd surprised him so many times, that even though he knew she couldn't cook, he wouldn't have been shocked if she'd exceeded his expectations.

Calista washed her hands and went to the silverware drawer with almost a skip. Yes, this was what he needed, but damned if Calista's scurrying feet and relieved expression weren't making him smile. He moved over to help Mom, falling into an old routine by her side. Mom was traditional, but she enjoyed him helping.

Calista went chair by chair, laying out the flatware while eying him. "You cook?" Her voice was shocked and her green eyes admiring.

He liked that. She wore that expression to varying degrees when he was on the ice, or they were in bed. Nice to know his other skills could provoke it. He'd definitely cook a full meal for her sometime, the two of them, candlelight, music, the works.

"He's single, he has to," his mom said. "He can't only eat out."

Calista shrugged. "We mostly do, supports local businesses." Calista sat across the table from Dad, who'd been checking sports scores on his phone. She put her heels on the edge of her chair and wrapped her arms around her knees. She was always more comfortable in small groups. "Tell me about Ronan."

"Great kid," Dad said, putting his phone down.

Calista looked fascinated, as if Dad had said that he had uncovered gold in their back yard at the age of five and had molded it into a hockey stick.

Mom pointed to the oven. Ronan flipped the switch to 450 degrees and slid the tray in.

"Geels powered back after their big loss to you guys. You've got them rattled." Dad sounded satisfied as if the one-point win had been a stomping. For the next forty minutes, Calista and Dad chatted hockey while he and Mom whipped up a salad and sides. Ronan listened and watched Calista more than he should, loving how animated she became over her favorite topic, though she more typically leaned toward quiet and still. He wanted to hug Dad for making her comfortable.

He tossed together a salad and spoke up when they focused on him, then the oven dinged and dinner was served.

Ronan took a seat beside Calista, and they all dug in.

"So good." Calista looked at his mom with admiring eyes. "You cook often?"

"Every night." Mom sat a little straighter and squared her shoulders, then her expression grew more subdued. "You haven't said what you do?" Some parents would know this from the hockey news. His were about supporting the game, not the front office.

Calista chased a pine nut with her fork. "Student."

Mom kept going. "And you're twenty…?

"Twenty-four."

Mom arched her eyebrows, though her questioning was this side judging. "But no paying job?"

Ronan almost choked on his bite.

Calista nodded. "I work part time at Dad's auto shop, but I'm taking time off to finish school."

"Ah, family business." Dad gave Mom a warning look. "That's nice."

"Oh, yes," Calista said with relish.

"And the rest of the time is school, and you're twenty-four." Mom was full-on judging now. "Oh, well, takes some students longer."

Calista looked down at her lap and flushed.

Ronan's protective instincts flashed to the surface, but he shoved them down. He wanted his parents' take on his relationship, and Mom had a process. He had to let this play out. He clutched the napkin in his lap and held his tongue.

"Nothing wrong with that," Dad said. "How much longer you got, kiddo?"

"One credit." Calista put her fork down as if the topic messed with her appetite. "I burned down a lab, so I have to complete a special project to graduate."

He hadn't heard that story. Ronan twisted to face her raw honesty. There was so much more he wanted to learn about her.

Mom arched her eyebrows as if she was the one feeling the heat. "Oh, my."

Ronan could tell Dad was trying to stay on the fence, but he was shifting over to Mom's side. "Tell us more."

Calista twisted her napkin in her lap, making him want to cover her hands with his own, but he resisted. She swallowed. "I work with fuel at Dad's shop all the time, so I was cocky. I just didn't realize how concentrated I had the stream."

How did he not know this?

"That's what insurance is for," Dad said, kindly. "When the project's done, you'll have your bachelors?"

Mom took a sip of her iced tea. "Back in my day, they called it a MRS degree. Are you looking for that? I got mine, met Mr. Stromkin at University of Washington and knew he was the one."

Calista crossed her eyes to him and mouthed. MRS? The acronym processed behind her eyes. "Master's in research science?"

Mom shook her head. "MRS. Marriage, dear, do you want to get married one day?"

"Oh." Calista giggled and relaxed against her chair. "Maybe, if someone could ever put up with me."

Mom looked sympathetic. Ronan's heart flipped

"My degrees will be two PhDs. One in mechanics and another in innovations."

Both his parents' mouths gaped. They'd definitely pigeon-holed her in a different box. Ronan loved the surprised looks on their faces. This was a fun change after years of girlfriends being fairly reactive to that question; Calista had taken the upper hand instead, surprising them like she did him.

"Do you want kids?" Mom plowed on with the full knowledge that she was being invasive. She was no longer even eating, just full-on interrogating.

"Depends."

"On?" Mom asked.

Ronan knew the questioning was wrong, but he wanted to hear Calista's answers.

Calista glowed. "If they're like Piper, absolutely. My sister's wonderful. Or like their dad, depending on who he is. Guessing I would pick him because I liked his traits." Calista looked dreamy.

Ronan felt a pang in the middle of his chest from her words. She had no idea how revealing they were.

Mom gestured to him. "What do you think of someone with a busy full crazy travel schedule like Ronan having kids?"

Calista lost her far away expression and nodded hard and enthusiastically. "Oh yes, lots of little Ronans would be amazing. As many as possible."

His parents laughed.

His heart swelled in his chest. He put his hand on her lower back.

Mom's expression melted. She nodded at Ronan.

Dad's face softened too. "He wasn't all that easy."

Calista shook her head, wearing an expression of denial. "I bet he was perfect. He's so amazing." She rattled off his stats with ease, and then went into his leadership skills, and spoke of how often he put the other players first and made time for them.

Ronan's heart filled, and he laughed. "Stop," he said, interrupting her recitation. He tilted her chin up because he couldn't help himself and kissed her lips. She tasted of a lemony iced tea and something uniquely Calista. He wanted to move further into the kiss.

Dad cleared his throat.

Right. Ronan lifted his head.

The conversation turned more normal as they all cleared the table while talking about the logistics of their quick visit and the game tomorrow. Calista insisted his parents ride with her and that she'd drop them off at the airport after the game.

Dad gave him an approving look behind her back.

They'd gone through all of that before he let his parents know to keep their relationship quiet. Which was fair because his head was spinning. *They'd both given him approving looks.* Over Calista, who couldn't cook, wouldn't be a traditional wife exactly, and he... he...*wife?* "We're keeping our relationship a secret. No one knows about us, so don't mention Calista being here." Ronan blurted the words faster than he intended.

Mom and Dad stared hard at him, and he realized he'd just stopped talking after telling them he was keeping his girlfriend a secret with no further explanation. They'd raised him better.

Calista rubbed her arms. "I'm having a meeting this week to see if my purchase of the Snowers goes through."

His parents looked uncomprehending.

"She's purchasing the Snowers," Ronan said, knowing the unexpected idea needed repeating. He rubbed his temple and steadied his breathing to wait for their reaction.

Calista nodded. "The seventy percent that's

available."

His parents had startled, but surprisingly, no questions or warnings came out. "You'll have to let us know how all that turns out," Dad said.

Mom gave him a side hug. "It's late kiddo, long day, long flight. We're going to head up."

Dad cupped him on the shoulder. "'Night."

They wished Calista a "Goodnight," and went up to the extra guest room.

He and Calista moved to the couch. Calista was tracing a design against the thigh of her jeans.

"What are you drawing?" Ronan brushed the silky strands of her hair aside so he could trace a pattern on her neck with his fingertips.

Calista shivered in reaction to his touch and shifted closer. "I've been planning a hotel connected to the stadium, with a section for singles and one for families. Fans can have all day outings, watch the game, and stay over. I was thinking about your parents coming up, having to pack just to see you. I want to add parent condos to the hotel, a wing of tiny apartments where they could leave their stuff. That way, they could come more often. Even if you were leaving the next day, they could stay longer."

Damn, she was going to make a thoughtful team owner. She was making the prospect of remaining in Austin an interesting, not before considered option. His heart pounded hard. He needed to talk to her and tell her about his intentions, discuss options with her. Not this weekend though, he'd enjoy their time together. He swung her legs over his lap so he could pull her closer.

Monday, an organizational notice came through on Ronan's phone inviting him to attend the upcoming arbitration meeting. The judge wanted to know who the starters would support in terms of ownership. Just like the front office to force them to show their hand.

His agent texted him within the hour. *"Know you must have heard about the hearing. They want the key players there. I leveraged this to your advantage. I let the Applebaum team know if they allow you out of your contract, they'll have your vote. They're on board. This came at just the right time."*

His skin chilled, and the hair on his arms prickled.

Shit.

As Calista and Piper walked through the door to the arbitration meeting, Piper bent her head to Calista's ear. "I went by the house to help you get ready for today."

Calista said nothing. Good thing Piper hadn't found her. Piper would have made her wear a suit like she and Dahlia were wearing. Calista was much comfier in her jeans and jersey, and today she needed all the empowerment she could get. Her hands were sweaty, and her brain spun with all the possibilities about how this meeting could go. Dodo could take everything and ban her from the stadium. Or she could take her seventy percent, sealing her position as owner, which would end her and Ronan. Calista drew in a shallow breath, then another in quick succession. Both options were bad.

Piper kicked her foot, making her hop and miss a step. "We both know what the house would look like if you were staying there." Piper's familial green eyes took on a big sister suspicious gleam. "You haven't texted me where you're actually staying."

Calista gave her big eyes and didn't answer.

"I will find out," Piper said.

They reached the conference room door. Noise buzzed from the other side. Piper gave her a quick hug. "You've got this."

Calista nodded, though she didn't have half of Piper's confidence. They moved through the door into the packed conference room. The usual chairs surrounded the table, but most people were standing. The star players were present and three of the dancers, along with Dodo and his lawyers, Dahlia, Olivia, Vivien, and the judge.

Piper joined Mikah while Calista hovered just inside the entrance, trying to steady her breathing while her mind bombarded her by rehashing possible outcomes. She could not make her feet move forward and inched backward until she could use the wall as support.

"Looks like we're all here. The honorable Judge Johnston calls the meeting to order." One of Dodo's lawyers said, as if they were in the courthouse rather than in the conference room.

Judge Johnston waved his hand. "None of that formality is needed Preston. But, yes, all take your seats please. For the sake of order, I'd like Dodo Applebaum and his lawyers on the right. The Amvehls and their people on the left. Lead dancers, Coach, and the Snowers' starters in the middle."

The attendees moved into place with a nervous energy, no one questioning the judge's authority. The judge who would rule on her future, based on what she had to say. Her throat closed up.

The judge grinned a professional, but sincere, grin in the direction of the players. "It is a true honor to meet the team." He went around the table and shook each player's hand before sitting opposite them.

"We'll talk later," Piper said to Calista in a low voice as they sank into their spots.

Calista nodded, too nervous to be concerned about anything other than this meeting. Was she the only one sweating? Dang. For once, she shouldn't have worn her jersey. Calista smoothed her palm over the bottom of the twenty-twos on her shirt front, and the motion helped. So did her group's easy demeanors. Olivia looked calm, Dahlia composed, and Piper wore a supportive smile. Vivien had dressed casually like her. Her pink t-shirt featured a llama with a gavel in his mouth. Would the judge find that disrespectful? Probably, maybe, he could think it was funny. She had to hold herself together. At least after today, the decision would be done. She snuck a glance at Ronan. His gaze met hers with gentle understanding.

Her breathing eased. She could get through this.

Judge Johnston flattened his hand on a brown folder. "I've had time to consider binders full of information. Your lawyers have been earning their retainers."

There were a few chuckles.

"I've received the signatures that you all agree my decision is binding." Judge Johnston spoke solemnly. "Now I want to hear from the invested parties personally. I want a 360-degree view of what the organization could look like going forward." He flipped open the binder. "Ms. Amvehl has lined up Czerski brothers Jakob, Conrad, and Zenon. This was welcome news to me."

Heads swiveled, and eyes stared at her, everyone's. Ronan's eyebrows arched, and he frowned.

Calista said nothing.

Olivia gave a proud and faux modest nod which shifted some of the attention off Calista.

Judge Johnston tapped the bottom of the page. "Whereas the Applebaums contend they never meant to let the team go, promise a continued running streak of wins, and solid management." He frowned. "But they've also agreed to release Captain Ronan Stromkin from his contract, per his request. This was unwelcome news."

Piper grabbed Calista's left armrest, and Dahlia

put her hand on the other one, caging her in support. Calista froze. She didn't need support. She'd misheard. Her gaze sought Ronan's, as did everyone else's in the room.

Ronan's face conveyed a million things, but none of them shouted that the judge's announcement was a lie.

He was leaving? Calista stared harder at Ronan, waiting for him to correct the mistake.

Ronan looked down.

He was leaving? Her chest tightened, cutting off her ability to breathe and stopping the whimpering mewling sound that wanted to emerge from her throat.

The judge was asking something, but all she heard was garbled speech. *Ronan was leaving.* Heat washed over her face and then fled, leaving her chilled all over. *Why? When? Why hadn't he told her? How long had he known? What would she do without him? Her? Shouldn't she be thinking about the Snowers? She was that far gone, that the team didn't matter?* Calista stared at the judge blankly.

"We need a minute," Olivia said. "This was not disclosed."

"This is not a trial," Dodo's lawyer said.

Judge Johnston was not unsympathetic. "I see this is news to you also. Why don't we take twenty?"

"We've barely begun," Dodo's lawyer shoved in, taking advantage of their weakness.

"Recess." Judge Johnston rose. "Reconvene at the top of the hour."

※

Everyone rose at once. The players went to Ronan. Her friends and family encircled her. The noise was loud and oppressive. Calista slipped around Piper, waved her off and jetted from the room. She headed straight to her favorite seats in the stadium and sank into her spot. She drew in a deep breath.

Here was one of the places she'd first felt normal. When a kid in her class had seen her at the game and given her a high five. When a fan had patted her on the shoulder because she was a fellow Snowers' fanatic. When the movement and energy had taken her out of her head and cleared her busy mind.

"Thought I'd find you here." Ronan came up the aisle and sat beside her. "Did you really seal an offer with Zee?" He sounded oddly neutral, as if he hadn't just upended her world.

She nodded.

"I'm captain, shouldn't you have told me?" His jaw tightened. "How long have you been planning this with Zee?"

Tears burned her eyes, and responses clogged in her throat. She couldn't answer. *He wanted to leave.* She rose.

Ronan took her arm and stood up in front of her. He moved closer and cupped her hip. "Calista."

They stared at each other, breathing heavily.

He could not be mad about Zee. Not when he was the one who'd had a bigger secret. She could tell from his blue eyes that he knew what this standoff

was really about. He'd just taken the offensive, like a
true sports star, aiming to win. She looked down.

"They're ready for us," Dodo called from the first
row. He was staring hard from one of them to the
other.

Anyone, absolutely anyone, would have been
preferable to Dodo Applebaum to come get her. He
likely knew that.

Calista squared her shoulders and went back to
the conference room.

They all sat down again in their same spots. Dodo
raised his hand as if he were in class. "Before we get
everyone's two cents, I want to speak up for Ronan
Stromkin and point out he should recuse himself."

Ronan's head snapped up.

"He's sleeping with Calista Amvehl," Dodo said.

Calista's face flushed hot and cold, but as before,
she couldn't make a sound.

All gazes shot between them, bewildered, doubting, confused.

Dodo nodded.

"Is this true?" Judge Johnston asked.

The chill moved into her bones, and Calista didn't
move, too numb over Ronan's news to truly react to
being exposed. Something that on any other day
would have deserved a reaction.

Willow snorted out a surprised laugh, which she
covered with her palm. "That's a stretch, Babe,

socially awkward and Ronan Stromkin. No one's going to believe that."

"Objection." Olivia leaned forward. "If Dodo lists which dancers he's slept with, we will allow this line of questioning, otherwise, we'll move on."

"Excuse me?" Willow said, her face turning the same red as her suit.

"Hey, now." Dodo shook his head. "No need to get into private matters. I shouldn't have said anything. Just thought my men should know, and Captain's vote should be weighed accordingly."

Willow stared at Dodo. "What did Olivia mean about the dancers? She's talking the past, right, like when you were with Dahlia?"

"Not now," Dodo said.

Willow rose and stomped from the room, leaving silence in her wake.

"It's true," Dodo insisted, pointing from Ronan to Calista. "Look at her jersey."

Calista crossed her arms over her chest.

"You're just being confrontational, like always," Dahlia said. "You know Calista took the purity pledge."

Yep, and then she'd burned it in Ronan's bed.

"No wedding, no bedding," Vivien started the chant, but reading the room, she let the words die off without adding another line.

Piper turned to Calista and cupped her mouth. "OMG. We *will* speak later."

Mikah straightened. "You know I've been staying out of this, but if you continue to throw out lies about my future little sister, we're going to have a problem. Not only will I be voting Amvehl, bigger than that, I will not re-up if the ruling is Applebaum."

The men erupted. "No Captain. No Czerski."

"Let's calm the temperature." Judge Johnston's eyes flashed around the room and slapped his palm on the table. Despite his expression, his voice came out calm and measured. "Twenty-four hours is reasonable. Let's compose ourselves and re-start tomorrow." He turned to Calista. "But I do need to understand. Would an Amvehl-run organization approve the Stromkin trade?"

A million emotions spun through her, and Calista still had no words. She looked at Olivia and shook her head no.

"Absolutely not," Olivia said. "Ronan Stromkin's contract is not up. We would not approve that no matter what another team offered."

Judge Johnston nodded slowly and rose. "We reconvene tomorrow."

Calista left the hearing, waving off her friends and family. A world of emotions weakened her and she couldn't even punch the ignition button on her SUV until a project popped into her head offering the respite of a distraction. Clawing onto the idea let her breathe, and she drove to the hardware store. An hour later, she parked in Ronan's driveway and got out her supplies. She loaded them into the portable wagon and rolled them straight to the front door.

She tapped in the code with forceful fingers, shoved down the knob, and strolled over the threshold. *He should have told her he wanted to go back to Washington.* That had prodded her the whole drive over. Anger was an easier emotion to handle compared to hurt, so she was riding high on that.

Ronan sat on his couch, his knees spread, his head in his hands. He lifted his gaze, and his mouth gaped. He looked at her with eyes just as cold and angry as her own. "After refusing to release my contract, you just let yourself in?" His voice was hard.

Calista stiffened her spine. "Your entry code is a four-digit number that you type in front of everyone. It's not a secret." She knew that wasn't what he meant, but she was relieved her words came out snippy and strong. Her voice hadn't cracked and she hadn't sobbed. She cocked her chin even higher.

"I'll change it."

"Weekly," she muttered.

"What was that?"

Calista stared at him because he had heard her, and he knew what she meant. When someone had to do something once, like change a code after an ex, that was life. When it was twice, they had to look inward. *It's not me, it's you.* Calista wanted to blame him for the anger screaming through her insides and shout at him, but the vulnerable words burbled up and stopped. "I had told Dodo I'd fix the drywall.

I'm here to fix the drywall. I do what I say." She continued wheeling the wagon out to the sun porch.

Ronan stared at her, then followed her. "I've always intended to return to my home team." Words he could have and should have said at some point during her stay. "You just shut that down, without having a word with me. While evidently speaking plenty with Zee."

Calista put on her N95 mask, plugged in her air purifier, and got the sledgehammer.

"What are you doing?" Ronan looked at the quarter-sized stiletto heel puncture in his drywall. "It needs a patch."

Amazing. Everyone always had opinions on how she fixed things. Maybe it was her. Some women broke things with shoes; she was more of a sledgehammer woman herself. Calista ignored him and tapped the blunt end of the tool in three solid hits above and below the circular stiletto hole. Vibrations pounded through her arms as she used more force than necessary, releasing some of her adrenaline. It *was* his wall, he should be consulted on the repair. She sighed and paused to explain her process. "You have to make things worse. Know what you are dealing with to make them better. I'm not a patch over it and move on person."

Ronan put his fists on his hips. "I'm a straight up guy. Say what you have to say, don't talk in metaphors."

Was she doing that? Despite the tension of the moment, Calista's lips twitched. She wouldn't have considered herself obscure. She wore his number across her chest. He was her favorite. At no point ever had she been okay with him playing for another team whether she owned the Snowers or not. How could he possibly think that? She dug another respirator from the package. "Put this on before I break the wallboard out. We don't know what kind of insulation is in this old house."

He put the mask on. "Calista." He said her name like an objection, as if to pivot her from her intentions. That wasn't how he usually said her name at all.

Calista pretended not to hear him. She put on safety goggles, took a claw tool and pulled out the sheetrock around the hole, revealing a relatively fresh column of brown paper-wrapped insulation. Good, there was no asbestos, ancient rotting wood, or stray wiring. She took off her goggles and mask and motioned that Ronan could remove his. Using both palms she shoved inwards, knocking down the insulation, which fell forward. She shined her flashlight into the dark space.

Huh?

She had not seen that coming.

CHAPTER 37

Inside was another room. The hair rose on her arms, and Calista looked over her shoulder. "What is this?" She whispered the question. Did she know him at all?

Ronan shook his head hard. "I don't know."

"This house was Dodo's bachelor pad?"

"Before he rented it to me, yes." He paused. "What do you see?" He truly looked like he didn't know what was behind the wall. Despite everything, that gave her some relief. She would have hated for the man she was seeing to have a secret boarded up room.

Calista breathed easier. "Another room." Calista lifted the sledgehammer, and this time Ronan didn't protest, but he held out his palm.

"Let me have a go." He took the handle from her and widened the hole. The pounding seemed to give him the same release of tension that the activity had done for her, a welcome outlet for the emotional turmoil. Once the hole was widened enough to fit through, Ronan looked at her and arched his eyebrows.

Calista nodded. She held the flashlight up, and he went in. She followed him through. The beam revealed a desk, a bookshelf, and an inner door across the square space. Calista found the light switch, flipped it, and overhead canned lights buzzed on easily, giving the room a cool blue glow.

Her mind went over what she knew about the layout of the house. This made some of the structural oddities make sense. She moved to the door and turned the doorknob. The door opened inward, readily revealing a row of insulation. She shifted it with her gloved hand to reveal new drywall. Okay. "We're in a small room which someone blocked up between the living room and the sunroom."

The room's overhead lighting, on its own, switched to a pale amber.

Ronan stood near a small desk. "I'm man enough to admit this is skeeving me out."

Calista took stock of her own feelings. After all that had happened during the last twenty-four hours, she should have been numb, but on this she wholly agreed. "Same." She was staring at an oddly thick bookshelf with conversely narrow shelves.

"Why would anyone want to hide an office?" Ronan cursed. "Am I living with some freaking shady tax records filed behind my wall?" Ronan opened the desk drawer and rifled through the items.

He withdrew a handful of storage drives and placed them on the desktop.

"That's one theory." Calista neared the shelf, eying the thick handle along the side. She grabbed the bar and pulled.

The room lighting turned red. She stepped back as the shelving dropped down, revealing a Murphy bed. The headboard was the type with thin rails. Two feather covered sets of handcuffs clanked down against the metal, and an extra-large tube of lubricant rolled across the black satin bedspread. "Secret sex room?"

Ronan cursed again. "No." Ronan shook his head, then ran his hand through his hair. He stepped back. "I mean, no judgement, I believe in a healthy sex life."

He also believed in secrets, like the fact that he wanted to return to Washington. "This room's not healthy." Calista let the tension show in her voice.

"We agree."

They agreed on a lot. Wasn't that important? Didn't he see that? "What do we do now?" Calista didn't know if she was asking about the room or their relationship or both. Her insides jangled with sick nerves. Maybe she was mysterious and obscure, but if someone knocked down her walls, there'd just find a solid structure and a sincere heart.

"I guess we cover the hole up, and I move into a hotel."

Calista pinched the bridge of her nose. *No. Don't leave, don't end this, don't go back to Washington.*

Stop.

Calista shook herself out of her head to focus on the moment. Ronan couldn't stay here. The setup covered over in Dodo's old bachelor pad was weird. Ronan had to leave. Leave this room, when his contract ended—their time together was really ending. The pain of their imminent separation felt tangible. Her palms ached. She wanted to hold his hand, she wanted a hug. She wanted all the reassurances he could give her. What did he want? She'd give a lot in this moment to have her sister's ability to understand men. "You could stay with me." The offer came out pained, her vulnerability open and on display.

"I..." before Ronan could answer, he frowned and flipped over three of the storage drives. "Check this out."

Her heart had stopped, waiting for his answer, and he wanted her to look at office supplies. If she were a screamer, she'd be yelling now, but her screaming was done on the inside. Calista closed the Murphy bed and moved to his side. The first storage drive read, *Jimbo Johnston's wife - Kay*. That riddle startled her from her own turmoil. "What's that mean?"

Ronan showed her the next two. *Warren's fiancée – Willow* and *Liam's girlfriend – Bianca*.

Calista stiffened. Dodo had better not be messing with her friend Liam. "I don't want to know what's recorded on those drives."

"Right, I'm just wondering if we should destroy

them or give them to the women involved?" Ronan shook his head. "I'm also incredibly pissed that we have to ask that question."

They agreed. She'd never been in a situation like this, but she knew who to turn to. "Piper's good with life stuff. Vivien's not judgmental and would know if it's a mutual...tape? Or could simply be information about the ladies, like a billionaire's background check on women in his life." She threw out the last to give Dodo the benefit of the doubt.

"That someone hid in a secret room?"

They shared a look. Neither believed it.

Still could be possible though. Calista shrugged.

Ronan pocketed the drives. "I'll give each one to the respective woman whose name is on it. Say I found the data device at my rental, and the truth, that I didn't look at the contents."

They searched another half hour but didn't find anything else that jumped out at them, so they turned the lights off and went back out. Ronan went to the wagon and got the plywood. He held it in place over the opening.

Calista secured the corners with a handful of screws and her drill. "Stupid of Dodo to have me fix the hole. He must not have known what room your ex's shoe went through."

Ronan rubbed his forehead. "I'll call movers and arrange storage, because Dodo will want me out as soon as the women hear about the storage drives and confront him. He'll figure out who found them and spoiled his secret." He met her gaze. "Your things are still here. We need to pack. I'll stay at a hotel for now."

Calista said nothing and went to the stairs to gather her stuff.

Ronan followed and touched her arm, stilling her. "You were mine. If only briefly." He swallowed. "Intensely. I didn't like that people didn't believe we were together."

That had hurt her feelings. Calista fought for the mature answer. "We're both good at hiding things."

"Being secretive, sneaking around, that's not how I want to live my life."

Calista opened her palms. She was potentially the new owner, and he was the star player. What else could they have done? Or was this about more, how weirdly quiet she could be? "I can't tell people everything that's in my head. No one can, and I'd bore them."

Ronan put his finger under her chin and lifted so his eyes met hers. "You've never bored me."

Calista's heart pattered and eased. He always surprised her with incredible words. She made a pleased sound. "Oh."

Ronan's expression softened, then hardened, and he dropped his hand away. "If the news is lifechanging it should be shared, like your bringing on Zee. I know you know that." He sounded jealous.

Calista pursed her lips. She did know that, and she did share, just not in the timeframe all her loved ones wanted. She blew out a breath. On the whole of things he could have asked her to change, that one was the most reasonable. Would he give her a chance to try? The only way that could happen was if he stayed. "You didn't tell me your news either."

"Guess we're both to blame." He looked at her steadily. "That should make our goodbye easier."

"Is that what this is?" Her voice cracked.

"I would never date the owner of the team I play for."

Calista breathed in and out.

"Or someone who'd put me last."

Calista felt her color drain and could say nothing. Spinning on her heel, she left without her stuff.

Calista went home that night to her empty house and stayed in her old room. She ignored her family and friends' calls when they rang to check on her. Ronan was the only one she wanted to speak with, and they weren't talking. She didn't sleep that night, and the arbitration meeting reconvened the next morning, though now she was even less emotionally capable of handling the outcome.

Calista arrived last. She took the seat between her cousin and her sister, and could feel their supportive stares, but she didn't meet their gazes.

Dodo checked his watch and then turned to the dancers. "I want to start today on a positive note. You know me, we love our Snowers dancers. I am making my position clear. I'd never cut the dance squad." Dodo wore one of his sharpest suits. He sounded bluff and hearty. In front of him were small turquoise bags, one for each dancer. The three women were representing the entire dance team, but Dodo had only brought enough bags for the ones here. He rose, placed a bag in front of each dancer, then retook his seat.

The first woman loosened the tie on her bag and held up a silver necklace with a diamond covered puck on the front.

Could the dancers be bought? Ugh, this whole arbitration hearing was about ownership. Of course they could. How would Dad handle this as a business owner? No one had ever tried to woo their mechanics away with jewelry, and that was the extent of her work experience. Calista sank lower in her chair.

Dodo spoke to the room at large. "The organization pays for our dancers to travel with us, their bar tab, cosmetic bills, and their monthly hair salon appointments. We also have a program allowing leave for enhancements if they are so inclined, fillers, saline double Ds or higher."

"Are we getting anything more? Anything new?" the head dancer asked.

Olivia nodded approvingly as the dancer took the opportunity to ask for more.

Willow pursed her lips. She wore an identical diamond-crusted puck necklace that hung low against her red silk top. "You'll get too many things for us to list here, but I have great ideas. Our future events will blow our past ones away, you know me."

Dahlia scooted her chair in closer. "We want to hear from you," Dahlia said to the dancer. "Then, we'll take the budget and decide as a group where the money benefits you most."

A blonde dancer who'd been quiet thus far spoke up, "I feel like these are non-answers, nothing concrete."

"You're right," Dodo said. "Dahlia's smooth, but MBAs are like lawyers. They say nothing, hint you'll have the world, but you never get satisfied. Whereas with me, well, you're holding something concrete in your hands right now."

Dodo's legal team didn't look put out by his words. The women pursed their mouths, not disagreeing.

Dodo gave a slight, *you're welcome* nod. "Enough about me. The purported owner should speak. Calista."

Yikes no. Why was Dodo always pushing her to talk? Because he knew she wouldn't.

The attendees waited.

Calista took a drink from her bottled water. "No thanks, Dahlia's got this, and Olivia." Her voice came out sleep tired, but at least she expressed herself. Why not, couldn't hurt worse than what had been said and unsaid in Ronan's foyer yesterday.

"The dancers' concerns weren't on the agenda." Olivia turned her legal pad around and tapped on the top. "Of course we can mock up a proposal, but the issues have to be disclosed first."

"See, MBA and a lawyer." Dodo held open his hands. He got a few chuckles, the loudest from Jerry.

Judge Johnston looked at Calista. "For the record, what do you have to say to the dancers' concerns?"

Calista stared back at him. She had no answers.

"The dancers aren't asking for a video presentation." Judge Johnston was professional, but insistent, and his voice had a slightly sarcastic edge that reminded her of Professor Terrence.

The blonde dancer spoke up again. "Are we getting new dressing rooms? Like the men?"

Oh, she should have considered that. Calista chewed on her bottom lip, and her mind mentally shuffled through the stadium blueprints. They could make that work. She nodded slowly.

"I haven't heard of any construction plans to that end," Dodo said. "Nor has Calista consulted with me about re-doing the dancers' space."

Everyone looked at Calista again.

CHAPTER 38

Calista honestly hadn't thought about renovating the dancers' changing room. She'd never even seen them. She fixed problems as they came to her. That was one of the reasons Dahlia was so pivotal. Dahlia had a dream for a big hockey family-friendly atmosphere, like with the costumes. Truth was, though, Calista had only helped a tad there, and hadn't really put in sincere effort. And what little Calista had done had been to support Dahlia, or in the case of the mermaid costume, to indulge her own interest in Ronan.

"We're waiting," Judge Johnston said. He had the sound of a person in command who was trying to give her a fair say but who was growing impatient. She appreciated that, but she also had the impression he was on Dodo's side, which was making this more uncomfortable for her. Or maybe that was her unfair assumption about him. Judge Johnston wouldn't be that happy with Dodo if he had any inkling Dodo had a thumb drive on his wife. She shared a quick look at Ronan.

Ronan met her gaze. His steady eyes offered no hint of direction, but he looked tired too. There were circles under his eyes. That helped somehow. So did the fact that he didn't toss the flash drives on the table. Being a shady blackmailer wasn't a role Calista wanted. Truth be told, the thumb drive hidden in the secret sex room still could be innocent. Calista held in her snicker. She concentrated on the problem at hand. "To be honest, I haven't given ideas for the dancers as much attention as I have for the hockey team and fans."

"See?" Dodo said. "Can you at least tell them if the dance team will exist if the judge has your contract stand? How much notice are you giving the dancers you cut?"

Cuts had never crossed her mind. Shock flashed through Calista as Dodo outmaneuvered her with his question, planting a false seed.

Lots of attendees started talking at once. One dancer got up and paced. "Will we even get two-weeks' notice?"

"Under the Amvehls? I don't know," Dodo said solemnly.

Calista's gut tightened. Job insecurity was one of the things Dad did his best to suppress. Auto shop work was physical, which caused limitations. Dad made accommodations where he could and transitioned some workers to the office when needed. She wanted to use Dad's model, not get rid of people.

Judge Johnston slapped his palm on the table. "Quiet." The room settled, but the tension remained high. "Ms. Amvehl, I understand you have an attorney and a business manager, but we all know major decisions come from the top. You are not under criminal investigation. There is no taking the fifth here. We are simply exploring the ramifications of a decision on this purchase."

This was sort of like the time Calista had explained about Liam's birthday plans. She could have slipped out of the conference room then, but she hadn't wanted Ronan to think she couldn't handle life. Truth was, she was like Dad, not a big picture project manager type. It was why Dad hired good people. She also knew addressing this huge group with ease and charisma wasn't something she could pull off convincingly.

On the other hand, Calista owed the dancers more attention than she'd given them. Calista got up and moved in front of the women so she could narrow her focus and be less intimidated compared to speaking to the full room. Her mind flashed to the dancers cheering her on in the Mer-tank. There, her tension eased. She'd speak with them with that in mind. These three women were potential friends, like Vivien and Olivia, well, more like Dahlia and Piper, but they were two of her favorite people in the whole world.

"Are you keeping the dance team?" the head dancer asked.

"Do you even like the dance team?" the blonde dancer asked. "Or..."

"Shh," the third dancer hushed her. "Let her answer. They keep asking her questions and then step in before she even has a chance to say anything."

"Yes," Calista said. And being able to spit out the one word freed her to speak further. "Everyone likes to be cheered on. And Dahlia has some family fun day events planned that the dancers could help with. I know the role of dancer is part time now, but I want to expand its responsibilities." She had no details there. Or of how future negotiations could go, other than to provide the example of the democratic choosing of the costume, but she didn't want to go down that road after facing up to her failing to give it her all, the way she had done with the players' upgrades.

There were a ton of murmurs, which was a fair reaction. As Ronan said, Calista was talking life upheaval. Calista swallowed. "I'll do better and put in the thought like I would for the guys. I'll improve your dressing room."

"Okay, whoa, thanks," Dodo said, cutting her off.

"Let her finish," the third dancer said. She shook her unopened jewelry bag.

Hmm, Calista wasn't the only one who didn't fawn over Dodo. Nice. "I don't have all my plans figured out. Dahlia is best at that, but my father has the auto shop on Henderson. I'd model much of the work here like he does his shop."

"You're saying we'll get a free oil change," Jerry

said. "Great, that's a hundred bucks. But now, you will have the dancers working overtime on your projects. That compensation doesn't remotely weigh even. I know I sound tough, but I'm looking out for the team."

No one had asked him.

Lots of murmurs sounded in the room.

Judge Johnston banged his hand again. She could tell he wished he'd brought a gavel. Though, as he'd said, this was not a courtroom, but a private arbitration.

"That wasn't what I meant." Calista flushed and didn't look at Jerry. Of course the dancers wanted to know about their salary. She should have led with that, but she had no idea how much money they made now as seasonal staff. "I'd make the dancers full time, year-around. I've lined up a financial advisor to work with the organization. I plan to start all staff from the cleaners up at a minimum of six figures."

The head dancer asked her to repeat that number.

Calista did.

"Dancers, concessions, janitors, those aren't six figure gigs," Jerry said.

"Shut up," the head dancer said.

"Turnover and unhappy workers cost companies more than they think. Dad says secure workers stay, which saves us money down the road. And once we chart your career path options, you know, after dancing, you'll know what next Snowers career to target." Calista held up her palms. "Training, Phys Ed, concessions, marketing...I know we'll need education stipends. Dahlia has ideas about merchandizing royalties for the players. We could create stuff relevant to the dancers." She wouldn't know where to start with that, though Dahlia would. She herself could speak to the dressing room remodel. The structure wouldn't be that different from the men's, but the women would have better vanities and a peg wall for appliances. Was this a good time to go over those details? Women weren't like men, they'd want a say in the fittings and that would take another meeting. Calista sought the eyes of the dancer who'd spoken in defense of her. "We could get lunch with Dahlia and Piper and strategize what we can offer better."

"Let's break here," Dodo said. "No need for the dancers to speak their piece just yet."

The head dancer stepped up and looked around at the other women. "No, I think we have the information we need. The Amvehls have our vote."

Ronan watched Calista's lips curve into a delighted smile as the dancers voted her way. He didn't know how he could be so freaking proud of her, and so infuriated with her at the same time. His own salary was transparent. He'd reached the level where his paycheck made sports news. He also had access to advice that other people didn't. He knew that and was grateful for it. One of the harshest truths about playing professional sports was that these careers didn't last long. When someone gave a sport their all, which they had to do to reach this level of play, it cut them to the quick when their career ended. He hadn't given much of any thought to the dancers' careers, what happened when they could no longer dance. This was a part-time gig for them, that's how he'd considered their work.

Not Calista. An Amvehl ownership would look different, better than Dodo's. Workers here would have options under her. Ronan was reeling, and they hadn't even scratched the surface on Calista's ideas. He'd never met a woman he wanted to talk with as much as he wanted to sleep with. Was that crazy? Was he thinking of staying? Letting go of his dream of Washington? Or would he still force the issue? Would she let him go? Or, in the end, was he only a Snowers player to her?

"I'd like to hear the players' opinions and their reasoning before making my decision." Judge Johnston waved his hand at the stars, indicating they should speak.

Calista drew in a breath, her chest knotting.

Saxon ran his hand through his overlong light brown hair and stood up. "I don't get to meet with the office much now. They don't explain or listen."

"Rookies." Dodo shook his head.

"We can set up weekly hour-long meetings,"

Dahlia jumped in. "And my door will always be open."

Saxon crossed his arms over his chest. "In that case. I vote Amvehl." He dropped to his chair.

"Rookies," Jerry said. "I vote Applebaum. In fact, I walk if there is any other conclusion. Like the Captain, I have other offers. Weigh that, why don't you?"

The judge hissed a breath and made a notation.

"Calista Amvehl had my vote from day one," Kiernan said in a simple, sincere statement unlike his usual flippant self.

The sentiment touched her, and she'd love to know how she'd gained his support.

Liam pointed to the hallway. "I need a private word with Calista first."

"Soften the blow, good man," Dodo said.

Calista rose, pushing her conference chair back, leaving sweaty palm marks on the arm rests. Great, at least the hallway would be private.

Liam jumped right in. "You spoke about new royalties?"

"I think that would be fair." Calista looked away from him. She'd been thinking about how best to help him since she'd researched him for his birthday but saying what she'd thought of required tact. "We could direct the funds to a trust for families or kids, then, when they want money, they can go through the trust, not the players."

"Why?"

"To take the pressure off. I hid my money for

years, but you guys have your salaries blasted on the news. I'd hate that if I were you."

Liam nodded, looking grim, and held the door for her to return to the conference room.

Calista went in, wondering if she'd over stepped, insulted him, and how to fix it. She liked the big Canadian. No way to smooth over the situation before the vote, but either way she'd want to make sure they were good after. She rubbed her arms, though the room wasn't cold, and took her seat.

Liam's serious expression fell away, and he grinned casually. "Calista got me maple syrup for my birthday. You had to know that got my vote."

Calista dropped her hands to her lap. The numbers were going her way. A flicker of hope strengthened inside her.

Kiernan punched Liam in the arm. "Yep, you're easy, bro."

"Mikah Czerski's opinion has been made clear." The judge faced Ronan. "Lastly, we'll hear from Captain Stromkin."

Calista's heart stopped.

Dodo held up his hand and looked at Ronan. "Before you speak, remember, I will allow you out of your contract to return to Washington."

The room got quiet.

"Still?" Judge Johnston looked at Dodo impatiently. "How will that help the team?"

Dodo crossed his arms over his chest. "That's how it is. We have twenty-two other players. Time to tap that resource and let someone else shine."

The judge frowned. "This has gotten off course."

"You know Calista can't handle running this team." Dodo's absolute certainty was deflating.

Calista pressed into the back of her chair.

"She got Zee Czerski." Judge Johnston didn't even lower his voice. "And she's keeping Stromkin. Do you know how that's going to play out? Do I have to say *Cup*?"

Dodo stiffened, but he didn't answer the questions.

The judge got it. Judge Johnston knew Ronan was destined to be a superstar player, and even though he and Dodo were friends, he was showing he could put the team first. Calista straightened, eager to hear more.

"Captain, I've followed your career," Judge Johnston paused briefly. "Your efforts transforming this team have been pivotal. Whether you stay or go, your opinion will factor heavily in my final decision."

Ronan turned and looked Calista straight in the eye. He wore a business professional expression. He was a man who wanted a straight response.

Calista swallowed. She should not find his tough look a turn on, this was not the time.

"Are you allowing me out of my contract so I can return to Washington?" Ronan asked in a tense voice. "I want to hear it from you."

Her heart cracked. He had to know the answer.

CHAPTER 39

Calista absolutely loved him. In ways and depths she didn't know she had. She wanted him to have the world. Calista could not lie to him, she had to do what was best for the Snowers. She met his beautiful blue gaze. "Never."

Ronan frowned, looking a combination of hurt and furious. "I vote Amvehl. Welcome to the organization, Ms. Amvehl." He sat back down, but he was looking at her like she was a stranger, as if he felt nothing for her.

Calista breathed out and back in too rapidly. Ronan voted her way. She'd get the team, but she wouldn't be able to have him. Her happiness was split in half by heartbreak, and the contradiction was beyond her emotional capacity.

Piper and Dahlia, on either side of her, each placed a supportive hand on her arms. Calista didn't look away from Ronan.

Dodo cursed. "Talent isn't everything. An organization has to run right. You know GM Hollis will walk. With things not working, how long are the men going to keep up their stellar play? Stressed talent fails, it's the truth. I thought the arbitration would settle everyone's concerns, prove the contract unworkable. All we're causing is division."

The judge tapped on the table in front of Calista, pulling her focus. "Dodo's not wrong. I'm leaning back and forth, and to be honest, I came into this with less than an open mind. Give me something here to show you can handle this responsibility not only to the team, but for the organization's commitments."

Just like freaking Project Genius. Show your work, tell us your plans. The re-piping, the new stadium seats, the family condos, the hotel... "There's a ton." Which part did he want to know? What would sway him?

Calista knew she was overthinking the huge important question, or underthinking it. She had to take this down to the core. The judge was concerned about the future of the organization. The GM role was critical. She could tackle that, just that one piece. "I have GM Olson Urqhardt signed if this goes my way."

Ronan jolted, and his chair rolled back.

Heads whipped toward her. All eyes, shocked with surprise, were on her. The judge whistled in the silent room.

Yeah.

Dodo's face flushed red, and he sank low in his seat.

Judge Johnston lifted a piece of paper and scrawled his name along the bottom. "Decision made. Seventy percent to the Amvehls."

Ronan breathed in the cool, misty air of home. He stared out at the dark green trees of the vistas from the backyard. Mom was setting out refreshments. Dad stood with him on the grass as he had done for the big dilemmas, the whole of Ronan's life. Ronan told them everything.

"Of course we want you back here." Dad pulled his hood up and moved under the patio. "Is it best for the Snowers team if you stay with them?" Dad had a reasonable, sympathetic tone.

"Yes." Ronan knew he sounded gruff, but Dad would understand. He joined him under the shelter.

"Is your staying best for the organization?" Dad continued.

"Yes." Ronan's word was grudging.

"Calista kept business and your personal life separate." Dad put his hand on Ronan's shoulder. "And you're angry, because you didn't?"

"He's hurt." Mom hooked her arm around Dad's waist. "He put Calista first. She put the Snowers first."

"Why?" Dad asked. "Why did you vote for Calista?"

"I love her. I wouldn't have done anything else."

Dad dropped his arm around his shoulders. "Not everyone has your clarity of purpose and moves, Son. Talk to her. Because despite Calista's decision, your Mom and I believe she loves you too."

The rock that was his heart eased, and Ronan nodded. He wanted to go back to Austin, to Calista. He just wished the decision had been his, not hers holding a contract, and forcing his hand.

Kiernan picked him up at the Austin Bergstrom airport in a black sports car blasting Irish rock music. Heads turned. Ronan pulled his ball cap lower and shoved on his shades. He dropped his duffel in the trunk and squished his body into the passenger seat. He never understood his fellow athletes who preferred cars more sized to fit jockeys. But he said nothing, because, hey, a friend wasn't something he was turning away today.

Kiernan slowed to take the corner. "Gonna say something? Or do I have to buy you a beer to pry the sulk out of you?"

Ronan rubbed the scruff on his jaw and dropped his arm against the door by the window, feeling the hot Texas sun on his skin where the cuff of his henley ended. "What's there to say? You know the deal, man, the front office is treating us like pawns, and in this case, blocking my move." He couldn't speak to the confusion on the inside, his men needed him to be stronger than that.

"Can't say I'm sorry. What do you think of Urqhardt? That's something, right?"

"I introduced Calista to him." Ronan expected his own words to sound bitter, but they didn't. With Dodo, they would have. Dodo would have used Ronan for the connection in a heartbeat. Not Calista, not on purpose, but she hadn't shared the fact that she'd hired his old GM, not with him.

"You want to play for your former GM?"

"Yes." That soothed him a touch. He couldn't put into words what having a GM like Olson Urqhardt meant to the big and little factors each player had to consider throughout the season. Urqhardt would have their backs, and they'd be free to focus their attention on the game.

"Your parents will still come down and see you play?"

"Yes." Of course they would. Ronan's chest loosened a touch more. Calista's thoughtful idea of the hotel apartments for parents hadn't even been brought up at the vote. The men would love that perk. Especially the guys on the lower end of the salary scale. This would be the literal game changer for the number of visits and home support they got. Calista had been sweet to think of that after meeting his parents. Many women wanted to make visits less convenient for the in-laws, not Calista. She was unique in the best ways.

Kiernan pulled up into the hotel lot. He put the

car in park and pushed the button to shut down the rumbling engine. He turned to Ronan and lifted his sunglasses so Ronan would see his serious teal eyes. "You had a hot, rich blonde in your bed?"

"Hey," Ronan said, tension ripping through him.

Kiernan's eyes hardened. "Calista's gorgeous, hot, and sweet. Most importantly, you're in love with her. Stop throwing away the win." He opened his palms. "Why am I always the sensible one?"

Holy shit.

Yep. Crystal clarity erased his lingering bitterness and confusion. Ronan knew what he had to do. He checked his watch. Calista would be in class now. "Can you drop me off at campus instead?"

Kiernan hit the ignition and shoved the gear into reverse. "You got it, bro."

Calista drew a square over and over until the pen tip tore the paper. Class had dragged today, even though Professor Terrence would be by to hear what they'd been working on and how they'd done the steps together without burning anything down. They'd fixed a locker room, created a maple syrup slide, bought the Snowers...Her friends could do the talking. She was rubbish with words that mattered. She stared down at the wood grain of her tabletop and traced her name.

"I'm not sure I understand," Olivia said from her window seat. She undid the button on her Peter Pan collar and squeezed the back of her neck. "Why are you upset? You got your dream come true—you own the Snowers. You got your ice hockey team."

"Seventy percent of them," Vivien corrected without looking up from her computer. "We can still spin it to sound great for hot Prof."

Calista rubbed her temple. She had hockey, yes, but no Ronan at her side. He'd left town, hadn't shown up for practice, and he hadn't called her. She'd sat in her old room, on her own comfy bed staring at their selfie, unable to think about school, or even relax into a game of hockey on TV, heart aching, mind spinning. Why? She'd gotten her way, all that she'd wanted. Ronan played for the Snowers. She could watch them whenever she wanted from her favorite seat and go home to her family. Alone.

The answer popped to the front of her mind. *Ronan meant more than hockey.* But she hadn't shown that to him. Her heart stopped and her breath caught in her lungs. That realization should have been clearer sooner. Calista shoved her papers and tablet into her backpack. She needed to get out of here. An almost giddy sensation settled inside her at having a direction to take, screw the final presentation, she needed to find Ronan.

"Where are you going?" Olivia asked, alarm in her normally measured voice.

"To find Ronan."

"You can't." Vivien looked up from her laptop. "We all have to be here to present."

Artie nodded, making his beef jerky strip bob.

A whirring sound emerged from the closet along with a mechanical burning smell. Someone should check that out. Not her problem. The mechanical puzzle didn't lure her like it normally would. She had human issues to contend with. Calista moved to the wall and raised the window to let in fresh air. There, she'd done her part for the class today, now she was out of here.

The whirring grew louder, and the closet door flew open.

A full-bodied, human-shaped robot rolled forward. The robot was Calista's exact double.

CHAPTER 40

Shock stopped Calista where she stood. The robot looked like her, but it was also not the same. From the jersey cut off under its huge double H breasts to the low-cut jeans fitted to the mannequin's narrower hips and bigger butt, she was a sexed-up version of Calista. Her wig was the same color as Calista's hair, and she had a fake sucker between her scarlet red lips that made her look as if she were puffing on a cigarette.

"Holy smokes," Vivien said.

The robot grabbed Calista's wrist in her rubber fingered grip.

Artie, sitting on the floor, held two remote controls. The one he manned with his left hand was spinning an arm around him on the floor holding a ruler.

When had he moved past the arm to a whole wheeled person? There were a million body parts in between. Confusion and so many questions swarmed through her.

Olivia thumped her pen against her yellow legal pad. "You do not have permission to use Calista's likeness."

"Kah-lees-tah is different," Artie said.

Olivia looked at Calista, comparing her to the robot. "Not that different," Olivia argued. She turned to Calista. "You didn't give him permission, did you?"

Calista gave Olivia a big-eyed look and shook her head. She pulled away from the robot, but the robot didn't let go. Calista found her words. "Release me, Artie."

"I'm working on it," Artie said in his voice that they all knew meant he was not working on anything of the sort.

Vivien confidently hunched over her laptop. "I'll hack it."

"Stay out of my code," Artie said.

How long would this take? "Hurry, Vivien." Calista pulled against the restraint. "I mean it, Artie. Release me. I have places to be."

Artie put the controllers down and lifted his phone. He hit a button on the screen. "Say it again, just like that."

Calista growled. Who knew how long this would last? Frustrated urgency pushed through her, and Calista got out her own phone and typed a one-handed text to Ronan. "*I, Calista Amvehl, release Ronan*

Stromkin from his contract." She hit send. Her heart lightened. This was either the most selfish thing she'd ever done or the least, she couldn't tell. Her breath whooshed out. She'd made a painful decision, now she needed to see Ronan in person to say the words to his face, and to apologize for not saying them at the arbitration.

Vivien typed hard on her keyboard. "The robo-woman is resistant to hacking."

"Her name's Kah-lees-tah," Artie corrected.

Now, he just wanted a slap. Calista turned a death glare on him. Artie had no idea how much he should not mess with her this week.

The robot tugged her two steps further back into the room.

Was the robot's receiver in her brain? Calista felt along the robot's neck underneath the rough strands of her wig. Maybe she could pop her head off.

The robot jerked Calista forward another foot.

Olivia scratched her pen across her notepad while reciting the date and time. Then she opened her phone to dictate the scene. "Attorney Olivia Hammond serving as witness." She shined the camera at each of them. "I'm making it clear, Artie, we will sue."

Sue, destroy his bandwidth, turn his creation to ash, Calista was on board. She shoved the robot's chin, but the head remained steady.

"I got it," Vivien yelled. The robot fingers loosened and then re-tightened. "Nope."

This went on four more times. Calista's impatience intensified with each attempt.

"Did you hear me? I will sue." Olivia pointed the phone at Artie. "Arthur Jenkins. Acknowledge that you hear my declaration."

Footsteps sounded outside and the door opened.

Ronan stood there framed in the threshold. His intent blue gaze searched for her. "Calista." His voice held relief as if he hadn't thought he'd find her.

His handsomeness, his sheer presence, was everything. *Ronan was here.* Calista's heart lifted, and she headed toward him. "Ronan."

The robot dragged her back.

Ronan's athletic stride brought him easily around the desks and to her side.

Her world was righting. She could explain now, fix everything, apologize, because he wouldn't be here if he wasn't open to hearing her out, right?

The robot clone grabbed Ronan's arm.

"Whoa, man," Ronan said.

Now, the tacky robot had one hand on her and one on Ronan. That didn't matter. *Ronan was here.* What did that mean? All she wanted to do was speak with him. Say all the words, but in private, just her and him. Calista tugged her arm until her skin pinched, and her bone bruised. The robot's fingers didn't budge.

Ronan tried the same to no avail. "Are you okay?" he asked Calista, his voice and expression concerned.

Calista nodded, staring up into his face.

"What is this?" Ronan checked out the robot, and his eyes narrowed on the robot's figure. He turned his head to Artie. *"What is this?"* He repeated the same question to Artie, but he lost the politeness that was normally in his voice when he spoke with people.

Artie, well out of reach, used his old, wheeled robot arm to roll a ruler up to Ronan's sneaker. Ronan stepped on the ruler, creating a loud crack.

Olivia held the camera low to get a good shot. "We've spoken about this, Artie. No measurements without consent."

Stilettos clicked on the tile outside. Willow came in, wearing a red sweater minidress and an angry expression.

Calista could have provided a list of names of who she thought she'd see today. At no point would she have guessed Willow.

"Calista." Willow's brown eyes were as unfriendly as they'd ever been. "You thought you could ignore my email? I went to school here too, you know. Finding your classroom wasn't hard." She took in the scene, paused, and then strode right up to the robot. She looked it up and down. "Are you kidding me?" She turned to Calista. "You Amvehls take and take until you have freaking everything. Don't you? You even get your own clone?"

Artie made the robot bug her eyes at Willow. They aimed at her boobs, lowered to stare at her legs, and bobbed back up to her chest.

"You get everything." Willow grabbed at the

robot's hips. The robot immediately released Calista and Ronan and clasped Willow's hips as if they were sharing a slow dance.

Calista and Ronan took advantage of their freedom and stepped back out of reach. Calista rubbed her sore arm and eyed the creature. "Like I want this. Get your own robot, I don't care."

"Maybe. I. Will." Willow huffed out the words while walking the robot backwards. Artie let her move it, and Willow reached the window. "Make it let go," she said to Artie in a domineering voice.

Artie used the larger controller and had the robot release Willow immediately.

Willow shoved the robot through the windowsill, and looked back at Calista with a smirk, as if she'd taken away something Calista had wanted. She planted her hands on her hips and faced the room.

Seconds later, a large crash sounded on the pavement outside.

Wincing, Calista met Ronan's gaze, and they hurried to the window to see. The broken mechanical parts spread across the sidewalk and into the grass, the female anatomy disturbingly realistic.

"Those pieces are obscene," Olivia said, looking out her own window, "but at least they don't seem to have hit anyone. That's important." She held up her phone camera.

Vivien joined them and shook her head. "We're going to lose so many points for that."

Artie wheeled the broken ruler over to Willow.

The jagged stick slid against her high heel and the engine revved.

"I said, not without consent," Olivia snapped. "Have you learned nothing in this class?"

Willow tilted her head and took in the situation quickly. "Consent? For a me-robot?" Her voice grew intrigued.

"You're like a sexy android." Artie eyed Willow's lean body up and down and then again fixating on her breasts.

Willow preened, arched her back, and ran her hands over her pixie cut.

"I could clone you. I mean." Artie cleared his throat and slipped a quick look at Olivia. "May I clone you?" he asked Willow.

A greedy light entered Willow's eyes. "Is this commercial? I'd expect a large percentage."

Artie nodded. "I'd want to record you, using that voice you used when you walked in."

Willow nodded and moved over to him. "For a price, that could be arranged—a big price." She sat down cross-legged in front of him. "Everyone would want to buy a robot that looked and sounded like me. We're going to be so rich."

Artie nodded. "Very rich."

Willow tilted her head to Olivia. "Write this agreement up. If he clones me, I want half of all royalties the Willow-bot brings in."

Before Olivia could respond, Professor Terrance came in, his face flushed. "I was having my afternoon tea, and I received no less than four calls about a ruckus up here. The whole point is to prove you can work together unsupervised. Is that wrong?"

Sort of. Maybe he should have been here and he would have known what was up.

Everyone was quiet, though Willow gave the professor an appraising look which he returned. Then he canted his head and sniffed the air. His gaze switched to stare at Calista. "Did you set a fire?"

"No." But she'd wanted to.

Olivia tilted her phone toward Artie, but she looked at the professor as she spoke, "I, Olivia Hammond am recording informed consent and a future royalty agreement." She punched stop. "We were just working."

"There was a commotion." Professor Terrence calmed a touch.

Calista's heart thumped, and she caught Vivien and Olivia's gazes. Their hanging out had made them understand what they needed to do with that one look—conspire together.

"No ruckus here." Vivien moved back to her chair and hunched over her laptop. She pulled up the hood on her llama jacket.

"Let me explain." Olivia gave the professor a well-moderated version of the events where they all cooperated together to support Artie's creation, draft a participant, draw up an agreement, and record the effort for posterity.

Professor Terrence nodded. "I knew Artie's project would bring all of you together. Artificial

Intelligence is the future." He frowned and waved his hand to the outdoors. "The situation out there? Explain."

"Clumsy robot balance," Calista said. "We'll sort out the kinks. That's the reason for beta testing."

The professor looked around the room. She couldn't tell how much he really believed them, but she could see how much he simply wanted out of there.

"Brilliant, this group has clearly earned their final credit." Professor Terrence now sounded pleased, as if he'd spent the weeks teaching them cooperative techniques, and they'd finally gotten it. "I'll go send in my recommendation now."

Whew. Her parents would be so proud. Relief and a tension she'd held since the class began let go of her. She walked over and bumped fists with her friends, and she skipped Artie in case he latched onto her again. Artie didn't notice, his attention was glued to Willow. That left Calista with her heart to deal with. Calista looked at Ronan, feeling a combination of shyness and hope. "You got my text?"

Ronan checked his phone. "No, wait, yes." He reached out to open the message.

Calista took his wrist like the robot had, but gentler, relishing the feel of him under her fingers. "Wait, I'll say the words in person."

Ronan cupped her face, sending warmth and tingles through her. "Me first. I'm sorry. I'm in love with you. I want everyone to know."

Calista's heart caught, and then shimmered with ecstatic hope and love, and she beamed at him.

Olivia pointed the microphone toward them.

"Dodo was right?" Willow sounded shocked.

The eyes of the room were on them. None of them needed to be a part of her and Ronan's moment. Not that she cared if they were public or private, just that they were together. Calista took Ronan's arm and led him into the hallway. Students strode past. There were posters pinned to a corkboard, the ambiance was not romantic.

Ronan put his arms around her waist in an affectionate hold, and this realm no longer mattered.

"My text lets you out of your contract. I love the Snowers, but I love you more." Calista pointed to the number twenty-two on her jersey. "Everyone has always known how I feel." Her heart bounced and danced and did all the things. The happy flood of emotions didn't stop her own words. "I love you too. Love-love, not just fan love, perfect love."

"That's everything I wanted to hear." Ronan grinned, gently brushed her hair back, and nuzzled her neck, causing quivers to flutter through her whole body and weaken her knees. "What do you want first for our perfect love? Candlelight and roses? Should we hunt for a house to share? Hockey should be in there somewhere, right?"

"What do I want?" Calista grinned, rose to her tiptoes, and cupped his face. She met his loving blue gaze. "Just you."

✻

Thanks for reading! Want more Snowers hockey romance? Well, hold onto your purity pledges, because Dahlia and Zee star in book three: *Passionate Love.*

ABOUT THE AUTHOR

Emily writes fun, happily-ever-after romance novels. She holds a BA in Psychology from Texas A&M University and an MFA in Creative Writing from American College Dublin. Her Adult Contemporary are under the name Emily Bow and Young Adult under Emily Evans. A native Texan, she loves travel, movies, and books and may be found at www. EmilyBow.com and www.EmilyEvansBooks.com.

ACKNOWLEDGEMENTS

Edited by Kella Carlton.

Thanks to my support, you're awesome: Michelle, Gail, Teresa, Veronica, Jennifer, Stacy, Joellen, Barbie, Wyatt, Nash, Brennan, Joseph, Megan, Wayne, Mishann, Rachel, Darlene, Jeff, Heather, Matt, Trevor, Mom, Dad, and all my supportive aunts, uncles, and cousins.

My Writers group: Dana Michaels, Dax Varley, Donna, Rhonda Brinkmann, and Deanna Roddy.

Made in the USA
Middletown, DE
22 May 2023